KOREAN
LITERATURE
NOW

Quarterly magazine on
Korean literature and translation

P9-DEW-974

© Choi Jisu

Korean Literature Now Magazine

Bringing You the Best of Korean Literature

Writer Interviews · Essays · Excerpts · Reviews

Vol. 42 Winter 2018

Poet Kim Sun-woo in conversation with **Christopher Merrill**

Writing Resistance: Voices from Korea and the US
Alexander Chee, Hwang Jungeun, Song Kyung-dong, John Freeman

Translation, Description and Gertrude Stein by Kate Briggs (*This Little Art*)

Seoul International Writers' Festival
Gender: Sight without Seeing

Have KLN delivered to your door four times a year for free!

Subscribe now at KoreanLiteratureNow.com

LTI Korea
Literature Translation Institute of Korea

KoreanLiteratureNow.com

GRANTA

12 Addison Avenue, London W11 4QR | email: editorial@granta.com
To subscribe go to granta.com, or call 020 8955 7011 (free phone 0500 004 033)
in the United Kingdom, 845-267-3031 (toll-free 866-438-6150) in the United States

ISSUE 146: WINTER 2019

GUEST EDITORS	Devorah Baum, Josh Appignanesi
DEPUTY EDITOR	Rosalind Porter
POETRY EDITOR	Rachael Allen
DIGITAL DIRECTOR	Luke Neima
ASSISTANT EDITOR	Francisco Vilhena
SENIOR DESIGNER	Daniela Silva
EDITORIAL ASSISTANTS	Eleanor Chandler, Josie Mitchell
SUBSCRIPTIONS	David Robinson
MARKETING MANAGER	Simon Heafield
PUBLICITY	Pru Rowlandson
TO ADVERTISE CONTACT	Charlotte Burgess, charlotteburgess@granta.com
FINANCE	Mercedes Forest, Josephine Perez
SALES MANAGER	Katie Hayward
IT MANAGER	Mark Williams
PRODUCTION ASSOCIATE	Sarah Wasley
PROOFS	Katherine Fry, Jessica Kelly, Lesley Levene, Jess Porter, Louise Tucker
CONTRIBUTING EDITORS	Daniel Alarcón, Anne Carson, Mohsin Hamid, Isabel Hilton, Michael Hofmann, A.M. Homes, Janet Malcolm, Adam Nicolson, Edmund White
PUBLISHER AND EDITOR	Sigrid Rausing

The T.S. Eliot extract in '#TeamBaddiel Vs #TeamBabel' by David Baddiel is taken from
'The Love Song of J. Alfred Prufrock', which first appeared in *Prufrock and Other Observations*.
Reproduced by permission of Faber & Faber. © T.S. ELIOT / ESTATE OF T.S. ELIOT

LOST CHILDREN ARCHIVE

A novel

VALERIA LUISELLI

Author of TELL ME HOW IT ENDS

"Impossibly smart, full of beauty, heart and insight . . . Everyone should read this book." **—TOMMY ORANGE**

kaddish.com

a novel

nathan englander

The Pulitzer finalist delivers his best work yet, a novel about a son's failure to say Kaddish for his father.

THE SOURCE OF SELF-REGARD

Selected Essays, Speeches, and Meditations

TONI MORRISON

Winner of the Nobel Prize in Literature

A rich gathering of her essays, speeches, and meditations on society, culture, and art, spanning four decades.

treat yourself to a
▶▶ GOOD BOOK

BLACK IS THE BODY

STORIES FROM MY GRANDMOTHER'S TIME, MY MOTHER'S TIME, AND MINE

EMILY BERNARD

An extraordinary, exquisitely written memoir that explores race in a fearless, penetrating, and true way.

AUTUMN LIGHT

SEASON of FIRE and FAREWELLS

PICO IYER

Author of THE ART OF STILLNESS

From one of our most astute observers of human nature, a moving meditation on impermanence, mortality, and grief.

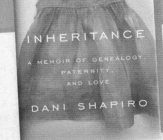

INHERITANCE

A MEMOIR OF GENEALOGY, PATERNITY, AND LOVE

DANI SHAPIRO

A new memoir from the beloved author of *Hourglass* about identity, paternity, and family secrets.

PRAIRIE SCHOONER

book prize series

PRIZES

$3,000 and publication through the University of Nebraska Press for one book of short fiction and one book of poetry.

ELIGIBILITY

The Prairie Schooner Book Prize Series welcomes manuscripts from all writers, including non-US citizens writing in English and those who have previously published volumes of short fiction and poetry. No past or present paid employee of *Prairie Schooner* or the University of Nebraska Press or current faculty or students at the University of Nebraska will be eligible for the prizes.

JUDGING

Semifinalists will be chosen by members of the Prairie Schooner Book Prize Series National Advisory Board. Final manuscripts will be chosen by the Editor-in-Chief, **Kwame Dawes**.

HOW TO SEND

We accept digital and hard-copy submissions.

WHEN TO SEND

Submissions will be accepted between **January 15** and **March 15, 2019**.

For submission guidelines or to submit online, visit prairieschooner.unl.edu.

AMERICAN RADIANCE

LUISA MURADYAN

PRAIRIE SCHOONER BOOK PRIZE IN POETRY

Better Times

SHORT STORIES

SARA BATKIE

Prairie Schooner Book Prize in Fiction

SOUTHBANK CENTRE

Hear acclaimed authors discuss their latest novels.

Marlon James:
Black Leopard, Red Wolf
Mon 25 Feb

Valeria Luiselli:
Lost Children Archive
Tue 19 Mar

Angie Thomas:
On the Come Up
Tue 12 Mar

Max Porter:
Lanny
Thu 28 Feb

LOTTERY FUNDED

Supported using public funding by
ARTS COUNCIL ENGLAND

Containing some previously unpublished short stories *The Cause of Humanity* brings together for the first time some 86 uncollected short fictions

RUDYARD KIPLING

THE CAUSE OF HUMANITY AND OTHER STORIES

Uncollected Prose Fictions

Edited by **Thomas C. Pinney,**
Pomona College, California

"These previously uncollected prose fictions bring us as close as we are ever likely to get to the working methods of 'the infant monster of a Kipling', as Henry James called him, and in Professor Pinney they have found their ideal editor."

Dr Phillip Mallett,
University of St Andrews

ISBN 9781108476423 | £19.99 / $24.95

Harvard

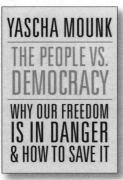

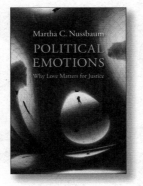

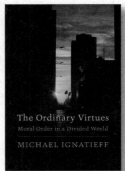

The People vs. Democracy

Why Our Freedom is in Danger and How to Save it

Yascha Mounk

"Provides a clear, concise, persuasive, and insightful account of the conditions that made liberal democracy work— and how the breakdown in those conditions is the source of the current crisis of democracy around the world."

—*The Guardian*

Political Emotions

Why Love Matters for Justice

Martha C. Nussbaum

Winner of the 2018 Berggruen Prize for Philosophy and Culture

"It is one of the virtues of Nussbaum's book that she neither shrinks from sentimentality, nor fears being judged philosophically unsophisticated."

—*New York Times*

Belknap Press | Paperback

The Ordinary Virtues

Moral Order in a Divided World

Michael Ignatieff

"Ignatieff combines powerful moral arguments with superb storytelling ... What is perhaps most interesting about *The Ordinary Virtues* is the contrast between the hopes and aspirations of the 1990s and the realities of the early 21st century."

—*New Statesman*

HARVARD UNIVERSITY PRESS | www.hup.harvard.edu

English National Ballet

SHE
PERSISTED

WORKS BY
PINA BAUSCH
ANNABELLE LOPEZ OCHOA
AND A NEW CREATION BY
STINA QUAGEBEUR
INSPIRED BY *A DOLL'S HOUSE*

4 – 13 APRIL 2019
ballet.org.uk/shepersisted

SADL
ERSW
ELLS

Sadler's Wells Theatre
sadlerswells.com
0207 863 8000

ARTS COUNCIL
ENGLAND

NatWest
Principal Partner of
English National Ballet

Dancer: Crystal Costa. Photo © Jason Bell. Art Direction and Design: Charlotte Wilkinson Studio

CONTENTS

Introduction

What should we do with our feelings? They've become so intemperate lately. A Pandora's box of furies has opened up and no one knows how to put them back. In such a climate, you'd be forgiven for thinking badly of feelings. When swept up in a feeling, we won't listen and we won't be told. We reject expert opinions because they're 'unfeeling' and elitist, preferring to derive our convictions from our intuitions. And our intuitions may sometimes serve us well, but they can equally lead towards historical revisionism, fake news and alternative facts: the mad maladies of our age. So it's easy to see why some wish feelings evacuated from civil discourse. Too much attention to subjective states can destroy common sense, leaving us in a world so fiercely divided that people on opposing sides are not only unable to agree on a solution to a given problem, they're unable to agree on what our problems even are.

Yet, troubling though they may be, feelings also tell us something about power and its limitations. The fact that repressing feelings so often makes them return more aggressively, for instance, suggests that to feel at all is always to be in some sense out of control, or even possessed. Feelings summon those parts of ourselves that seem strange, dubious – foreign. As such, whenever we pronounce certain people too emotional to participate in politics, we should consider who historically has been labelled thus: ethnic minorities, for example, or women. So if being emotionally overwhelmed intimates that one's power to act has been curtailed in some way, our feelings could well be our bodies protesting by endeavouring to move us.

In this special issue we begin palpably, therefore, with the literal feeling of feeling. In a stunningly original account of how the sense of touch in China has been transformed as the country has itself transformed into a market economy, Poppy Sebag-Montefiore traces the intimate relation between our personal and political bodies to reveal how profoundly immersed our physical capacity for feeling is within history, geography and the political cultures we inhabit. Politics likewise coalesces in extreme bodily affects in Margie Orford's visceral rendering of how South Africa's histories of racial and sexual oppression are materially rooted – in the flesh. Disclosing the 'shame' that's been her lifelong companion, Orford contrasts that feeling's embodiment to its verbalisation by white South Africans who wield the word like a nervous tic to refer to almost anything other than the shameful reality itself.

Words appear similarly unhinged in David Baddiel's deep dive into the vortex of the head-spinning feedback loops of online reactivity, here around anti-Semitism. While participants of online conversations get no closer to understanding one another, they do get readily triggered into evermore solipsistic denials and enragements. Burrowing down with him into just one of these rabbit holes, you laugh because otherwise you'd cry. Whereas in William Davies's trenchant analysis of the role sense of humour plays in the politics of populism, we note how joking, especially online, can equally function as a signalling system for groups seeking to conserve their privileges by shutting out those earnestly seeking representation.

A sense of exclusion may lie behind a great deal of the hysteria coursing through our times. But for all its shriller expressions, mightn't this sense of exclusion admit of another more muted feeling? In Hisham Matar's extraordinary meditation on the threads connecting two great writers in exile, Edward Said and Joseph Conrad, he suggests that these towering authorities in English literature were both afflicted by a sense of their own untranslatability: a feeling of perpetual estrangement and non-belonging, sustained even when one becomes a master of the very language that yet leaves one feeling forever a guest, never altogether at home. So who feels at home? In Olga Tokarczuk's enigmatic story 'Borderland', translated from the Polish by Jennifer Croft, we enter a zone whose rites and laws are intended to shore up national identities through the exclusion or appropriation of outsiders. It's because they're so permeable that borderlands can arouse such fanatical self-certainty, though here it seems that even the greatest proselytisers find themselves prone to estrangement.

While Tokarczuk offers a boldly imagined vision of life at the edges, in Yvonne Adhiambo Owuor's 'Distilling Existence' we meet the reality: a devastating portrait of life lived *in extremis* in Kenya's Mathare Valley – 'what Middle-earth would have become if Lord Sauron had won' – seen too in Bernd Hartung's accompanying photographs. And yet as Fabián Martínez Siccardi's moving memoir of his Patagonian childhood, 'Feeling Southern', reminds us, zones of exclusion aren't always that visible: one's own story of oppression may itself be an overwriting of other, untranslated stories.

We first feel changes in the weather at our extremities, but the sensations that begin at our nerve endings will soon be felt by the rest of our body. The same would seem true of the political body whose extremes are increasingly affecting the mainstream. Zones of exclusion may be less exclusive than supposed. Peter Pomerantsev's 'Normalnost' explores how what once appeared the exclusive culture of post-Soviet Russia – the denial and distortion of facts and their replacement by fantasy and feelings – turns out to have been at the vanguard of a politics now mirrored by the West – a West whose ability to sustain its own ideological mythos without the bolstering opposition of its Cold War foe has simultaneously collapsed.

Alongside the changing political weather are changes in the actual weather: two climates that can no longer be logically separated. In Diana Matar's bewitching photoessay, 'American Orchard', she disports a take on the pastoral vision that, as Max Houghton's introduction recalls, has long since captivated American writers, artists and dreamers. Through Matar's lens, however, we see that the remaining traces of that idyll are at risk of vanishing, the meteorological and political weathers together creating a climate that is destroying that land, and with it those dreams, taking us into a future of desertification both literal and felt. So how did we get here? If 'American Orchard' depicts the consequences of a culture so derelict in its duty that it has ceased to care for the people and places over which it's charged, in Josh Cohen's 'Lazy Boy' we consider that Trump's appeal may consist precisely in his showy disregard of all feeling for others – I REALLY DON'T CARE. DO U? Such dissoluteness, when mirrored in the heart of the anguished liberal, then turns to creeping apathy: a crushing sense that resistance is futile.

Among the myriad insights to be gleaned from our extended interview with Adam Phillips, there's the speculation that when a fascistic wave feels so energetic as to seem invincible, that must be how it works: by making a persuasive show of its own libidinousness. Resistance, then, is critically a challenge for the imagination. Now is the time to imagine new ways of getting together and being political. To do so we must relinquish some of our lazy-boy presuppositions about who it is we are by admitting more of our own ambivalence and complexity, as indeed our feelings themselves invite. If we're feeling '*Beside ourselves*', as Alissa Quart writes in 'In Ballard', we're 'upset but also / *outside our "I"* '. And we sense this too in Anouchka Grose's hilariously honest account of how hatred and murderous rivalry for her sibling animated her transformation into a goody-two-shoes Social Justice Warrior. Such subtle attention to the unsentimental within sentiments can likewise be discerned in Benjamin Markovits's fictional rendering of the micropolitics underpinning relationships both romantic and familial. One could deem cynical the recognition of how a kind of unwilled calculus may be inscribing the logic of power and negotiation into even our most intimate feelings, but it's by means of such self-reckonings that we can engage with not only who we are, but who we might come to be as well. We could, for instance, discover that we're *less* cynical than supposed. Thus, as Joff Winterhart graphically portrays, while ready-made social projections can provoke instant fear, fury and outrage, such certainties can just as easily give way to wordless confusion when our fantasies are tested by the reality of actually meeting those about whom we've only fantasised – in one of the ever-dwindling public places where such encounters remain possible.

Imagining new forms of sociability is what teenagers have always done best, usually by ignoring the warnings of elders to cross borders and meet different people in alternative spaces – and particularly nightclubs, to soundtracks attesting that if this *is* an experiment in politics then it's one full of feeling. Such feelings have lingered for Chloe Aridjis whose Mexican adolescence she beautifully evokes in an essay recalling one particular night that, though already infused with the baroque lawlessness that has gone on to engulf her country, also contains the passionate hopefulness of young people coming together to protest a world of walls and barriers out of a desire that dwarfs even fear – the desire to meet each other, dance with each other, touch each other. The inspiration for making changes both personal and political is, for Hanif Kureishi too, related to the recovery of the powerful feelings aroused by music. Sharing his own past efforts to overcome a state of depression associated with the isolating effects of a political and economic system built on competition, he credits music, specifically musical improvisation, as both the resistance and the cure.

Sensitive creatures that we are, we're wont to react to each other, mirror each other and catch each other's feelings like a contagion. But we could experiment more with our responses. In this special issue, facing down the furies means, in the first place, reimagining them. Or surprising them. As Nick Laird has it in 'The Politics of Feeling':

> If someone despises
> you, the work is still to do nothing despicable, to be oppositional but
> patient and cheerful as your own mother – if she wasn't pretending –

For however fanatically certain or dizzyingly uncertain they may make us, our feelings needn't only be a problem for politics – they can equally be a resource, and maybe even a solution. ∎

Devorah Baum
Josh Appignanesi

**SCHOOL OF
ADVANCED STUDY
UNIVERSITY
OF LONDON**

What's on

Talks, seminars, exhibitions, and summer schools highlighting the latest research across the humanities

**Exhibition – Staging Magic:
The Story Behind The Illusion**
21 January – 15 June | Senate House Library

**Repatriation, Peacebuilding and
State-building in Burma/Myanmar**
20 February | Refugee Law Initiative

**Warburg on Luther and Dürer:
Media Wars and the Freedom to Think**
20–21 February | The Warburg Institute

**Britain and the British in Novels and
Memoirs by Refugees from Nazism**
27 February | Institute of Modern Languages
Research

Oral History Spring School
11–13 April | Institute of Historical Research

**The Brontës: Nineteenth Century Study
Week**
20–24 May | Institute of English Studies

London Rare Books School
17–21 June, 24–28 June, 1–5 July | Institute of
English Studies

T. S. Eliot International Summer School
6–14 July | Institute of English Studies

Senate House | Malet Street | London WC1E 7HU

sas.ac.uk/Granta

National People's Congress of the People's Republic of China, Great Hall of the People, Beijing, China, 2011
Courtesy of the author

TOUCH

Poppy Sebag-Montefiore

Between 1999 and 2007, I lived in China on and off. I worked as a journalist at the BBC bureau in Beijing for some of that time. I wasn't there for the job; I was there, and the job helped me stay longer. The first story I covered was the launch of China's first manned spacecraft. We broadcast astronaut Yang Liwei's message that crackled and fizzed back to Earth: 'All's well,' he said, as he orbited our planet alone. The good lines may have already been taken, but it was 2003 and China was transforming from a socialist into a market economy, from a developing country into a global superpower. Our news cycle turned between the thrills and promises of development and the fallout from such rapid modernisation: pollution; unequal rights for migrant workers in the cities; people beaten when they petitioned the state for compensation over land illegally confiscated and sold off by local officials. It was an epic story, but the lows were distressing. By the end of my time there, I'd interviewed so many people who were in such a state of fear that I began to catch it, and after being detained a couple of times, I was paranoid. I'd check behind my curtains when I got home.

Before reaching that point, I was having my own passionate relationship with China. Just to be awake was to absorb – the language, ways to live – like a baby learns the world. Every day

I was touched. Many times, by friends, by strangers, by the lady who swept the street by the courtyard where I lived. By the water sellers, the restaurateurs, by old men playing chess, by people I didn't know. Most I would never meet again. I was handled, pushed, pulled, leaned upon, stroked, my hand was held. And it was through these small, intimate, gestural moments that I began to get a hold on how macro changes imprinted themselves onto people's relationships and inner lives.

Touch had its own language, and the rules were the opposite of the ones I knew at home. Beijing's streets were scenes of countless gestures of touch. If people bumped or rubbed arms as they passed in the street there was no need for an apology, not even a flinch. Strangers would lean their whole body weight against one another in a queue. Everyone seemed to have a certain kind of access to anyone else's body. Shoppers and stallholders would hold on to each other's arms as they negotiated with one another. People would pack in together around a neighbourhood card game. In the evening, women would hold each other in ballroom embraces as groups waltzed on street corners.

Touch in public, among strangers, had a whole range of tones that were neither sexual nor violent. But it wasn't neutral either. At times, yes, you'd be leaned on indiscriminately because of lack of space, or to help take some weight off someone's feet. Yet other times you'd choose people you wanted to cling on to, or you'd be chosen. You'd get a sense of someone while haggling over the price of their garlic bulbs and you'd just grab on to each other's forearms as you spoke or before you went on your way. Touch was a precise tool for communication, to express your appreciation for someone's way of being, the brightness in their eyes as they smiled, their straightforwardness in a negotiation, a kindness they'd shown.

I felt buoyed and buffeted by this touch. I sometimes felt like I was bouncing or bounding from one person to the next like a pinball, pushed and levered around the city from arm to arm. If the state was like an overly strict patriarch, then the nation, society or the people on the streets were the becalming matriarch. This way of handling each other felt like a gentle, restorative cradle at times. At other times all the hands on you could be another kind of oppressive smothering. But usually touch was like a lubricant that eased the day-to-day goings-on and interactions in the city, and made people feel at home.

I wanted to document this unselfconscious touch. To keep hold of it. I could tell that this ease between the bodies of strangers might not survive rapid urbanisation. This touch was so visual, so visible. I freed my camera from the head-and-shoulders interview shot and took it out to the streets.

A few weeks ago I found a tape of video footage that I'd labelled TOUCH I and shot in Beijing sometime between 2005 and 2006. Low sunshine glows pink-gold on people's faces. An open-fronted clothes shop blasts a techno beat out onto a giant pedestrian street near the centre of the city. There's a long queue of customers waiting to go inside. My camera is on the closeness between the people standing in this line.

I focus on two men in particular. One is older, perhaps in his sixties. He's wearing an army-style jacket and grey woolly hat. In front of him is a man probably in his forties; he's wearing a mauve jacket, spattered with tiny flecks of yellow paint. These two men are leaning against one another. Neither notices particularly. The man in khaki now bashes into the man in mauve several times as he turns to look at how the queue has grown behind him.

They get closer to the front of the queue. I move with them and the music booms louder, a heart pumping, like a soundtrack from the inside of the body amplified onto the street. The man in mauve starts to bop. B-boom, B-boom goes the music, left-to-right goes the man in mauve. Each time he steps to the beat – he's dancing, he's keeping warm; he's standing sideways in the queue – his right arm bumps into the man in khaki's belly, repeatedly, rhythmically, again and again. The man in khaki doesn't flinch, he's welcoming it as much as he doesn't acknowledge it at all. He's comfortable. Watching, it now seems to me that it's impossible that these two men don't know each other, in fact they must really be quite close: friends, workmates, family even. Most likely they are father and son. Just as I'm about to fast-forward the tape to skip to the next vignette – the two men get larger – I'm approaching them with my camera – their faces fill the frame, and I hear myself ask: 'Where are you from?'

'Hebei,' says the man in mauve.

'Hubei,' says the man in khaki.

Hebei means north of the river, and Hubei means north of the lake. These are provinces about six hundred miles apart.

'How do you know each other?' I ask.

Their voices overlap:

'We don't know each other,' says the man in khaki.

'We don't,' says the man in mauve.

Up a dingy staircase, above the Lucky House Mini Market on Shaftesbury Avenue in London, there is a traditional Chinese medicine clinic. Dr Fan is in his sixties, he left China about thirty years ago and tells me, when I'm back in London, that this touch I'm describing is a rural way of being together: the touch of peasants. I've struggled to find people in Beijing to think about this touch with because it's so obvious to them they can hardly see it. But Dr Fan tells me, as he pummels the sole of my foot with his knuckles, that intellectuals and the ruling classes have always kept a respectful distance from each other, have always been more self-contained. During the period I lived in China – that time of mass migration and urbanisation – Beijing was a city of villages piled on top of and around each other. Dr Fan said it was true that under Mao everybody did come physically closer to one another. Especially within the sexes, men with men, women with women. Mao sent people from the cities, the 'educated youth', down to the countryside to learn from the peasants. Maybe all hands that know each other's work, know each other.

Touch is an important part of China's traditional medical practice. Doctors feel their patients' wrists for six different pulse lines to make a diagnosis. Massage is used for preventative health and as a cure. Pressure points on the skin relate to specific internal organs and touching them releases toxins and reduces inflammation. Once I had stomach cramps on an eleven-hour boat journey from Shanghai to an island in the East China Sea. A lady on the next bunk, whom I'd never met before, took my hand and found the acupressure point that corresponds to the uterus and began to press it for me. Gradually the pain dulled away.

Yang sheng 养生 means 'nourishing life'. It's an active pursuit of health through the medical arts – massage, exercise, food. Think wellness – if wellness was less about gym memberships and spirulina shots, and more about a set of ancient ideas for how to cultivate your body's energy to improve your health and sense of well-being. It's combined with a fear for your life because of the lack of health-care welfare, and the necessity not to be too much of a financial burden on your one child in your old age. When I lived in Beijing, *yang sheng* wasn't so commercially inflected among the older, urban generation. It was a bodily intellect, a tuning-in to the needs of the body: at times carefully considered, at times instinctive and ingrained. It's what brought people together for ballroom dancing in the evening, and exercising in the park together in the morning.

In many ways this kind of coming together on the streets to attend to the needs of the body felt like a form of resistance to the state, a complicity among people. Although this kind of solidarity may in some ways have been made possible and encouraged by socialism, taken into people's own hands, it felt like a form of personal autonomy. In a place heavy with censorship, where published and broadcasted words can't necessarily be trusted, this was a public sphere of the senses, a way to feel one another out. Being together like this was also a way to derive pleasure and vitality from each other, without asking or taking anything from anybody. Instead, it's a reciprocity, an openness, an attention to a personal need.

I remember the first time my boundaries dissolved to accept the confident, unselfconscious touch of a stranger. I was standing in the audience at a Tibetan Buddhist festival at Labrang monastery in the yellow-grey mountains of China's north-western Gansu province, and a man, probably in his eighties, came up behind me and wrapped his arms around my waist. I turned round affronted at first, then bemused. He didn't even look at me but craned his neck over my shoulder towards the show. I saw that his grip around me meant nothing to him but to be able to stand and see without toppling over. He was using my body as if it was part of his. Once I'd checked out whether there might be anything sordid going on, and realised there wasn't, I remember I couldn't help but feel delighted by having this man hang on to me. I was a bit ecstatic about it. An elderly man could use my body to help him stand and see. And it was lovely. I made my friend take a photo of us from behind and from the front. My face is beaming. It could be compared to the invigoration you get from standing in front of a painting that you love. But this touch is more powerful: it can happen at any time, often when least expected, and it's personal – the medium is another living being. It gives you something of Freud's 'oceanic feeling' – when the baby doesn't know the contours of its own body, before the ego, when it's one with everything else.

I sometimes wonder if there's a shadow side to this touch. If the accessibility of everyone's bodies can be mistaken by those with power as a right to them. Could it be partly why local officials can be quick to hire thugs to beat petitioners as a way to deter them from complaining to the 'higher-ups'? Does the easiness and informality between people encourage corruptibility among officials, leaning on other leaders to sway them?

At that time, touch in China between friends and peers of the opposite sex, of all ages, was restrained, almost taboo. If I tried to hug or kiss my male friends as we parted, they'd be embarrassed and squirm away. But within the sexes, friends and colleagues, especially younger ones, would lounge all over each other. Women would often walk with their arms linked. Guys would walk with their arms across each other's shoulders. Men on construction sites would sit on one another's laps.

Platonic touch had its own erotics. It imbued you with a direct hit of the love, energy and camaraderie that you get from friendship. Perhaps touch between friends was partly set free, and came to the fore, because sexual touch was prohibited by the Communist Party under Mao. Sex was confined to marriage, and even then wasn't supposed to distract from the love for the revolution.

Among the older generation, who grew up under these ideas, couples are fairly formal with each other physically in public. When I spoke to older people sitting by Beijing's Back Lake about the kinds of touch they shared with their spouses in their homes they were matter-of-fact. Sex was sex, one lady told me, it never involved kissing. An elderly man told me of his relationship with his wife: 'I rub her back, she rubs mine.'

In a bestselling Chinese short story of the late 1990s, 'I Love Dollars' by Zhu Wen, the narrator, also a writer called Zhu Wen, decides the best thing he could do for his father, who is visiting him in the big city, would be to help him get laid. Zhu Wen muses: 'Thinking about it, I realised Father was a person with quite a libido, just that he was born a bit before his time. In his day, libido wasn't called libido, it was called idealism.'

The sense I had was that the mainstay of physical, intimate life for the older generation in Beijing was felt on the streets.

After I moved back to London, I would return to Beijing for a couple of weeks each year. In 2008, I went back during the summer Olympics. I'd been there in 2001, the night Beijing won the bid. A spontaneous street party sprang up. People abandoned their cars in the middle of the road. They were euphoric. They'd been accepted by the world. Now, seven years later, Beijingers seemed to be putting up with the Games with muted acquiescence. Much of the Beijing of 2001 had been bulldozed. A modern city had replaced it. And in elaborate preparations for the Olympics, Beijing had been cleaned up. In the immediate run-up to the Games, anybody vaguely questionable had been removed. The city's Spiritual Civilisation Committee had banned certain behaviours: spitting, disorderly queueing, the indiscretions of the body. Volunteer elders were given official red armbands and a phone number to ring if there was trouble. They'd sit on stools on the pavement with a good view of their patch. The city was straitjacketed. I didn't go to the Games, but I did get out my camera to record the ways that people would touch one another. It was hard to find instances of the old touch. Now along the boulevards my viewfinder filled with the clasped hands and interlinked arms of young couples and lovers.

Touch was relocating from the street to the home, from public to private life. It was becoming privatised and sexualised. The younger generation now performed a newly liberated sexuality on the streets. They offered each other different kinds of tenderness, attention and care, sometimes with gestures that resembled the globalised, romantic Hollywood way. In 'I Love Dollars', the father reads some of Zhu Wen's writing and complains that it's all about sex: 'A writer ought to offer people something positive, something to look up to, ideals, aspirations, democracy, freedom, stuff like that.' Zhu Wen responds: 'Dad, I'm telling you, all that stuff, it's all there in sex.' Where for his father's generation there was a forced sublimation of sexuality into idealism, for Zhu Wen the new and potentially difficult ideals are sublimated into sex.

The city had sped up. People couldn't shuffle past each other in the same old ways. The new middle class had places to be. Supermarkets were taking over from street markets, where there's no bartering, or need for much communication at all, in fact customers were often on the phone to someone else. Migrant workers now lived in the city in large numbers but were usually sequestered away. They slept in dorms on their construction sites and didn't have the same rights as urban residents. Where previously I'd barely been able to distinguish between rural migrants and urbanites, now the differences between people who'd arrived from the countryside and the city residents were striking, visible in fashions, faces, how beleaguered they were. Now urbanites kept their distance. There was a growing fear of migrants, that they might want what urbanites had. People began to talk about migrant workers as dirty, dangerous, people to stay clear of. They were untouchable.

Somehow the bland, fatigued Soviet-style rooms – a portrait of a leader on a white chalky wall, paint that brushed off on your clothes – had been a background for people to have a certain social command over their bodies. But the architecture, infrastructure and public spaces of late capitalism – sparkling malls, privately owned and patrolled, steel towers, underground trains – were all spaces that encouraged more public formality, better behaviour, more self-consciousness, wider gaps between strangers.

I went for reflexology in a clinic I used to go to in Beijing, an offshoot of a large traditional Chinese medicine hospital, and for the first time the masseur wore plastic, scratchy gloves. It's for hygiene purposes, he told me, there are so many people in the city now.

Suddenly massage and acupuncture weren't the only therapies. Psychotherapy talk shows were appearing on television. Rather than healing through touch, people were now interested in sitting in a room with a therapist with strict boundaries against physical contact. As this was a brand-new profession, in the absence of a psychotherapist whose experience people could trust – some who felt they needed to understand more about their inner lives began to train to be therapists and analysts. Over the next few years, 400,000 psychological counsellors would qualify in China's main cities.

When I moved back to London in 2007 – I missed that public sense of touch. I continued to bump into people on the street. Friends walking beside me would be embarrassed and apologise on my behalf as the people I'd pushed into would be annoyed and I wouldn't notice. But soon I readapted to London streets and grew as irritable about the clamour and crush of strangers as the next person. And then I did what everyone with a sensory project did at the beginning of the twenty-first century. I went to talk to a neuroscientist.

Francis McGlone's work centres around nerve receptors in our skin called C-tactile afferents. They've only been recently discovered in humans. They lie within our hairy skin, and are particularly concentrated in our back, trunk, scalp, face and forearms. They respond to slow and light stroking. None are found in the genitals. When stimulated, through stroking, the C-tactile afferents produce pleasure. It's not a sexual pleasure, but the kind of feeling brought about by the touch between a mother and baby. Neuroscientists call this 'social touch'.

These nerve fibres are ancient, they existed early in the life of the species, long before language, and even before the receptors that tell us to move our hand away from pain. This is a sign that they're vital for the protection of life and health. In early times we needed people nearby throughout our lives to help us groom and to clear us of parasites. The reward for sticking together was pleasure.

McGlone is interested in moments when modernity overrides what he sees as evolutionary processes. He believes that we need C-tactile stimulation from birth for the social brain to develop. When I told him about what I noticed in Beijing, he said that it might be that poorer people gather together more than richer people because they rely on each other more for survival. He describes his world of science where everybody tinkers away alone to get their work done. Social distance, he says, has its uses – it allows the brain to get on with other things.

But Francis McGlone does bring people together. He runs the Somatosensory & Affective Neuroscience Group at Liverpool John Moores University for scientists and psychologists working on the relationships between C-tactile afferents and our emotional lives. He invited me to present my anecdotal observations from Beijing to the group. Jayne Morton, a massage therapist and occupational therapist for the Cheshire police force, said that my descriptions reminded her of where she grew up in the Wirral in the 1970s. Her parents ran the social club. Men would be in one room lounging on one another, and women in another room, arms linked, sitting squashed together. The men had finished National Service and needed a closeness with people who'd gone through similar things. The women, used to the men being away, spent time with friends who were also home with their children.

When the church closed down in the early 1980s, so did the school and the club. Everyone dispersed. People spent the evenings with their families. Then the Wirral became more diverse and multicultural, but without a big hub for meeting. In the 1980s, Jayne said that organising events for parents at the school had become more difficult because of higher divorce rates – step-parents and parents often wouldn't be in a room together.

This made me wonder if, when communities break apart, the relationship between the couple becomes overdetermined. Does the pressure for all the different kinds of erotics that I found on the streets of Beijing fall on just one other person? In the group, perhaps we are able to replay some of the intimacy of our infancy, the gentle touch of our mothers, that kind of care we must still long for. It makes us feel good, part of the world around us and with people we trust – even if that trust is calculated in an instant.

Francis and I shake hands as we part. We didn't touch when we met or when we said goodbye after dinner the night before. We'd spoken for hours, straight-faced, professional. But as he guided me down the purpose-built university corridor he did pat me on the back of the shoulder blade. The pat gave me the impression that he thought I was all right. It was nice.

The shock of the UK's Brexit referendum result when it happened caused intellectuals and cosmopolitans to reflect on how 'out of touch' they are. Academics called themselves out of touch, a presenter admitted that the BBC was out of touch. London was declared way out of touch. And now words are barely trusted. We're post-touch, post-truth. How will society communicate now?

Could it be that anxieties and fears are stoked when people are so far out of reach from each other – not only from establishment elites, but from the rest of the majority of the population too. Church halls, community centres have been closing down; work places with zero-hour contracts offer limited opportunities for socialising. There are few spaces where people can jostle together, to share and make the world with our hands.

Perhaps this atomisation means that some people feel threatened by the idea that immigrant groups seem, at least, to have something that the majority population don't have: functioning 'communities'. New migrants often do create expat networks for work, spaces to gather for faith, to eat, to speak native languages, live close to each other. They need each other to survive. The thing about touch is that it's visual, visible. And if there isn't enough integration then people who already feel isolated will feel excluded from the perceived closeness of immigrant communities, and then too from those bonds that enable us to come together and help one another thrive.

The most acute moments of life – birth and mourning – require us to live at increasing distance from those we are closest to. The distances and proximities at which we live from our loved ones, and everybody else, are also modulated by macro forces: economy, ideology, identity. The metropolis imprints itself onto the intimate details of our lives. Wherever that leaves us, my experiment (sample size: one) says – we aren't stuck like this. It takes just a few months in a different world of ideas and our bodies respond, adapt, and the space between us can change again. ■

BORDERLAND

Olga Tokarczuk

TRANSLATED FROM THE POLISH BY JENNIFER CROFT

I've set aside the morning hours for writing, when the sun rushes into my room in a great bright column that crashes over the edge of my table and pools luminous all across the wide stone floor. For that is when it's brightest, and it's when your head is clearest, too. I intend to write regularly, because regularity is the very thing that matters most. Father Basil taught us that. Repetition is the true engine of the world, he taught, and evil comes from chaos, which idles the engine and causes confusion. But my head hasn't grown accustomed to thinking just yet. Nor have my fingers yet taken to writing. Which is why I'll strive to capture what it is I have to say in the fewest words possible, especially since all these thoughts come to me just exactly as they please. I have no power over them – details awaken in my memory with no warning and form elaborate sentences at the absolute worst moments, when my hands are full of different dyes and I can't reach for anything to write with, or when it's my turn to play with the children, a thing I really like to do, in fact I prefer it to every other occupation.

But since accepting the need to write – this was after Father Basil's death, when it seemed all would crumble and be ruined – I've lost my old peace and know it to be lost forever. Not even sleep can grant me rest now – even my prayers are in tatters, fluttering with nothing underneath. I can no longer dive into them like one would into a snowdrift. Now the sentences can come at any moment, banging down the door of my poor brain, demanding an audience. Only after I've written them down do I get any peace, and then they're gone.

In his great wisdom Father Basil must have known that despite writing slowly and lacking in words I am still the most suited out of all of us to perform the task. While he was still conscious, in his muted and diminished voice and in front of everyone, he relieved me of my numerous responsibilities so that I might have time to write. He unburdened me of cooking, a hated obligation, and from cleaning. He had all the paper in the Borderland brought to me and all the available writing tools, though many of them had dried out and could no longer be used. I do have a whole box of colored pencils. When we discovered moisture in our stores after last winter, I went through the reams of mildewed paper, sheet by sheet. Not much of it was able to be saved. But that paper was old already anyway, from before the Repartition – it even tasted sort of different when I bit off a clean corner and investigated it by means of mastication. It tasted like Communion – the purest and holiest and most refined of all Communions.

I think of what I write here as just a first draft, so I replaced those unsalvageable reams with a box of strange long sheets of paper printed on one side, almost illegible with age, and now when I reach for one I don't even concern myself with which side's up and which is down, I just write. It must hail from a golden age, since it's been used on one face only, neglecting – a haughtiness today incomprehensible – the reverse, clean, unwritten white page that wallows in the sin of sloth and inactivity. How could those sides be granted silence while their reverses bear witness to events, agreements, plans and ideas . . . A variety of words are noted down upon those quadrangles. Then on the right side, figures. For example:

Starting balance 2,355.89
Debt limit 5,000.00

And underneath:

Total discretionary transactions 11,812.00

I don't know what it all means.

And so I write, two hours every morning, warming my feet in that pool of light, having submerged myself in the dry and bracing air that flows over the river from the steppe. At times – but not often – my concentration is disturbed by cannon fire as our garrison aims over at the other side, mostly just in case, I think, since those on the other side have long ceased to bother us. On the table I have the treasured possessions Father Basil had entrusted to me: the scissors, the colored pencils, the pen I myself make ink for, the candles, as well as something I received from her, I mean Udina, before she disappeared. It's a beautiful and complicated thing, made of eleven slender sticks bound together at the bottom by a metal wire and connected by a thick white paper, now unfortunately sullied. But when you spread out the little sticks, the paper unfurls, and you can see across it these expressive designs in black ink, which must be the symbols of some exotic writing. I unfold and fold this object when I lose my train of thought – like now – and it helps. It is a handy and attractive object. It gives you pleasure to hold it in your hand. You don't really need to know what it was used for in order to feel that pleasure.

Like all of us, I wound up here thanks to Father Basil, although I couldn't say precisely how it happened. I was only a few years old, and all I can recall – as though through a fog – is the old woman who took care of me. Father Basil told me it was my grandmother, who died. He often told us how after the Dimming came great chaos and collapse. But before that happened, people had a tremendous capacity to move about and even speak with one another at a distance. Long ago, in the cellar, he demonstrated a device that, when a person wound its crank, could bring illumination to a fixed little bubble, but then that small machine quit working, and the transparent bulb broke.

At any rate, the war and chaos destroyed such things, or they were stolen by the savages, and then everything but everything was gone. Father Basil would sometimes sit with us and sketch a range of different things that apparently people used to own. Some of them were so strange that I thought – may he forgive me – they might be fictions. But then Father Basil stopped dispensing those lessons intended to remind us – and himself – of what that world used to be like. He would tell us every day that, living in the Borderland, we had the most sacred of duties: to defend our civilization against the barbarians, and that instead of yearning for the past, we ought to concentrate on what there is. And what there is is our Borderland, the Prut River that separates the civilized world from chaos, as well as what remains of the garrison, where every so often someone will sink some straggler in a rowboat trying to come across the river. Above all there is the Holy Virgin, Mother and Queen of the World. It is Her we unfurl in the face of Chaos every year. And so it shall continue, until the civilized world is once more reunited under Her guidance, and it all goes back to how it was before the Repartition.

In the beginning, I was a Kalfaktor, handling odd jobs – all initiates begin this way – alongside the other boys like me whom Father Basil had taken in, and we supplied the Borderland with firewood, which was already difficult to come by since migrants had cut down all the trees. We'd set out in little packs and head off south, and there, far from here, at the foot of the mountains, we would chop what we could, while the older boys floated the logs back down to the Borderland, on the current of the Prut. This project took all summer. Then, in winter, which is sad and oppressive here, Father Basil taught us to read and dye thread and embroider weave. As I found physical labor taxing, I would look forward to those winter nights when we would all be gathered around the fire, exercising minds and hands. And we would learn by heart all of Father Basil's prayers.

He once saw me carrying wood down to the stores and took pity on me. I don't know what I did to draw his favor, but he unburdened me of that hard work and assigned me to dyeing, and then to writing

– perhaps it wasn't anything I did. Father Basil always looked on everyone with great benevolence, squinting slightly, which is no doubt a sign of sympathy. He had me look after the fires in our ovens. I ran up and down the stairs in the mornings, digging out the ashes and scattering them around the fields, though the west wind threw gray clouds of ash directly into my face, so that I went about filthy, and was a laughing stock.

Back then the Borderland was more populated than it is today. There were still groups of people dragging up here from the west, and some would even make their way to us, although we'd never let them in, only offering our stables and our lawns. Father Basil didn't want them interfering with our minds. Those people would look at our high bank and at that other one across the river, wild and flat, incredulous, until finally they'd just turn around and go back to wherever they'd come from. On that side, too, there was a greater commotion back then. Foreigners could come up from the steppe, and when they did, they were like herds of dead-tired animals, and they would try to cross the river at any cost. But shots would fly at them from the garrison, and they would scatter in great haste. The ones from the west, our people, who spoke our language or at least something like it, would stand out on the high riverbank, and it was as if the sight of those flat, monotonous terrains on the other side brought them back to reality: this was the end, there was no point in going further – here was the seam of the world, long since torn asunder, never to be mended again. So they would stay with us for a while, and then they'd slouch away in disappointment. In the evenings they'd light fires and make a great big circle around the whole of our courtyard. Songs in many voices all together rose up to heaven, to the Holy Virgin and Child. Meals were served from great big pots atop the driest of the wood. Back then I thought the smell of pea soup was the most beautiful smell in the whole world.

I don't know if it's my memory that pictures those scenes as more together and pure and close. There was more of everything then – the sun, the light, the smells, the details, even objects. The linen we wove with was sturdier and smoother, the colors of the thread more vivid, the pencils less worn out and the paper brighter and more resistant to wear. The knives were sharper, and the doorknobs would spring their latches right where they were supposed to, the lids fit the pots better, and even some shoes still had fine strong laces, instead of floppy strings made out of linen hemp. I could go on. Something strange has happened to our world now – it's like it's broken, like it's lost its freshness. Like it's rotted.

But I can't deny – for this was taught to us on winter nights by Father Basil – that we can only see the world through our own senses, only through our own selves, and of course, I'm now twenty years older, and from a lost child I have grown into a man, a guardian of the Borderland – a member of this holy family, admittedly much smaller than before, but still a family; and I have changed so much I sometimes think I'm someone else entirely. So perhaps it would be best if I had no desire to understand the world, limiting myself instead to my own sensations.

But all the same I consider that Father Basil did make one mistake: he didn't require we take regular note of what he told us. Now I feel that certain teachings of his will fade into oblivion. Our steward Mateus the Second, whom a dying Father Basil designated as the one to carry on our winter studies, was broken by the void left after Father Basil's death, vanishing last spring, like several other of our brothers. Those who remained turned further inward, and now it's hard for us to be together in that good way we used to. Sometimes I see how many of Father Basil's tales I've forgotten, how his stories get mixed up in my head, how many important details I have lost, little asides he would make during the most ordinary of our daily tasks. For instance I no longer recall the names of the Lord's siblings. I only know that there were twelve of them, the same number as the books in our library.

W hen Father Basil died, which happened shortly before dawn, at the very start of January, at the nadir of that long, gloomy, difficult winter three years ago, we took his heart out from his body and placed it in a box, burying the rest in a pretty spot by the wall outside, so that he might have a good view of the west he had yearned for so long. However, the next evening three of the brothers, Marek the Fourth, Mateus the First and Marek the First, opened the box and cut right into the heart. They had in mind Father Basil's words: 'The Lord's cross is deep within my heart.' And indeed, in his heart, larger than the hearts of others – so said Mateus the First, who knew about such things – they found something akin to a small cross, made of something similar to bone. And our hearts soared, for we knew this to be evidence of Father Basil's holy soul. In the darkness, in the cold, in our isolation, we decided to investigate the entire buried body. And this then yielded a real miracle – in the gall bladder there were three round objects, which we recognized as emblems of the Trinity. Inside Father Basil we also found, made of his flesh, a crown of thorns, a whip and nails. We guard these relics closely now.

W ith Brother Mateus the Second's departure all our knowledge of the weather and the calendar vanished as well. This was a painful loss, and since it occurred we haven't really been able to calculate the spring and summer solstices. Instead we work by approximation based merely on what we see. The Great Night of the Rebirth is now celebrated by day, when the ice over the Prut has melted, and we celebrate the Birth once it's become so dark and cold that it is unbearable, and we are drowning in sadness and despair. But our most important holiday – Standard Day – is commemorated when the world is most open to sun and life, when the sky is clear and friendly, and the transparent wind carries our images far across the steppe.

In Father Basil's time, this was truly a great holiday, the whole garrison joining in, many divisions firing their weapons all day long in honor of the Standard. On the other side of the river, the savages took fright and were astonished. Father Basil would claim – and it almost seems to me that I saw it myself, as a child – that once the barbarian hordes fell upon the earth in holy terror the Standard shone bright, almost like a second sun. But for the last few years the savages have not come as gladly – they have scattered, evidently giving up, although of course now it would be so much simpler to take a boat across the river.

This is why I have to break off my writing from time to time, because, as I mentioned, the Standard Day preparations are already under way. I need to check on the dyeing of the threads, see if the linen is soft enough and whether its different shades all complement each other. The Standard became damaged last year, and this past horrible winter we repaired it, centimeter by centimeter. Certain sections had faded or decayed from the moisture and had to be replaced. We decided to make the most of this, and took the opportunity to enrich the Standard with innovative elements. Of course I also have to take care of our two children.

Our children are Peter and Paul, except that Paul's a girl. I was the one to name them; until that time they'd been known by their barbarian names, which were hard to pronounce or remember. I wanted them to have civilized names so that they could fit in our world a little easier. I called their mother Christopher, but she wouldn't go by it, and it sometimes even made her laugh. What she called herself was Udina, and whether we liked it or not, we were eventually forced to do the same. This was a shame because Christopher, as Father Basil told us, was a great man, and he carried the Lord across a river when He was still young and before He had learned to walk on water. I felt proud I had glimpsed the similarity between their stories, because Udina, too, had come to us in early spring, right before the Day of Rebirth, carrying children on her back and stomach, wrapped up in solid cloth. She had moved from one ice floe to the next and only by the skin of her nose escaped drowning in the freezing water as she made her way up to our bank. I still don't know why those in the garrison did not shoot at her. Perhaps they were drunk, or maybe they got scared upon seeing such a strange figure. By the time she made it to us, she was almost lifeless, as well as very dirty. The children were in the same state. A terrified clutch, blue from the cold and from hunger. Those in the garrison, on learning what had happened and that we had some foreigners with us, came quickly in order to reclaim them and take their lives, this being the law of the Borderland: no man from the other bank is ever permitted to stay. It was I who took full personal responsibility and managed to convince them that these three people, only barely still among the living, posed no threat whatsoever to the civilized world, and that as soon as their health was restored, we would get them on a boat and send them right back where they came from.

Udina was the only grown woman I had ever seen. So I can now say I am familiar with three distinct stages of feminine variation: my grandmother, whom I barely remember (above all the squeeze of her dry, bony hand), Udina as the mature form, at the height of her development, and now Paul, a tiny woman who has only just discovered how to walk but who does not differ in any particular way, aside of course from those bodily signs, most surprisingly, but praise be to God, they are concealed from the gaze of outsiders.

It's hard for me to write about Udina, because every memory of her fills my heart with suffering and sadness. We did the best we could for her here, gave her a warm room and food. Although it was difficult to communicate with her, since she spoke the language of the savages, we took her in like a brother among us. I taught her to dye and to light a fire with a little piece of glass. I taught her to embroider and to choose the threads. She had long, dark hair and beautiful hazel eyes. Her face was smooth. But Udina was a savage. She feared us. In the evenings, she would barricade herself inside the area I had allotted her along with her children, and by day, whenever one of the brothers just tried to go up to her, she would shriek in a terrible, piercing, shrill voice. I must say honestly that I was the only one she trusted, and we were even able to converse, gradually establishing the rules of our common language, which was made up of individual words and gestures. Sometimes she would laugh joyfully, when it would come to pass that we both knew some word. 'River,' I would say and indicate the Prut, and she would repeat in a manner sounding almost identical. I liked her laughter very much. It was important to me to make her laugh as much as possible, and then I, too, would be joyful. I gifted her a piece of good canvas, and she made herself a long shirt out of it, and delighted by our colorful threads she embroidered herself a vivid fish on it. She knew how to braid her hair into complex configurations, thereby introducing us to a new custom. Now almost all the brothers wear their hair in this way. She also taught us a special dish – you have to make a dough and then squeeze it up into very thin discs, and then envelop within them boiled potatoes with cheese. But when the ice started to melt, and the banks of the Prut got green again, she wandered out to the wall more and more often and she just stood there, stock-still, staring off into the steppe. She missed it, that was clear. Missed them, missed her fellow savages. Just as I missed Father Basil. I know how painful that is, how heavy it weighs on the heart, how deep it gets inside you. You want to do something, to rip that pain out of your body, and at the same time you know there's simply nothing to be done. At least she could run away somewhere. But how about us? Where could we go to get just one more glimpse of Father Basil?

I must have somehow sensed that she would run away, although I didn't even realize it myself yet. I wanted to prevent it and judged it would be best to show her the thing that was keeping all of us here, what inspired us to awake every morning in the same place and not give in to the madness of uprooting ourselves and ceaseless travels – what separated us from the savages. For us constancy and order are, after all, the pillars of civilization. The civilized world exists because of an attachment to a place, by being more like the tree than the birds. Such were Father Basil's teachings.

I took her down into our stores, and there, unveiling the windows, I showed her our Standard, spread out across the floor. Udina must have been impressed by its great size and grandeur, and the colors, even though here and there some of them had faded. She circled it, keeping her breath in. Yes, I had been right, for she fell under its sway, its charm, its power – as everyone did. Then this woman crouched and examined up close the appliqué patterns and the stitches, touched regretfully the intermittently jagged edges, the abrasions and discolorations. I must confess her absorption made me happy. It meant that from then on she would rather come down and labor over this great miracle instead of standing on the battlements and looking out, unable to see the steppe. And indeed – she requested from me a real metal needle. Then for several days she mended the edges of the Standard. It was good to watch her slim, skilled fingers as they brought order into chaos. From then on we would sit in the afternoons with the other brothers, too, and we would sew and stitch and embroider. In her rough language she would tell stories we only understood in part – about animals, marching, hunting, great deserted cities somewhere to the east, mountains at the ends of the earth, a great sea that might be to the south of us and into which flows our Prut. She talked about great boats powered by the wind, about iron roads. She showed us moving lights that travel through the evening sky and then, after she left, I started calling her a moving star in my mind. In the end she asked me to embroider in a corner of the Standard the same fish she had done on her shirt. And I agreed. Why shouldn't she be able to leave behind her trace? Why couldn't all of us do that? So each brother thought up some animal or other, outlined it and colored in the outline. There was a heron, a hedgehog, an owl, even a snake. I chose a dog, because it seemed to me a dog would be the closest to what I do: like a dog, I am a guardian. Udina assembled a beautiful fish, completely covered in colorful scales, with a great eye made out of the glass for starting fires, with a fluttering tail. She embroidered those scales one after the next, each out of a different piece of dyed linen, until the fish looked alive.

And then, once it had gotten completely warm outside, she disappeared. Father Basil said that the savages are the way they are because they get bored quickly. That is why they travel, why they don't belong to the civilized world, because they lack our values – attachment to a place and regularity.

At first I thought she would come back, and then it was me standing on the wall and watching the steppe, mistaking every moving dot for Udina. How did she get across the river? I don't know. Maybe she went the other way, to the west. Maybe the Standard awoke in her a longing for something different, something unknown, and maybe we have that longing, too, but we don't have the courage to admit it – that somewhere out there other places exist, other ways of standing guard. She left her children with us, which is the real reason I think she will come back. She was in fact quite attached to them.

The children are active and joyful creatures, we all fell in love with them. The brothers even prefer taking care of them, having that be their duty, than working the fields or dyeing and spinning the threads. Brother John the Second is teaching them our language, as well as other civilized capabilities – setting down the letters of the alphabet, reading, growing herbs in the gardens and making cheese. Mainly Peter, since Paul is still a very little girl. They also assist us in our labors of the Standard, for the holiday is rapidly approaching – the days are getting longer. It's because of them that we decided to add yet another figure to this year, and not an animal figure like before, but a human one. We determined that Father Basil would have praised this decision, for now the Standard will feature a true Trinity, and as we know, he had one in his heart.

That labor continues. My hands are dyed blue and red, and my fingers have been pricked to bleeding with the needle. We arise at dawn so as not to squander so much as a single ray of light. Our tomatoes are already ripening, so we are subsisting on them and cheese alone, because to light the ovens for bread would just be wasteful. Today Brother Lucas the Fourth reminded us as we were all working what Father Basil said about the Standard – that long, long ago, before the Dimming and the Repartition, the wonderful Standard was shown every evening. Back then it was completely white, pure as the Virgin, and yet in total darkness colorful moving images would appear on it. The Standard had a voice back then – the figures spoke, moved around, sang holy songs. Multitudes would visit it and in their reverence were witnesses to that miracle, every evening. Yet in a world that was falling apart and drowning in chaos, the Standard fell silent. That is why with our needles we must persuade it to hold forth once more, must nudge it, must suggest to it new images.

Oh, Udina, oh, Christopher, walking across the water, if you were here, you would see how we are performing our task with dedication and devotion: how we ready our babes, better overlaying their skin, how we clean the long trumpets done from angelica stems, while in the garrison they're readying the cannons, and their freshly polished barrels gleam, how the frenzied fuss goes on. A sturdy stand has already been erected on the battlements so we can hang the Standard facing east, and perhaps it will draw in once more our barbarians from the steppes, used as they are to the annual show. Do they know, do they assume, that we do this for them? For the Great Virgin to gaze upon them, that queen of the civilized world and of all the borderlands and steppes. And now she's even more powerful, because we've added a second little child beside her, so that now she shows herself in all her glory, holding one child close, the other by the hand.

And I even dare to harbor the slight hope that somewhere in the distance Udina will notice it and won't be able to resist turning around and coming back for us. ■

LAZY BOY

Josh Cohen

For two years my daydreams had been haunted by an image, more accurately a GIF, looping on the inside wall of my skull. It showed me slumped against the lip of the sofa in a rumpled shirt, hair matted, eyelids drooping, left temple propped on my curled fingers as I stared over the top edge of the TV screen. A ribbon of numbers and words, headline statistics of the June referendum or the November election or some monstrous hybrid of the two (FARAGE EDGING ELECTORAL COLLEGE), streaming indifferently across the screen's base. Around me, scattered alongside misshapen aluminium takeaway trays slick with palm oil: a smartphone low on battery, a laptop low on memory, unsheathed pens set on the open, soiled, blank pages of a notebook.

I couldn't stop recalling this scene, undeterred by the fact that it hadn't occurred; I'd slept through both those nights in some misguided gesture of defiance, as though disaster could be averted merely by refusing to pay attention to it. But what was the source of this moving tableau, if not my own memory?

In truth, I don't know. An appealing if preposterous answer came to me in a flash a few months ago, as my eye fell on an illustrated plate of Albrecht Dürer's celebrated 1514 engraving, *Melencolia I*. It appeared in a book I was reading at the time on *acedia*, the medieval term for the spiritual torpor induced by traumatic recognition of the vanity of worldly life.

There she was, Melancholy, the image of exhausted dejection I'd seen a thousand times, staring moodily into the middle distance, surrounded by the same array of discarded technical instruments, still fiddling distractedly with the pair of compasses pinned onto her skirts. It occurred to me that now, 504 years later, my unconscious, like some personal fake-news farm, had insinuated her into my bodily memory. For my daydreaming self, giddy with self-importance, it evidently wasn't enough to be a mere person; I had to be an allegory of my age.

In his seminal 1943 monograph on Dürer, the German-Jewish art historian Erwin Panofsky interprets *Melencolia I* as a departure from the traditional iconography of melancholy. More than the personification of a generalised 'gloomy inertia', his figure of Melancholy is an image of a metaphysical affliction. Her slumped despondency is the effect of intellectual exhaustion, not laziness: 'work has become meaningless to her,' writes Panofsky, 'her energy is paralyzed not by sleep but by thought.'

Melancholy is tired and emotional. The geometrical or practical instruments scattered round her – the hourglass, the hand plane, the scales, the saw – can take precise measure of Earthly time and space; but her weary gaze is directed beyond the visible world, not at it. She radiates defeat by the 'insurmountable barriers which separate her from a higher realm of thought'.

Panofsky quotes Dürer himself: 'The lie is in our understanding, and darkness is so firmly entrenched in our mind that even our groping will fail.'

Around me too, sources of limitless information and instruments of thought that do nothing but return me to the same exhausted refrains: 'I can't', 'It's all too much', 'No. No.' I am sleep-deprived and sluggish, drained of any capacity for surprise or hope, my deadly inner lethargy a form of impotent solidarity with the world itself. There is no symphony of histrionic lament, only a hiss of white noise.

Darkness is firmly entrenched in my mind and yours. The metaphysical lie of the sixteenth century has found its correlate in the political lie of the twenty-first. That, surely, is what my daydreamed avatar intuited in those early-morning reveries, casting his bleary eye over sickly old men wreathed with medals, rejoicing through tears that they had their country back, or over blowhard frat boys swollen with beer and triumph, whooping in menacing chorus.

Did my unconscious turn to Dürer's Melancholy in search of an analogue for my own feeling of humiliation? That, at any rate, is what I now see in her expression of bitter helplessness: the grim understanding that she understands nothing. She resents those impenetrable heavens, just as I do those jubilant, laughing crowds, infinitesimally close and infinitely distant, celebrating their victory over me and all the other pathetic losers.

It must be humiliating to master, as does Dürer's Melancholy, such a vast body of scientific knowledge only to find it redundant before what you most want to know. I'd thought I knew something too. Over how many acres of commentary had my eyes wandered – on the mounting hatred of the political establishment, on the cultural dispossession of white men, on Rust Belt hopelessness and the forgotten North of England and the losers of the neo-liberal consensus, on all other stock phrases that by now tripped so effortlessly off the tongue?

It wasn't as though the diagnosis of these real historical grievances was incorrect, any more than the metrics of compasses and hourglasses were incorrect. But Melancholy's predicament is that in their very correctness, they miss something more elusive and more essential.

For the liberal world order to buckle so precariously, something had to compound those wounds and hostilities. It was something I could see radiating from that gurning face, whose long-term residence in my daily consciousness I was now grimly anticipating: an anarchic pleasure in upending meaning, in the gleeful scission between words and things, actions and consequences. *I could stand in the middle of Fifth Avenue and shoot somebody and I wouldn't lose any voters, okay?*

It's one thing to attack civilisational norms, another to turn them into empty phrases. The former might induce anger and resistance; the latter induces humiliation, at least for me. I find it hard to invoke concepts like environmental responsibility or minority protections or human dignity these days without feeling the prickly heat of mockery on my neck. That I could allow myself to feel mocked, that my inner grip on the substance and meaning of these terms seems so fragile and vulnerable, only deepens the humiliation.

It occurred to me at a certain point that the Fifth Avenue comment wasn't so much about the lemming-like credulousness of the base, more about an air so thick with indifference and disgust as to render the act of shooting someone publicly, in cold blood, as arbitrary and meaningless as squirting them with a water pistol. In theory, holding to meaningful values should confer on me a talismanic righteousness before the nihilism that faces down all values with an indifferent smirk.

But it doesn't, which may be why I needed the daydream – to give voice and visibility to an obscure region in me that feels as defenceless as a sleepless baby, unable either to shut or to open his eyes, bereft of the slightest clue as to what to think or say or do.

In the established narrative of 2016, a loose network of global operators harnessed the political capital dormant in the unheard and unseen anxieties and vulnerabilities of the 'left behind'. We repeat this potted analysis with the same coiled enervation with which others rub worry beads, all the time suspecting it may not really be doing anything, that 'darkness is so firmly entrenched in our mind that even our groping will fail'.

We, metropolitan guardians of the waning liberal order, want to enlighten the new populist constituencies. Palms pressed exasperatedly to our foreheads, we asked our conveniently silent and invisible interlocutors of Dudley in the West Midlands, or Knox County, Tennessee, if they really thought these venal fuckers cared about them, or that they were going to put them back in control or make them great again.

No one, we kept reassuring ourselves, elects for chaos and insecurity and division. Now, called out twice on our smug, uncomprehending complacency, we clung by our fingertips to the conviction that we knew something they didn't, that if only they could just see . . .

We'd thought the rally crowds, baying gleefully at journalists and slugging protesters, were just the sad dupes of false promises. We were too fearful or unimaginative to suspect that it was the sheer emptiness of his words and gestures, the exhilarating licence he gave people to believe in anything and nothing, that really roused them. We'd assumed we were in the contest of substantive forces we used to call politics, where versions of justice run up against one another. Now we stare confusedly into the middle distance, bitter and exhausted, unable to navigate the weightless space beyond. 'The lie is in our understanding.'

An August 2017 cover of *Newsweek* shows him slumped in a leather recliner, one hand listlessly pointing a remote at the TV, one leg balancing a bag of Cheetos, a few of which sit unclaimed on his chest and protruding stomach, the spare hand holding a can of Diet Coke. He stares at us glassily. Across his shins, a headline punning on the recliner's famous name: LAZY BOY. The familiar bored, pouting petulance, the pastiche-Rockwell style, the trashy snacks and of course the recliner itself, all referencing the so-called 'base', forging a not-very-subliminal link between white working-class rage and the posture of slobbish entitlement.

The visual allusion to Al Bundy, hero of the 1980s sitcom *Married . . . with Children*, supposed forebear of this slobbish white rage, further confirms the smug class prejudice, as though the real objects of fear and scandal were the cheeseburgers, the diet drinks, the tacky furniture, the laziness, as though all that's really wanting is a good dose of the Protestant ethic and a dash of metropolitan style.

Faced with the creeping forces of authoritarianism, misogyny, racism and environmental vandalism, *Newsweek* bravely called out the truly unforgivable offence of being an overweight, vulgar slob.

It serves as a nice illustration of what we might call liberal double-consciousness. On one side of a diptych, the media's hand-wringing claims to have learned the lessons of 2016, and their intention to renounce past complacency and contempt for the flyover states, 'we're listening and learning!' On the other side, the Lazy Boy.

Yes, as an exemplary othering of the so-called base, this image is nakedly contemptuous and therefore contemptible. But what is othering if not an exercise in projection, in the ascription to you of everything I hate and fear in me? Because I don't see him staring back at me from the La-Z-Boy, I see me, I see a crystalline image of my own burned-out soul; of the redundancy of anger, of satire, of action. I see my daydream given startlingly objective form. Lazy Boy, *c'est moi.*

Notwithstanding *Newsweek*'s intimations, the 'Executive Time', the golf, the petulant boredom and brazen ignorance of policy have nothing to do with the harmless indigence of the slob. The aversion to hard work is not a symptom of the 'low energy' for which he so liberally tweets contempt.

On the contrary, hard work in his universe is the fate of the low-energy inhabitants of the world, the losers condemned to the domain of what Freud called the reality principle. Where its counterpart, the pleasure principle, is premised on the immediate coincidence of desire and its satisfaction, the reality principle teaches that desires can be fulfilled, if at all, only by means of patient labour. But who among us is granted exemption from the rule of patient labour? Only the possessor of the phallus, the fantastical organ ensuring there is never a gap between my desire and its satisfaction.

The reality principle is what kicks in when I make the painful discovery that I don't possess the phallus, that its reality is purely symbolic. There neither is nor ever was one for me to possess. Of course, some of us do possess the organ known as a penis, but it's hardly the same thing; the confusion of that vulnerable pendulum of flesh with the magic talisman of omnipotence is the source of a good deal of the world's troubles. The realisation of this non-possession announces the endemic crappiness that is both the bane and the meaning of human existence, that we must endure endless obstacles between ourselves and what we want, not least our ignorance of what we want.

Recognise the sovereignty of reality and you're consigned to the company of losers. You are low energy not because you're lazy but, on the contrary, because life is hard work, because your faltering, self-doubting will is subject to the constraints of time and space and the existence of other, competing wills, all of which are bound to tire anyone out.

One way out of this impasse is to wield one's will as a phallic battering ram, to model one's very being on the primal father, the terrorizing patriarch who in Freud's weird origin story is licensed to grab all the pussies while his loser sons cower in awed and envious submission. Then you can tear laughingly through the world, unimpeded by law or limit.

That the phallus is an imaginary entity without substance is no objection, is in fact precisely the point. A phallic order is itself without substance; it is the fantasy of the abolition of Earthly reality, licensing its master to bend, break, slash and burn its contents with gleeful impunity. It is the world conjured by Faust, who need only speak his desire to see it come miraculously into being, the cartoon world of Tex Avery and Hanna-Barbera in which time and space bend deliriously to the creator's whim.

It is the world conjured by the rallies, where all the intractable social, economic and political realities weighing down the crowds evaporate with a word, inducing those rushes of shared ecstasy. All the anxieties and humiliations of work and money and status liquefied in the universal solvent of greatness.

It can only be exhilarating to enter a version of reality in which all our insomniac agitations are lifted, in which the abuse, corrosion and burning of human, institutional and planetary bodies are revealed to be nothing, deep-state myths purveyed by low-energy losers. Perhaps that's what he meant about shooting someone on Fifth Avenue – that the body would dematerialise even as it bled out. What you're seeing and what you're reading is not what's happening.

Notice that this last statement offers a serviceable definition of the experience of a work of art. Theorists of art from Socrates to Wilde have scorned or revered art's capacity to create and destroy worlds from the weightless matter of words, images and sounds. This was what we thought distinguished the imaginary from the external world; in the latter, action is made difficult and unwieldy by the resistance of mass and gravity, so that you couldn't just do what you wanted.

Now we're being shown that the external world can be treated as though it were as weightless and malleable as the imaginary one. Words are floating free of the obligation to bear a shared reality. Masha Gessen has recently observed that the term 'fake news', more than sow doubt about the accuracy of mainstream news stories, is intended to drain the very distinction between the real and the imaginary, to turn words into bubbles inflated with their own nothingness.

The speed with which truths can be made and unmade under this new verbal regime is exhausting, violently so, for those of us whose turn it is to be left behind – in the sluggish time and space of the old, disappointing reality. ∎

POLITICS IN THE CONSULTING ROOM

Adam Phillips in conversation
with Devorah Baum

DEVORAH BAUM: Do you think psychoanalysis has a working definition of politics or the political?

ADAM PHILLIPS: There's presumably a variety of definitions, depending on which kind of psychoanalysis you're affiliated with. There's always been a question in psychoanalysis about how significant politics is, which is strange because in a way there's only political life. There's only group life and conciliating rival claims. So, the material of psychoanalysis could only be political because it's about people and their lives, how they live together and so on.

But I think psychoanalysis has been treated, on the one hand, as a refuge from politics, and on the other hand, I think it's been overly politicised in a way that's rather diminished something about it. Because certainly in the psychoanalysis I was trained in there was a wariness of psychoanalysis becoming ideologically committed – as though the risk would be that it would be a version of a Maoist training camp, but in the subtlest possible way, and that people's individual personal histories would then be used for some kind of political activism. You might ask, 'What else could they be used for?' But I think that the aim, at least in the psychoanalysis I learned, was that the psychoanalytic setting was a place where people could reflect on these things and have a different kind of conversation, one that was private. So it wasn't actually that the psychoanalytic setting was a refuge from political life, but it might be where you would go in order to return to politics with a different sense of what that can be about.

BAUM: So the idea would be not to change your politics but to change your understanding of what politics is?

PHILLIPS: Yes, I think so, and your embeddedness in social life. Because there's only social life.

BAUM: I'm really interested in the idea that people feel the need of a refuge from political life, or from an understanding of the social as inherently political.

PHILLIPS: Obviously each individual is going to be different. But for a lot of people, the political world seems unintelligible, overwhelmingly complicated and frightening. And yet everybody feels implicated or involved in it, even if their involvement is a retreat. So one way of envisaging psychoanalysis is as a place where one could go to have conversations untrammelled by the fraughtness of political life. In other words, a place where there are fewer people, fewer points of view to consider, and where you yourself could be listened to – whereas of course in any group of more than two people, there are too many competing claims. From a psychoanalytic point of view, not being able to bear the excess of politics can also be seen as a projection of an unwillingness to bear the complexity of one's own mind, the multiplicity of competing claims and interests and tones and temptations that you are composed by. You may need a sympathetic, less clamorous place to consider all this.

So one of the things that psychoanalysis has institutionalised is the possibility of being listened to on a long-term basis. That's very unique and extraordinary. But you could also say that, if we were democratically minded, then one of the things that we would need to be educated in would be the capacity to listen and to bear contradictory points of view. So it would seem to me that one of the things that psychoanalysis was invented to do was to enable people not to simply be obedient subjects or objects.

BAUM: So psychoanalysis has an anti-authoritarian, subversive character?

PHILLIPS: Yes. An anti-dogmatic character. In the kind of developmental theories that I was taught the question was: how do you get to the point of being able to acknowledge that there really are other people in the world? That being a very difficult thing to achieve. Once you acknowledge that there are other people in the world, then you have to acknowledge the fact that you can't control the other people on whom you are dependent. And then you're in political life. The end of solipsism is the beginning of politics, presumably.

BAUM: It reminds me of the philosopher Emmanuel Levinas's idea that the ethical relation takes place between two people, but the moment there's three, you're in the domain of justice, politics, negotiation and compromise, which is interesting if we think of psychoanalysis as a refuge from politics by going back to the idea of just two.

PHILLIPS: If you believe that there are ever just two – whereas in fantasy, and therefore in reality, there's always a third. Because you and I may be sitting in this room, but there is a world there, and there are all the people that we're related to and so on. So you never have a pure couple. What you can do is create the artefact of a couple in which the other people are thought about differently.

BAUM: When living through dark times, as we are now, it is hard to think of a more appealing idea than psychoanalysis as a refuge from political life. And that idea can lead us in a number of directions. One of them is to think of psychoanalysis as a space in which you're finally with somebody who has no agenda . . .

PHILLIPS: Yes, although there's a risk in that too. When external reality becomes unbearable, people begin to have elaborate internal worlds. So a risk of living in politically tormenting times is that there's going to be a retreat, which is itself self-destructive. One could become, as it were, fascinating to oneself at the cost of engaging politically.

But in reality it's impossible to meet someone with no agenda, even if their agenda is to have no agenda. Anybody who comes to see a psychoanalyst is walking into that analyst's personal history – not explicitly, but no one can absent themselves beyond a certain point. So psychoanalysis is an opportunity for you as the patient to find out what you're expecting is going to be expected of you: what you think the agenda of this person's going to be. And that can be useful, interesting and revealing to think about.

Because, yes, the analyst has an agenda. The analyst has a sense of what the good is. But at its best it can be negotiated or discussed or considered from different aspects. For example, your analyst may believe that it is a moral and emotional good to be able to free-associate, to be able to see the way in which you actively narrow your mind. To see the way in which there's a part of you that attacks your own development. So psychoanalysis can never be a neutral space, but it can generate a different kind of conversation.

BAUM: It's not a debating society.

PHILLIPS: Exactly. The analyst is not as forthcoming as somebody in a pub or at a dinner is. But one of the things that the analyst may be trying to discover is what it would be, from the patient's point of view, to be kind to them. Because obviously we all have our own ideas of what it is to be kind, but what a particular person believes kindness to be from their point of view is a fundamentally political thing.

BAUM: I imagine quite a few people who come to psychoanalysis want to test whether they can break the codes of political correctness by stating a position they think they can't declare elsewhere – to state it without being hated or exiled for having that thought in their head . . .

PHILLIPS: Yes, they do. And the experiment from the point of view of the analyst is not to take flight into inner superiority, retaliation or cynicism. So the patient can rely on the fact that you will be able to take in what they say, whatever it happens to be, and think about and consider it by talking about it and looking at it from different aspects without pre-emptively judging it. But the patient always has to deal with what the analyst herself can't bear to listen to, just as he did with his parents. Analysts, like our parents, are born of their own political and emotional histories. Analysts have just entered into these histories in a slightly different way.

The implication of free association is that there's a huge amount of pre-emptive judgement going on before we speak or indeed feel anything. And so I think the more oppressive, punitive and coercive a culture is, the more people are going to use psychoanalysis as the place where, and people often say this explicitly, 'I can't say this to anyone else but you.'

BAUM: It's really the hallmark of resentment, isn't it, to have a strong sense that you've been silenced and a sense of who the silencing people are?

PHILLIPS: And you will hate, and sometimes revere, I think, the people who demand you inhibit yourself or demand you become reticent, cautious, careful, polite – unless you identify with the people who oppress you in order to manage your fear of them.

BAUM: One of the political conversations that I guess may be raging in the consulting room right now is #MeToo. Do you get to hear a lot about how people feel about moments of sexual revolution and how that impacts particularly on those who sense they're guilty or not quite 'on side'?

PHILLIPS: I think psychoanalysis was partly invented to address people's terror of their own misogyny. Misogyny is structural. From a psychoanalytic point of view, the absolute nature of the initial dependence on the mother has got to be formative. The person that can make you feel fabulous can also make you feel like shit. And you can't recover from that easily. And everybody is terrified of their own misogyny because you want to kill or torment the thing you love.

So it would seem to me, if we take a figure like Harvey Weinstein, that we're not going to solve this problem by humiliating him. A punitive response is a dead end. Therefore the question is: if you don't punish people who do unacceptable things, what else can you do with them, or to them? Because the risk is always that misogyny gets escalated by the way in which it's punished. People have to be accountable for what they have done; and they must not, in any way, be celebrated for doing terrible things. But what punishment can never fully acknowledge is that actions can't be undone, that time is irreversible. We tend to punish people when we don't know what else to do with them. Punishment is a failure of imagination and people must take the consequences of their actions – both the punishers and the punished.

So that can be where psychoanalysis comes in, because you can go to your psychoanalyst and say – to some extent – all the things you might feel about women. And you might be able to have the kind of conversation in which you have a sense of where these thoughts and feelings come from, but also what you might want to do about these thoughts and feelings. Because this isn't like having the flu. It's not just going to go away or get better. But you *can* behave more or less well. You *can* be more or less cruel. And that matters.

BAUM: I imagine you've been hearing a lot of grievance lately from, for instance, the misogynist man who feels aggrieved because he perceives that the rules have changed. But I imagine there are also a lot of women . . .

PHILLIPS: I was going to say, yes, because in some ways the women I see have more to say about this than the men. I mean they want to talk about it more. And what they have to say covers the whole spectrum, including the fear that people will be so radically inhibited that nothing will ever happen between men and women any more: no one will dare to initiate anything, no risks will ever be taken.

BAUM: Do you see anyone who feels that their politics have just been confirmed or that they've been liberated by what's happening in the world, so much so that you're no longer necessary somehow?

PHILLIPS: I think there is a bit of that, but I think those people are people who wouldn't come to see someone like me.

BAUM: In the first place?

PHILLIPS: In the first place. I think with politics it's often that way round – that people enter psychoanalysis who feel they don't know what they want or how to go about agitating for what they want in the world outside. I went to Chicago recently and just happened to have a conversation with some people who said that they can see the drawbacks of Trump, but actually he is a very liberating figure because he's somebody who says what he thinks. So he represents something that is powerfully affecting to people, people for whom the political situation is their personal solution.

BAUM: And it's true that there's an analogy to be made between what he's offering and what a psychoanalyst offers: the idea that you don't have to repress anything.

PHILLIPS: Yeah, people could potentially claim that Trump is fostering free speech, including the freedom to lie, which is a very human thing.

BAUM: So could one say that certain Trump supporters, on the very opposite shore from #MeToo, have their own sexual revolution going on? There seems such a tremendous libidinal energy and enthusiasm released at Trump rallies – huge crowds of people really letting go and enjoying themselves. It's one of the reasons I think I find the pictures of those rallies so disturbing, because of how orgiastic they appear.

PHILLIPS: I think it's the psychoanalytic idea of sexualisation that can be useful here. Lots of things can be sexualised or experienced as sexual that aren't necessarily. So sex is then being used to do what it wouldn't usually do, which can make things that are deeply unpleasant seem very exciting, for example. So it's not really that sex is everywhere, it's that sexualisation is everywhere. And it works like alchemy: it radically transforms the nature of the experience. And when we do that it's because we live in a world with other people who frighten us, and we're continuously in all sorts of conscious and unconscious exchanges with them. There's therefore a huge amount of regulation going on, including distance regulation through judgement, and there's tremendous fear about the bodily self and what we might do or be capable of if we're not being controlled, under surveillance, punished and so on.

It's like the story Jean-Paul Sartre tells of the young married couple. They come down for breakfast every morning. The wife makes the husband breakfast. He leaves and goes to work. She sits by the window crying all day. When he comes back, she perks up. The obvious interpretation of this is that she has a tremendous separation anxiety, but Sartre suggests a better interpretation is that when her husband goes to work she's free, and she has a terror of her own freedom. So she sits by the window crying and doesn't do anything.

I think we could redescribe this anxiety about freedom as an anxiety about desire itself. What do we imagine we might want when we're not under surveillance? Or under surveillance from a variety of different kinds of people. We tend to imagine ourselves as under surveillance from the usual suspects.

BAUM: So are you saying that the key psychoanalytic question is who would you be and what would you do if you didn't feel yourself under surveillance?

PHILLIPS: And what would you want?

BAUM: And that's the key political question also?

PHILLIPS: Yes, working out what you want if there was no one to inhibit you. Although you'd also have to acknowledge that in reality you always *would* be under surveillance. But it's still a useful way of imagining things: the self unoppressed by others – that there *could* be a world of collaboration, and not simply competition and punishment.

BAUM: One of the problems with democratic politics is the supposition that everybody should be able to speak freely and represent their own wishes. Psychoanalysis appreciates that not everybody knows themselves quite so well. So what looks like a level playing field really isn't one. People who feel they know what they want get away with an awful lot on the basis of other people not having a clue where to begin, even though this freedom is apparently theirs for the taking.

PHILLIPS: And that seems to me to be a very challenging thing: how do you imagine or describe a politics that includes the idea of the unconscious, or the idea that people don't know what they want? Because politics is all about telling people what they want or eliciting what they think they want. You could think about this on the basis of the idea of self-ownership. The idea that, 'I know what I need. The question is just: how do I get it from other people?' As opposed to thinking, 'I don't know what I need and the point about relationships is not how to meet my needs but to discover what they are'. Then it's a collaborative, unfolding process. So I'm not already armed with my needs. They're made up in exchange, in a relationship.

BAUM: You said that people come here and they have a lot of projections about what they think you want of them and what your agenda may or may not be. So I imagine you find a lot of specifically political ideas are ascribed to you too?

PHILLIPS: Yes, there's a bit of that, but also I'm perfectly willing to have the conversation, not that that solves the problem. So if I'm asked, I will say. I may also say, 'I wonder why you're asking.' But I don't think we should be exclusive here. And there's something silly about not disclosing your political positions. But political positions have to be provisional to some extent because they're always circumstantial. And it has to be clear that you don't need people to agree with you.

BAUM: But there must also be a degree to which the people who seek you out are probably quite aligned with you politically. Is it fairly rare for you to see somebody who's wildly opposed to your politics?

PHILLIPS: Yes, it is rare. This is one of the differences between working in the National Health Service and working privately. Because when I worked in the NHS, there was a huge range. And in basically middle-class, private practice, it's a narrow band. People sometimes come to me because they assume we have a political affinity and they're often right.

BAUM: Is that a problem?

PHILLIPS: I think it cuts both ways. The problem is the assumption about collusion: that of course we agree about X, Y and Z. But the good bit is the solidarity and like-mindedness. There are psychoanalysts that are terrified and suspicious of the idea of like-mindedness. They usually belong to identifiable groups.

BAUM: And I imagine some people never mention politics?

PHILLIPS: Yeah, ostensibly they don't, as though they were leading a sort of apolitical life.

BAUM: Would you raise it with those people?

PHILLIPS: It depends because it's so circumstantial and specific. But if I think there's an active repudiation or refusal of something – and I would assume that if you need to believe that you're not leading a political life that there are a lot of other presuppositions that go along with that to do with your involvement with other people generally – then yes, I probably would.

BAUM: When I was in analysis I imagined I could notice on the face of my analyst when he agreed with me and when he didn't. In particular I sensed that my obsession about my Jewishness must have seemed really pathological from his point of view – the way I'd keep bringing it up in all kinds of situations. And so I imagined him thinking that I'm a fairly reasonable person, but with a madness in that direction.

PHILLIPS: As though it was like a sexual perversion or something.

BAUM: Yeah. I'd try not to bring it up, but then I would again. And I'd think he's right on the one hand to view it as a sort of mania. But I'd also think he just doesn't get it, that I do have this extrasensory perception that's linked to my Jewishness – which I guess does sound pretty mad . . .

PHILLIPS: Élisabeth Roudinesco was once asked, 'Why was it that so many Jesuits went to see Lacan?' And she said, 'Because Lacan had a great regard for people's vocations.' And I find that really wonderful and interesting: the idea that people *do* have vocations. They have real preoccupations that profoundly organise their lives. And on the one hand, in analysis, you can work out what the preoccupation is a self-cure for: what it might be a solution to, what it does. But also, it's true: you are preoccupied by this, and that's integral to who you are. And of course it can be looked at from different aspects, but it would be a shame to think, 'Oh God, here she or he goes again.' Every reiteration is always somewhere an improvisation.

BAUM: Perhaps too it's to do with not quite knowing where to situate this part of myself. With feminism, and right now in particular, I feel I sort of know where it's situated, politically. I know how to call on allies. I've never really felt that with my Jewishness. And so I've never really felt my thoughts about it have been legitimised by a public discourse – or at least not one I'm comfortable identifying with. So that sort of feeling of political homelessness it gives me is probably one of the reasons why it makes me so insecure, and why it matters to me so much.

PHILLIPS: That tolerance of uncertainty may be one of the differences between politics and psychoanalysis. In politics people think they know what they want, and in psychoanalysis the assumption is that they don't know. And so it's very difficult to put these two things together because in psychoanalysis, at least to begin with, decisions don't have to be made, whereas in politics they always do.

BAUM: That seems to me the tragedy today – that the people who know what they want are in the minority, but they're the ones who are controlling what's happening because the majority haven't got a clue what they want, so they sit by the window crying and doing nothing.

PHILLIPS: And what's exposed, then, is that not knowing what you want is like an invitation to a certain kind of authoritarianism – or simply to somebody who knows what they want and so will organise your desire for you.

BAUM: Since the Brexit vote this country has never seemed to me more divided. And that conflict is taking place within families, within political parties, within social classes, within regions of the country, and between generations. So how are people addressing that when they come and see you?

PHILLIPS: As a source of conflict. Yet you could say that Brexit is also sanguine because it actually exposes the country in which we're really living. A lot of people may have been living in a sort of pastoral myth about our relative harmony and so on. But certainly Brexit has had tremendous impact on the people I see. It's very singular in everybody's account, but most are horrified by the scale of the xenophobia that it exposes, and by how much social hatred there is. And by how much people seem to want, in a sort of fascistic way, to get rid of the thing they're troubled by as opposed to thinking about and discussing it. Where have people got the idea, the assumption from, that scapegoating is a good thing, that blaming is one of the best things we can do?

And although Brexit is of course not necessarily the return of fascism, I think a lot of people have been shocked into disbelief that fascism is happening again, as though fascism is not by definition something that recurs as a desperate political and personal solution. So it could be that one of the things that's traumatic is that we *are* shocked – it's a bit like discovering we've been living with a false picture of reality. And so this seems incredible to people like us. Well, it *is* incredible. But *why* is it incredible? Or what have we been assuming social reality is really like such that this seems such a devastation? A lot of people I see feel that the country they thought they lived in has been taken away from them.

BAUM: It has felt like that to me. But again, it really matters who you are. I have friends who don't particularly come from the margins who find these conflicts all a terrible shame and rather annoying but the terrors of this moment, terrors that are so palpable for others, just haven't been noticed by them somehow. If anything, they're suspicious of people who mention politics.

PHILLIPS: Yes, they want that conversation to stop so they can get on with their lives. But for me, and I don't know if this is your experience, it can exacerbate one's sense of Jewishness because we now have to think of ourselves as more Jewish or differently Jewish than we had thought of ourselves before. My parents never denied being Jewish, but they wanted to be English, and they valued Britishness, and they thought this was a good country. They didn't think of Britain – broadly speaking – as anti-Semitic. And it's not that it has suddenly become anti-Semitic, but I think in a more obvious way now there's the sense that it is and can be.

BAUM: But I wonder about the idea that this was always there and just needed triggering. Is it not possible that it got invented somehow, that people have had a latent sense of discontent that could have been shaped in any number of directions?

PHILLIPS: Oh yes, I agree with that. I don't think this reveals anything about human nature. I think it just reveals something about a particular political and historical ethos. And it seems to me that in capitalist culture there is a possessive, acquisitive individualism and there's profiteering and scarcity. And what that invents for us is a picture of people desperate for minimal resources with no sense of a commonwealth, with not enough experience of the pleasures of collaboration. And the fact that we know how just a couple of people own nearly all the world's wealth and so on. And what's amazing is that we sit with this knowledge or even nod along to it – because it's totally startling.

And so what's happened in the last 300 years, and certainly in this bit of the world that we live in, is astounding. It's astounding that it can be the only game in town; that really profiteering is what life's for. It's amazing. I mean if this was the fifteenth century and you went down the street and asked people what they want, they'd say they want to be saved. Now people would say they want to be rich and famous.

BAUM: Because they think that will save them.

PHILLIPS: Yes, there's still a redemptive fantasy somewhere.

BAUM: But do we even know how to oppose it? One of the ways I imagine psychoanalysis can test our dreams and ideas is by questioning whether the positions we think are opposed are really all that different from each other. Profiteering may be a capitalist principle but it's hard to find any space in modern life, including spaces of putative resistance, where people aren't in some sense on the make, having to self-promote, prove themselves, or basically honour the idea that time is money. Can psychoanalysis interrupt that relentless demand to capitalise as a sort of psychic drive?

PHILLIPS: I think in a way. It's like a relationship with the National Health Service. When I was growing up and when I worked for the NHS it was a sort of reliable mother. When and if we became ill, somebody would look after us with a certain degree of care. And now psychoanalysis in the NHS barely exists. And so there is a kind of terror. There's no backdrop of reliability or assumption that we're all in the same boat or that we have any sense of a shared world. There's not an identification with each other's vulnerabilities. That's horrifying to me. There are plenty of people who think this competition is exciting. And plenty of people for whom this is neither here nor there. But it seems to me to be terrifying. There are good accounts in child psychoanalysis of children needing the backdrop of a more or less reliable mother, of how the child can only experiment with growing up in an environment he can trust enough. Without that environment – without the as it were good-enough-mother of the NHS in the background – people become 'violent and strange'.

Donald Winnicott has the idea of the family as a kind of commonwealth that allows the child to experiment with his own greed and aggression and vulnerability, but without the fear of retaliation, or too much retaliation. If the child can give the father and mother the full blast of his aggression – often born of frustration – and the parents don't reject him, he can then believe in his parents' resilience, and not experience his aggression as the end of the world. When Winnicott says 'the object becomes real by being hated' he means that when people survive our hatred of them, when people can more than bear our aggression and our desire, we find out what they and we are made of. The most interesting experiment in living is finding out who we can be in relation to other people, which is finding out what people might want from each other. That is what politics is for. If you live in a cultural ethos of profiteering and triumphalism – a culture of intimidation and retaliation and the idea of winners and losers – you severely circumscribe what is possible between people. Once envy is promoted as the only game in town there can be no fellow feeling, no real politics. Real politics *is* fellow feeling: the refusal of scapegoating, not allowing one's sympathies to be waylaid; not allowing anyone to, as D.H. Lawrence wrote, 'determine the being of anyone else'.

BAUM: You spoke before about people suddenly feeling they're no longer at home in a country they'd assumed *was* their home, and feeling shocked to discover there are many people out there who might like them gone, or even destroyed. I imagine they've also been frightened to discover their own capacity for hatred *for* those people. Is that something people have wanted to talk about?

PHILLIPS: Yes, definitely. Two things are exposed. One is a world that is much more frightening than they want to live in. But also the possibility that the things they hate in other people are a part of themselves as well. I think that the risk always is that psychoanalysis can be a bit glib about this when it says that of course the things you hate in others are also in yourself. Actually sometimes they are, and sometimes they aren't, in my experience. And in the ideal version of this encounter it can sometimes bring out the best in people by mobilising them to stand up for things that really do matter. So it can reveal that there really is solidarity, there really is collaboration. People *are* actually capable of being kind to each other. These things do happen.

BAUM: That's reassuring. Yet when I went to the anti-Trump demo the other day, the moment I showed up I felt I wanted to go home because I found all the affirmations and banners implying that we were strong and unified in our resistance untrue. I felt very far from everybody else.

PHILLIPS: The risk is that we're just living in a culture of righteous indignation, and that liberal education is an education in righteous indignation.

BAUM: Whereas you've been finding that the space of psychoanalysis can be a space of political creativity, of imagining new forms of collaboration?

PHILLIPS: Yes, and new forms of sociability.

BAUM: I don't know what those are . . .

PHILLIPS: But you could think, 'Of course you don't – we don't.' That's exactly the point of the conversation. You can't imagine a new kind of poem being written, and then somebody turns up and they write one. It's a bit like that. Things do happen. In the nuances of relationships, new things occur and people find different ways of being together. Not as a social movement, but I think that it happens in moments.

BAUM: So would you say that, over the course of these last years where every day we read of another horror, by listening to people you have been finding reasons to be hopeful?

PHILLIPS: Well, yes and no. More hopeful in the sense that I really do believe in good experience and in the solidarity of people that I love and like. And I know there are good groups. And there are groups of people and individuals who embody things that matter to me a lot. But I do think things are cataclysmically bad.

BAUM: It's so interesting that word 'solidarity'. It has a political lineage. So it's quite hard to imagine using that term to describe your relationship with someone whose political views you find completely abhorrent. But presumably, if you're seeing them professionally and that is your word for what takes place between you, you have to reimagine what solidarity might be . . .

PHILLIPS: I think you're right. But one of the ways you imagine this is, for example, you know that the person you're speaking to has been a baby, that they've had parents, that they've grown up in what may be a completely different way from how I have and so on. You know there are some fundamental experiences that they've been through. Now they may have come to different solutions to all these things, but I assume that, while not everybody's development is the same, there is some commonality here. There are certain things that everybody's had to deal with or has to go on dealing with by virtue of being the kind of creatures we are. So I think psychoanalysis is a kind of moral education. Of course I hear things that might really horrify me, but I assume that if somebody comes to see someone like me, it's because they're troubled by those things too. If they weren't, they wouldn't be here.

So if somebody comes to see me and tells me that they hate black people, I assume it's a probe, that they're saying it to me because they want to know how I'm going to react to it. And I'm going to react to it in a variety of ways, none of which would be to endorse it. But my assumption would be that if they hate black people, there's something they're very, very frightened of. Just as if they came to me and said they have a pigeon phobia. These are of course vastly different issues, but they're on a spectrum somewhere.

So from my point of view people come to talk about how they manage the things about themselves they cannot bear. And my assumption is that there are better ways of doing it, and I'm going to promote some of those better ways. Not as a programme in the first instance, but . . . I think my assumption is that the more we talk and the more we elaborate, the more we find that there are different kinds of thoughts we might have. We always displace our terrors about ourselves.

BAUM: I do think politics has a peculiar place in our culture. I might just be narrating my personal experience, but I find hearing a political idea that I disagree with unbearable. I'm usually open to what people have to tell me about their sexual preferences, about their religious ideations, and about all sorts of other controversial topics. But then I hear a political position I don't like, and I'm suddenly not open at all. I'm so disturbed that I just want to shut down the conversation.

PHILLIPS: But isn't that feeling a version of the truth for everybody, which is: we can take in all sorts of things, and then there are things we can't. And that's where the action is, if you take the psychoanalytic idea seriously. Because at that moment, you're saying, 'No, that's not me. In fact, I can't be me *and* take this thought or idea in.' So then the psychoanalytic question would be: why do you need to dissociate yourself from this? And thinking about that could be very enlightening. Not that you can learn to happily become a racist or anything like that, so much as you can see what it is about racism that you need to dissociate yourself from. And that can be enlivening.

BAUM: Have you had that experience of people?

PHILLIPS: Yes, I have. But not only that experience, because it can also be horrifying. To experience psychoanalysis is not a wonderful story intrinsically, whereby you appropriate all the bits of yourself you disown and feel better. You might also feel a lot worse. And that's the risk of psychoanalysis. It's the risk of being alive. You can never know in advance how much of yourself and your history you will be able to bear. And you can't know the consequence of these acknowledgements.

BAUM: My sense is that my own hostile response to political disagreements is very culturally pervasive right now.

PHILLIPS: Oh it is, absolutely. It's almost a description of politics.

BAUM: So it's a description of politics to declare that these are my limits. As though politics is a new word we have for what's sacred . . . Why do you think it is that politics has moved into that place?

PHILLIPS: I don't know of course, but you can imagine that it might have to do with the number of people we are called upon these days to either know or know about – so we are being presented with more parts of ourselves than we feel we can bear.

BAUM: So really it comes back to your idea about democracy, or the difference between the dream and reality of it?

PHILLIPS: Exactly. It's always a question of how much of our own complexity we can deal with or enjoy. And from the looks of things right now, not very much. People of course vary hugely. But the experiment in living that psychoanalysis induces is discovering what it might be like to live if you could bear more of your own complexity. What kinds of relationships would you then have?

BAUM: So that new understanding, to be politically meaningful, would then need to become an intervention. Who can show us how to bear more of our own complexity?

PHILLIPS: I would have thought that the art that appeals to us, appeals to us either because it confirms who we are and want to be, or because it adds something new. It brings some news, and it's news that we want. It may disturb us, but we want it.

BAUM: So it would be in the arts that one would find this inspiration . . . not in politics as such?

PHILLIPS: No, but it's weird that we can't find it there. Because you would think, if we're just dividing this up, there are religion and politics and the arts. And why would they be delimited in this way? Why would it seem that political life involves gross oversimplifications? As though when people get together, they can only get together by simplifying things or making them crude. It doesn't seem to me that that has to be the case, but it looks like it's often the case.

BAUM: I'm always interested in how people use words in the vernacular. And when people say, 'Oh, it's getting very political,' very often they're not talking about big-P politics. They might be talking about the culture of their workplace, for example. And what they normally mean by politics then is that people have been behaving cynically.

PHILLIPS: Yes. People were behaving badly with the available resources.

BAUM: To me that idiomatic idea of politics is someone effectively telling me, 'I have to play my cards close to my chest. I appeared to be on the side of this person, but it was only because my own advancement would have been jeopardised otherwise.' What does that kind of talk suggest to you?

PHILLIPS: What I would analyse, so to speak, is all the ways people have of being strategic and self-promoting. Because I think that's estrangement. That's my presumption. So if someone is telling me they're working very, very hard to get ahead, to be successful, to be more prestigious, more attractive, more intelligent, all that stuff, I know that this is a false lure in some way. It's like a misrecognition of the problem because it's the difference between fantasising about a meal and eating one. Some things are more nourishing than others. And the problem with fantasy is, when it doesn't lead you to a better relationship with reality, it's enervating. It's like a black hole: it draws your energy away.

That would be my criteria here: that anything that's about, in this case, my need to dominate other people is fundamentally estranging. Dominating other people can be exhilarating but it's not heartening. Or fortifying, or really reassuring. We should stop asking how intelligent people are, and just ask who we really enjoy talking to.

BAUM: But your patients would probably want to tell you that this, in their view, *is* reality.

PHILLIPS: Of course. But it's often the case that people come to me with, say, a sexual perversion and they want to persuade, in this case me, that really I just haven't got the guts, that *they're* the ones in touch with reality, that this is what sex is *really* like. Sex is really exciting, but you've got to be up to it. And that isn't true. It just isn't true.

So I always sense the workings of ideology when patients want to assert that they know more about reality. They certainly know more about *their* reality than I can. But if somebody is sitting or lying there promoting a version of sadomasochism, I can question it because I just don't believe this is the best way of living. I don't mean that I've got an ideological project setting out to cure you of your sadomasochism, but I just think as a way of organising your world, it's too frustrating. It's actually intrinsically enraging. But what we're being offered culturally, broadly speaking, is a sadomasochistic solution: the idea that I'll feel awfully strong if I can make you feel weak, or vice versa.

BAUM: And that's similar to people complaining about the politics of their workplace, when they're telling you that they had to go behind the back of a colleague? You're suggesting that you don't have to play that game of realpolitik because there *is* another way of doing politics?

PHILLIPS: Yes, I definitely am. And I'm sort of saying or implying that they might have been entranced or a bit hypnotised by a false picture of reality. And I think I'm free to do that because they're coming to see me – implying that clearly the picture they've got isn't working for them. So however omniscient they're sounding, they know somewhere that if they really were as omniscient as they think they are, they wouldn't be talking to me.

BAUM: The best essay I've read about our contemporary moment is Theodor Adorno's chapter on Freudian theory and fascist propaganda in *The Culture Industry*. He was talking in 1951 about American fascists but it seems as though he's writing about right now. And he's having that same glimpse of clairvoyance himself when looking back at Freud's writing about group psychology and the analysis of the ego from the 1920s. He's wondering how Freud seemed to know what was to come. And his own Freud-influenced meditation on how fascism occurs is brilliant but also terrifying because it appears to show how invincible it is.

PHILLIPS: And the dangers of identification. The wish to be like someone else can be a way of hiding or occluding the ways in which one is different from them. The question, from a psychoanalytic point of view, is: what is this identification an attempted self-cure for? What is it about yourself you don't want to know?

BAUM: Milo Yiannopoulos claimed before Trump was elected that the alt-right is seeking a cultural revolution, not an economic one. It's the cultural nature of it that somehow makes it feel invincible.

PHILLIPS: It's as if these are stages in the rise of a kind of organic fascism. And Freud was at the beginning, and it has carried on. It must be part of the way it works, to make us feel it's invincible. Because in a way the ruling ideology has got to set the limits for what seems possible. And that's part of the tyranny, because we don't actually know what's possible. So it's almost like thinking that they've set the bounds of the possible and the impossible, and then we who are not satisfied by this have to think of other possibilities. Slavoj Žižek has said it's easier to imagine the end of the world than the end of capitalism. And that's true, but that fact itself is terrifying.

BAUM: Adorno says what enrages fascists most is anybody calling for introspection, because group identification can't work if its members are looking inwards.

PHILLIPS: Introspection and also scepticism, because now you could look back and think the rise of scepticism must be partly about how you deal with fascist states. What's the antidote to a culture of being dogmatically certain?

BAUM: It is telling that under totalitarian regimes psychoanalysis has been pushed underground or been co-opted. But there must have been moments when psychoanalysis has been more ready and willing to enter public and political debates than it often appears to be now.

PHILLIPS: It seems to me that psychoanalysts have, broadly speaking, retreated into their consulting rooms and their institutes. Why aren't they, we, marching, writing political pieces in the *Guardian*, or whatever? It's a question that assumes, on the one hand, there's a sort of grandiose psychoanalytic interpretation of politics in which it's as though psychoanalysis is some sort of key supreme fiction for understanding things. But on the other hand, I do think clinicians have an anxiety about speaking in a larger context – an anxiety that it will expose their vulnerability and that of psychoanalysis by subjecting it to a greater array of criticism. The question is: would they survive? Or: would they go on being able to give an account of themselves that seemed viable? I think it's a fear of humiliation in some ways. But also, psychoanalysis is based on privacy. So it's a question that concerns the relationship between the private and the public.

And I think there's also been a fantasy of purified transference. The idea that if you're a psychoanalyst who is in any way in the public realm, you've already corrupted the practice because people are already having fantasies about you, whereas you should be a private, reticent, quiet, withheld person, so people can come and see you and invent you. It's not true. I could appear in a film or I could never meet anyone outside my consulting room, but people are still going to have their fantasies about me. There's *no* neutrality because even if I don't speak, the question is: who am I that I don't speak? You cannot not express yourself.

BAUM: Have you ever taken a political stance in public?

PHILLIPS: As far as I know, I haven't fought shy of it, but I haven't been so moved politically that I've then written a piece stating, 'Here's what I think in the light of what I do.' I think that's my, well, complicity and sort of embeddedness in the profession. But I felt that working in the National Health Service *was* doing something political. And therefore I was really dismayed and disillusioned when it was no longer possible. That for me was a kind of watershed for all we're seeing now.

BAUM: And what do you think of those psychoanalysts who've come forward publicly and diagnosed Trump long-distance by saying that, for instance, 'Trump suffers from a narcissistic personality disorder' or whatever else?

PHILLIPS: I hate all that. I think it's really disreputable to analyse people who are not in analysis with you. It shouldn't be done publicly, because it's really character assassination by other means.

BAUM: There are political thinkers or academics who work in politics who *are* wondering if they can get some fresh insights from psychoanalysts. I think they do want the help, actually. And I think they want to know where it can serve and where it can't serve their purposes.

PHILLIPS: They're right. There's a lot of really interesting thinking and description in psychoanalysis. It's not everybody's cup of tea, but it can be very illuminating. The trouble is that the psychoanalysts who've intervened in politics have been very quickly pathologised. For example, Wilhelm Reich, who did some interesting things and wrote some interesting books, like his *The Mass Psychology of Fascism*. And there were free clinics in Berlin and there were analysts who spoke out against Nazism and so on. And it seems to me clear that the British Independent Group is sort of socialism by other names in a way. The trouble is they didn't say that. The political world is about explicitness, whereas psychoanalysis is very often about implicitness. But I think we *should* say what sort of political organisation we believe in and why.

BAUM: And what about the idea of the family as a matrix for understanding political relations, given how central the family is to psychoanalytic investigations? Are you as a psychoanalyst inclined, for instance, if you hear somebody declare an extreme political position, to then focus on whether they're the oldest or youngest sibling, or if they lost their father in their early childhood, or that kind of thing? Because isn't it true that information like that *is* often telling?

PHILLIPS: It is telling, but it isn't decisive. There's the Joan Riviere idea that socialism is the religion of younger siblings and that sort of stuff. And of course there's something in it, which is why it amuses us, but it's never the whole story. It's not an explanation but a restatement of the problem.

BAUM: And when people come to you who do obsessively talk about politics, do you tend to view politics then as symptomatic of something else, i.e. something non-political that they find themselves unable to talk about?

PHILLIPS: Yes, but you can have this both ways, because I think it would be misleading to assume that it *is* something else. Because it is itself, whatever that means, and it also has roots and analogies. Otherwise the interpretation's oversimplified. There have got to be lots of connections between your family history and your political affiliations. But one thing doesn't equal the other.

BAUM: And finally, this special issue of *Granta* is called The Politics of Feeling. Do you have any sense of the politics of feeling or the feeling of politics?

PHILLIPS: I think feeling is intrinsically political just in terms of acculturation. We're born not speaking, we have a very intense bodily experience and so on, and gradually over time things are named. And this comes from the culture, and the culture is a group culture. So all of what we think of as feelings could only be caught up in a political world.

So there's no such thing as non-political feeling. But it's partly a question of languages. I think the feeling for politics is a very interesting thing. What might make us or anybody think, 'Politics really isn't my thing', and yet we might have preoccupations that are profoundly linked to what are called political questions that are couched in political language, but we don't go on marches, or we don't vote, or we don't particularly talk about trade unions or whatever is nominally political. And I think it's a very interesting question where anybody gets their feeling *for* politics from and what they think the feeling is.

I grew up in quite a left-wing home where people talked about politics a lot. And in Wales of course it was all about mining. And then there was South Africa. For my bar mitzvah I was given a biography of Aneurin Bevan, for example. That was the world that I grew up in. So I never thought there was something else called 'politics', but when I discovered literature between the ages of fifteen and eighteen, I thought literature was much better than politics. I wanted to read novels and poems. I wanted a more nuanced life. I didn't want to read Marx, Lenin, Trotsky. Which was why Ruskin and Raymond Williams were such a discovery. I thought then, and I think now, that it was a bit of a way out, a refuge from politics – or at least I thought that literature was a way of reincluding what politics tended to leave out.

BAUM: So have you noticed any pattern regarding what seems to lead people *into* politics?

PHILLIPS: No, I haven't. But I wouldn't have thought it would be worlds apart from somebody becoming an artist or a priest. It must have, as it were, profound roots. Something to do with what people do together. Some fundamental feeling of injustice. ■

Nick Laird

The Politics of Feeling

(For Bannon, Conway, Kelly, McConnell, Mulvaney, Pence & Ryan)

I'm going to level with you now about the despicable phoniness of those
who declare they're going to level with you now: also, let me make it
abundantly clear that those who say let me make it abundantly clear

are shitting in your milk. There's a sickness at the core of this but
let them scream whatever they want: we will size it up beautifully,
we will size it up without frenzy or sloth or pretense. And let it be

noted that it has been noted. I am sitting here very still in the question
of myself, and by the time this poem appears I expect I will be even
whiter. As you are aware the Irish only recently got to be white,

but some of us seem to be liking it an awful lot. My sandwich is finished
but I sit on in the middle of the square, decentered by the lassitude of
Thursday and this recurring sinus infection. Abroad remains the trio

of affinities – the body one inhabits; God, the cause or lack thereof of
all level of outrageous detail; and the other animals who walk around
me endlessly in circles. The day is a massacre of clarity: clouds erupting

out of their skin, whiteness on whiteness over the dogs in the dog run
growling and sniffing and crapping, over the jet of the fountain
    endlessly
replenishing the crest of itself in whitely continuous effort. The curled up

leaves at your feet, desiccated reds and browns, patches of exhausted grass,
the Japanese jazz band, the texture and temperature of the bench. Why
    is there
this? For sensation? For pleasure? See if that stands up. I hold in my palm

a few at a time the facts of cashew nuts from the bag of facts of cashew nuts.
Everything already is fraying at the edges if not completely gone. Everyone
is mourned in turn and that stench is the stench of decay from the trash
    can.

Something rotting in a bag of skin. Look at it and away. If someone
    despises
you, the work is still to do nothing despicable, to be oppositional but
patient and cheerful as your own mother – if she wasn't pretending –

but what then? What is next? I no longer find it surprising that one of
  the Wi-Fi
networks coming up as my home option is ClassWar5G. Yesterday I
  noticed
another had appeared named PatrioticSocialist. I am telling myself to
  get up

and go when a guy slopes past pushing his kid in a stroller like I used to,
the lovely dullness of those intervals just shoving the stroller into the
  future.
On the next bench a squirrel surveils us, sits on its hunkers, munches.

I flick half a cashew off my sleeve and into infinity, and snap the
  Tupperware
container shut, and stand up to brush myself off before walking out
  into
Manhattan like a good European as the rich get richer and the poor
  get fucked.

Wilson Amunga prepares the cooling pipe for distilling the liquor.
Mathare River, Mathare Valley, Nairobi, Kenya, 2018

DISTILLING EXISTENCE: A STUDY WITH WILSON AMUNGA

Yvonne Adhiambo Owuor

Photography by Bernd Hartung

M athare Valley in Kenya is what Middle-earth would have become if Lord Sauron had won a scorched-earth war strategy. Vestiges of a deformed, defiled, distorted and wounded sublime Shire are much in evidence: the shadows of softly rolling hills, landscapes that were once terraced, a natural amphitheatre interwoven with streams, and a once-splendid conflux where two Nairobi River tributaries merge, the Mathare meeting the Getathuru. The vapour and spray, now darkened, from that falling-into-each-other of rivers suggest a long-ago season of light-hearted beauty. The tributaries that once exchanged fish species are now slow-moving swamps that compare sewage notes.

Among the 750,000 occupants of this dystopian Eden – the internally and, mostly, permanently displaced of Kenya – is a choir of voices tinged with a nostalgia for lost beauty mingled with despair at inestimable loss. The former hustler who recalls how clear the waters in which he swam as a child used to be, fishing for tadpoles, the colours of the lingering birds – honeyguides mainly, and the dragonflies of many colours. 'The river was once an endless song.' We stop to gawk at what humans have made of the river. It is a dark, dense green sludge carrying the detritus, debris and dirt of Upper Nairobi. Condemned plastics have created eyots midstream. The 'bridge' that links the two sides of the valley is, appropriately, a giant dull blue sewage pipe carrying Upper Nairobi's excrement into and over the lives of Kenya's discarded souls. If the river makes a sound now, it is a drawn-out moan. Here is the dirge of what structured, systematised violence woven into governance structures produces, this horrible transmutation of life, this negative sacrament.

The most resilient evil in the valley is one called 'extrajudicial killings'. Every day is hunting season, and you are a target if you're a male within the thirteen to forty age range. The national blood sport, the thrill-killing season often coincides with the rising of political temperatures in Kenya. Yes, there are young men and women who, backed into a corner watch their peers cruise past in Lamborghinis and later drop three million shillings in one nightclub hour. Some decide to seize for themselves the benefits of Upper Nairobi living, the violence has deep tentacles: carjacking, robbery with or without violence, rape, sodomy, slaughter.

After the private funerals, the stunned mourning, there is always the special Kool-Aid of collective amnesia. The security apparatus in this valley is intricately committed to the delivery of death, sometimes for no known reason, operating under a gruesome 'moral' code that is able to plaster over the evidence of state absence and neglect. The valley dead do not count; they are barely registered. At least five funerals take place in the valley each day, and three of the corpses are more often than not young ones, and two of these are almost always young men in the prime of their lives. The keening of the wretched rises and falls only in the valley, as the rest of Nairobi loses itself in a hamster-wheel life of hustling, hysterical night-partying, and hapless pontifications on social improvement programmes that are never going to be implemented.

Along a harrowed river's banks chugs an alchemical and menacing presence; large, round grey-black vessels belching fire and vapour. These are tended mostly by men, who move like agile phantoms. They shuffle inside, along, into, out of the green-black putrid stew that is the Mathare River. In intervals, a dramatic hissing erupts, spewing brown steam into the atmosphere, perfuming the atmosphere with an unexpected sweetness. And then the passing wind mixes the aroma with the stench of human disorder emanating from the river and drives it into our nostrils. At least we now know what Nairobi really smells like. Pipes and tubes lead into other black-brown metal canisters, these former oil cans. This is 'The Base', a restricted area. The elixir being distilled is called *chang'aa*, in regular Kiswahili. In the valley, it is known as 'cham' or 'steam'. The set-up is mesmerising.

Ubiquitous yellow plastic containers, in all sizes, former cooking-oil vessels, now serve other functions that extend their lives: water carriers, sitting stools, storerooms. Walking down precarious steps into the valley, the yellow plastic containers are impossible to miss. The valley is a place where things acquire new forms, habits and purposes. Recycling is a fine art here. And like the Inuit with their fifty names for snow, there are many ways of water here, categorised by the water cartels: cooking water, drinking water, clothes-washing water, cutlery-washing water, plant and tree water, *chang'aa* water, bathing water. Different costs. There are also water-support services: delivery, transportation, distribution, fetching, carrying. Yes, there are pipes leading to blocked taps that are meant to carry water. But nobody knows who shut the water off, or why in a city of at least 20,000 plumbers the blockage in the pipes cannot be fixed.

Vapour from the *chang'aa* brewery, 'The Base', taints the area with an eerie mist. It has been raining in the city so from where we wander we can see how the river has breached its boundaries. The sun is up today, fierce and focused. There are souls flitting by the river, shrouded in smoke, shadow beings darting to and fro. We make our way towards our destination, leaping across narrow streams with pockets of clear water; a startling, oddly hopeful sight. Glimmers of old purity, future possibility. Four goats browse on a green patch over which twelve eucalyptus trees loom. We are waiting for *mpishi*, the Chef. It was he who planted these trees eight years ago.

A man lopes towards us.

It is he, Wilson 'Amush' Amunga. He is a beautiful man by any human standards. His eyes are probing and direct. It is this that a person first notices. He is a slender, sinewy man with glowing midnight-dark skin and high cheekbones. He has a firm handshake and appears a little shy. His is a reassuring presence. This is conveyed by how he stands in his world. Unintimidated. Alert. Whenever an emergency arises, there are the 'run-to' people whom others turn to automatically. Amunga is a 'run-to' person.

'*Karibuni*.' Welcome, he says, shaking hands with us all before he leads us to his home. Just then, a long-limbed woman, youthful, with large eyes and angular cheekbones that somehow mirror Amunga's, appears. Amunga's voice acquires light. 'This is my wife, Caroline Medeva.'

We gather around to greet her.

Medeva's faded flowered skirt and loose white blouse do little to reveal how arresting she is. She wears a stillness that should suggest serenity, but is belied by the intensity of her watching, her barely restrained restlessness.

Amunga and Medeva are each other's protector, a carapace of family for each other. They have made of their relationship a bulwark against a mad, bad, capricious world that does nobody any favours, that would destroy the most vulnerable without blinking. Their children have inherited the character of family quietness. The gentle atmosphere in that odd-shaped home softens our own voices, simplifies our questions.

We arrange ourselves on the yellow plastic water containers that serve as stools. The rectangular room is neat. The spaces – kitchen, bedroom, areas for clothes – are separated by a piece of blue cloth. A single light bulb is tucked into the wall. It is not enough space for a man, his wife and three children to occupy. Amunga pays almost 1,000 shillings for the privilege of squatting in this shack.

During the 2017 bloodletting season also known as the Kenyan elections, Wilson Amunga's house was set alight by those who had mistaken his political affiliation. Amunga is a fiercely apolitical man. A neighbour had rushed to warn him: '*Toa vitu wanakuja kuchoma*,' 'Remove your things; they are coming to set this place on fire.' Amunga managed to escape with his wife and children. He had watched the life he had carefully built turn into ash. He has had to rebuild a new place out of the debris of the former.

Wilson Amunga will start at the beginning in response to questions we put to him. He stumbles, and then speaks more firmly of being born unwanted. He tells us of his abandonment by a mother who deposited him with a cherished but impoverished grandmother before disappearing for good. His voice lowers as he remembers the woman who raised him, his grandmother, as if she is the only soft cushion in a cold, hard universe. He has memories of being treated as a mistake by his immediate family, of always searching and yearning for a father who had never tried to find him, of imagining what might make a mother dump her son and never look back. He tells us of his ache to go to school.

'But we were so poor.'

He took himself to class after class, having put together different versions of a school uniform. He recalls how he sat in different school classrooms until he was thrown out, sent to fetch parents who were unavailable, sent to raise school fees when none was to be had and none were offered, of time passing and leaving him behind. Still, Amunga is proud of his mathematical ability. 'My arithmetic skills are good,' he states.

Silence.

And only then the hint of a dream held so close to the soul that it has grafted itself onto the man: 'What I would have become had I gone to school.' He returns at once to his default stoicism, looking away, embarrassed, as if he has been caught dreaming in public. His voice is tight. 'My children go to school. They will study. As long as I live, my children will go to school.'

The next part of the telling becomes unexpectedly difficult for us, the observers, the eavesdroppers, the story-gatherers, the citizens of Kenya. Amunga says, 'There are days when the family must choose between having a meal and paying school fees.' Amunga's smile is wry. 'Sometimes school must win.'

In the rectangular home we have crowded, our silences are specific and loaded. A quick glance around; all our heads are lowered. One of us scratches the ground with a twig, studying the plastics covering the floor as if they are the oracle. There is no way any of us can escape a sense of indictment. There are no innocents in the fact that even one citizen in the Republic of Kenya has to undergo an hourly existential battle to garner for his family the basics of life. This is a country where, with allowances included, the average parliamentarian takes home at least seven million shillings a month, where one of the chief executive officers of a national bank earns 27 million shillings a week. Where oil and rare earth minerals exist, a country that delivers to the world the finest rubies and the most exclusive tsavorite. Where salaries are taxed at 45 per cent, and a minister's son can spend one million shillings buying drinks for acquaintances in a Nairobi nightclub, where seven-million-shilling billboards advertise SportPesa gambling opportunities over the valley; in a country that moves billions of dollars borrowed on public goodwill into private bank accounts, a nation that squandered the treasure of its supposed 'independence from colonial rule', in such a country there is no excuse, no reason, no justification for a citizen, almost sixty years later, to daily have to choose between living and dying.

We look away from Wilson Amunga and his son, and from each other, because his is the face of national betrayal. In the years that now exceed the season of the British sojourn that developed the Kenya idea, a 'post-independent' leadership has managed to oversee the wilful destruction of the nation-building ideal, has predated on the country's most vulnerable, generation after generation, and devoured the future of its best souls. The one time the Amungas and Medevas of this country count, is during election season when they become useful numbers in a ballot count.

We citizens pretend that we do not know what the smoke rising from the burning shacks of Mathare means. We pretend that the wheelbarrow ambulances that rush the valley's mortally wounded to clinics and hospitals are justified, as are the hardened backs of men, boys and mothers that carry the dead to be mourned in the hovels they are forced to call house and home.

W ilson Amunga has found a kinship with soil. He loves the earth. In his words, 'It rewards the work of my hands. Soil is honest. Soil gives you back what you give to it.'

In 1999, he had his first work assignment as a gardener in Kitale. He earned his first salary, and used to store his earnings under his mattress. He lived and worked on the farm for three years before one of the friends he had made, Arif, convinced him to come to Nairobi, where he would make his fortune.

'*Uko na fare, twende,*' 'You have the fare, let's go,' Arif said.

Amunga had saved 750 shillings. He used it all to travel to Nairobi.

He disembarked in the city that evening. He recalls his shock at the sight of the famed city.

'I had expected a magical place, a green city of wealth. I thought everybody in Nairobi worked. It was a disappointment.' He shakes his head at the naivety of that young man. He soon realised that he needed to find work, or die. He moved to Mathare and settled in the Sokomoko area, Hospital ward. On his way to the first of his dwellings, he watched people hurry up and down the hill hauling water. The Mathare water crisis would give him his first job.

Amunga hauled water, day in and day out. He carried water for the workers at 'The Base'. For every circuit he made he earned 20 shillings. He also took up other odd jobs, to earn some extra survival money. His water-hauling introduced him to new neighbours, and one day, it brought him the woman, Caroline Medeva, who would become his wife.

'I was at the water point, fetching water, dressed in rags. She saw me and thought I was a *chokora* – a street child.' He laughs. He mimics her voice, 'You are a mess, a bum.'

"No, it is just work," I told her.'

Medeva giggles and grins over her shoulder at him. She is seated on the floor, facing the door, seemingly basking in the afternoon sun. But she is listening to us, protecting her husband in her quiet way. Her other two children play by her feet.

Amunga's eyes are distant, remembering. 'She then told me to continue with it. She liked that I was a hard worker.'

His son strokes his face. He looks down at the child.

We wait.

'And soon we were together,' he adds.

Another soft laugh from Medeva.

'Everything changed. Together, we decided to stop drinking. I stopped because of her. She stopped because of me.' Amunga glances at me. 'But I still like *miraa*.'

Amunga seemed to be settling into life. Soon after, again through Arif, he obtained work with a tailoring company and quickly acquired sewing skills. 'I am good. I have an eye for design.' His clothes proclaim the truth of that statement. Amunga is not boasting. He is a man with no time for false humility or wasted words, who understands what he knows and what he does not. 'And then Caro and I had our firstborn.'

Amunga goes suddenly still, as if the import of his words and their meaning have struck him anew. It is as if all his existence had been leading to the moment when a new life would arrive, life that was dependent entirely on him. That child clings to his father's thighs.

Trouble pounced on Wilson 'Amush' Amunga in 2006. At the height of one of the now-normalised Kenyan blitzes against its able-bodied young men. Amunga was in a *matatu* returning home from work when it was stopped by the police. All the young men in it were forced to disembark and were arrested and charged with being members of a 'proscribed criminal gang', in this instance, Mungiki. Amunga's cultural origin and profile are as far from Mungiki as the east is from the west, to use a biblical analogy. Mungiki, a pseudo-religious-political gang, is strongly associated with those from central Kenya. Its methodologies, rituals and allegiances would be abhorrent to a man of Amunga's orientation. There is no pretence or shade of grey about this. Still, such is the nature of justice for the targeted voiceless; a miscarriage of justice would occur. Wilson Amunga was found guilty and was fined 200,000 shillings, or prison for two years. His grandmother would struggle for more than a year to raise the fine by selling her pride, the cows she had worked to raise for her upkeep. After Amunga was finally released, his employer at the tailoring company wanted nothing to do with him.

The story is appalling for far too many reasons, yet there is no anger in Amunga. Here is a citizen who has no illusions about the extent of the law or justice for the likes of him. Here is a man still anguished at the thought that his grandmother, the only mother he had known, had to give up even the little she had saved to pay for the laziness of a judge, the amorality of a prosecutor and the venality of a system that is indifferent about grinding the bones of its young men into dust.

After Amunga left prison, he retreated to his shack and found refuge in Mathare. He had a family to support, and not enough to support them with. The memory of his season in Kitale came to his aid. There was a neglected patch of space in the valley that was filled with debris. It was a mess. Amunga cleared it, centimetre by centimetre, and planted vegetables and trees. He supplemented his gardening and the sale of his produce with his old water-fetching job. He reserved some of the water for his garden. Amunga teased life into the plants and trees that, to this day, stand tall and green and provide shade and aesthetic relief to the many.

There is one gladiatorial arena where Wilson 'Amush' Amunga has implemented a Faustian pact in order to guarantee a different life for his children. It is the place where Amunga has acquired the sobriquet of the Chef, *mpishi*. This is the *chang'aa* distillery, at 'The Base'. This is an open-air 'factory' that in another world and culture might be looked upon as an impressive living-art installation. Amunga's water-carrying excellence, coupled with traits that he repeats as a personal code – '*bidii*' (diligence), '*nguvu na kazi*' (strength and hard work), '*hesabu*' (capacity to count) – secured him the job. Access to the distillery is a privilege. No stranger is allowed close to the site. Those invited in must have a capacity to be steeped in and shelter its secrets. Amunga was called across the threshold – an uncommon vocation – not by God, but by the phantom powers that wield power over the valley. They had noted and needed his focus, intelligence, relentless capacity for hard work and steel will. He took the *chang'aa* brewer's job because his children need to go to school and his wife needs to feel safe, and they all need to eat, and he is a man and father who believes he must provide for his own.

Bidii, nguvu na kazi, hesabu.

A code.

It has made of Amunga *mpishi*. The Gardener is the Chef, distilling a toxic city river into an alchemical potion that the city's wounded, sad, lost and fragmented can consume, exchanging their souls for a moment of forgetting and carefree laughter. Apart from testing the quality of his brew, neither Amunga nor his wife imbibes the fruits of Amunga's labour.

T he ingredients: dry firewood to light and keep the fires going. Water to be carried from the top of the hill to the bottom five or six or seven times by a slight man with big shoulders and a will for his children to live another kind of future. A fetid, blackened river that only forty years ago had storks and herons squabbling on its banks as they dove for fresh fish. Yeast (different kinds used; brewer's secret). *Kangara*: fermented molasses mixed with water, sugar, ground sorghum and yeast in perfect portions. Light the fires and raise the temperatures. An impressive fire dance unfolds. *Mpishi*, 'the Chef', stirs, tastes, scents, times, watches the temperature, stirs, watches. 'You must use your eyes, know what to look for.' *Mpishi* has his ways of seeing, of noticing colour and the pressure of the steam. 'There is an art to fire,' the Chef observes, his gaze lost in the imagination of his alchemy. 'Fire can make or break a brew.' Here is a master of the science of distillation. 'The secret is in the stir.' Now he ponders colour, swirls some liquid in a glass, inhales the bouquet, sips, holds, spits. 'There is an art to tasting.' If he was offered the vocabulary of tastes, he might rhapsodise over flavour palettes. But he is a distilled man with no breath for bullshit. 'Balance,' he insists. 'Always balance.'

He is a man who is fascinated by the technology of production: the pipes, the copper. He explains how the blend heats up and the alcohol steam passes through a distillation system, a rig with copper pipes through which the distillate passes, and through which the vapour is released as if a fire-breathing creature stirs. What remains flows down a coiled pipe into a recycled oil can sitting in the putrid river that cools it down, condensing steam into liquid. A pipe carries the pristine liquid into another of the yellow plastic containers, ready to be graded, distributed and sold. From that moment on, everything is out of the Chef's hands.

His work is done.

A squadron of middlemen, vultures and proxies descend like migrant locusts and coalesce around the product. The ecosystem of scavengers in action: gurning, grunting, sneaking as they receive their unmerited cut, the benefits from an intoxicating nectar created out of the debris of human souls. The ecology has a coded name for each one of them according to their categories of greed. The Chef must be cautious because it is not impossible that one of these might decide to jail him and his kind.

When *chang'aa* is referred to in Kenya's official circles, it is prefixed with the adjectives 'illicit' or 'illegal'. The references are accompanied by a wrinkling of noses and variations on the bellows of Old Testament prophets. Nothing turns the officious as apoplectic as decrying the distillation, distribution, sales and consumption of *chang'aa*. As with many human enterprises, *chang'aa* has its counterfeiters who adulterate the product with all manner of substances, including embalming and jet fluid either to extend the life of the product, amplify the hit, or make a little go a long way. The consequences are often devastating: blindness, impotence, massive organ failure, death. And still even the adulterated products have their clients. A bottle of beer in Nairobi can cost up to 150 shillings. Half a glass of *chang'aa* is available for ten shillings, and it is more potent than pure whisky.

The origin of the word *chang'aa* seems to have been lost in a retelling that is now accompanied by sound, fury and finger-wagging. It does not mean the ridiculously prosaic 'kill me quick', as some alien journalist misreported. Like *busaa*, another alcoholic beverage brewed in Kenya, *chang'aa* is probably rooted in one of the cultures that moved into the magnet city that is Nairobi. One anecdote suggests that *chang'aa* as a word emerged out of an inside joke among illegal distillers and their clients of Luo cultural origin, who learned to ask (with a wink), '*Cha ngaa?*' – 'Whose tea?' Code name for another kind of 'tea' on tap. It would also be a homonym for 'there, who?'

There are many ways of brewing *chang'aa*, but the core ingredients and its chemistry are consistent. Expertise and precision are required, and a master brewer, like Amunga, even if he is immersed in a stinking river, is regarded with awe.

Climate, quality of water, source of ingredients, temperature gradations and the skills of the distiller inform the output. The output is graded according to colour, sweetness, dryness, smell, flavour, palate, blend, clarity and origin. As with wine, beer, coffee and other spirits, *chang'aa* connoisseurs exist who can explain with zeal the nuances and advantages of a variety that comes from Korogocho as opposed to the Kibera kind.

The finest Mathare *chang'aa* has a distinctive smokiness with strong earthy undertones. I am told it is particularly heady. Given the state of the river that supplies its water, and the analogy of the distillation of a city's sinfulness, I believe this. A master distiller from anywhere in the world would find the *chang'aa* procedures familiar.

The primary differences are in perception management, brand and an effective cover story (myth). Standardisation, scale, detail, public relations and guilds provide the rest of the padding that separate *chang'aa* from Absolut Vodka. A creative entrepreneur may one day emerge to package *chang'aa* as a high-value, distinct, revenue-generating base distillate for sale to the wider world.

Kenya's annual 'war on *chang'aa*' is a manufactured farce, with all the ingredients of a bad theatre play. Everyone involved knows that this is a vast ecosystem whose shareholders and bosses, *'wadosi'*, include those in the highest echelons of the Kenyan state. It is no secret that members of the police, the military, the environmental and health offices and politicians are all in on the take. The real owners of the distilleries are high-end businessmen. The availability of cheap alcohol for the people at the bottom of the pyramid is required to mute the rage of those who would otherwise be on the streets demanding their rightful due from the neglectful state. It is in nobody's interest to shut down the distilleries that operate in the open, visible on the ground and from the air, and that can be approached from all directions.

The immense profits from this 'illicit' business quickly flow from the hands of the distillers on site to those stretched in all directions. The least of the beneficiaries are the men who labour close to the fire, alchemists like Amunga, who are in constant risk of death through explosions (there is no safety equipment on site) or indentured servitude.

Amunga has just emerged from a three-week absence for having lost a drum of the brew as he worked at night. (When pieces in the brewing system go missing or get damaged, the cost is borne by men regarded as being on the lower scale of the cycle.) In debt to his employer, Amunga got into further debt when he had to borrow money from 'Eastlands Shylocks', loan sharks in his neighbourhood, to pay rent, feed his children and send them to school. It does not bother him that he had to forgo meals in order to settle those debts. Meanwhile, the distillery runs day and night. It is only inactive on the days of the year set aside for 'The Raid'.

'The distillery is in the open, there is no secret about its presence.'

'Correct,' replies Amunga.

'But every year, for the past, what . . . thirty years . . . we have been treated to images of dramatic raids on *chang'aa* dens.'

Amunga laughs out loud. 'Correct,' he says, wiping his eyes. He then glances at the calendar on his wall. 'In fact "*they*" are late this year.' His eyes glimmered in mischief.

'Aren't you worried? Won't you be affected?'

Amunga shrugs. 'We shall hear about it a week in advance.'

That is the extent of Amunga's contribution on this topic. He needs to keep the trade secrets. But afterwards we will consult with others, the 'connoisseurs' who were curious about our visit to the area. They were happy to supply more detail.

Before each raid, an informant linked to the police will alert the brewery 'owner' about the impending action. The owner will inform the manager/supervisor at the site. The site manager will activate 'The Plan'. He will arrange for his crew to collect scrap oil drums, which have been kept aside for just this purpose. They will be placed as if they are in active use. Close to the day of 'The Raid', they will be filled with river water. The press will have been tipped off so that before 'The Raid' their cameras are already rolling in readiness for the 'surprise' action. Young men paid to act the different roles required will take their positions. These include the distiller and the *chang'aa* clients, complete with red eyes and swollen lips who still have enough wits about them to flee as the police and officials raid the base and chase after them. Crying dragon tears on television, in what might be the finest performance of their lives, are officials from the agencies that for the rest of the year are not to be seen: various security officers, people from the National Authority for the Campaign Against Alcohol and Drug Abuse (NACADA), the ill-named Kenyan Slum Upgrading Programme (KENSUP), the National Environmental Authority (NEMA) and any number of non-governmentals and religious groups that need to show evidence of their commitment to Mathare Valley sobriety. Once the lights have dimmed and the pre-packaged story (complete with alarming statistics) has run, the *chang'aa* business resumes. The gullible public will see officials in action on the 7 or 9 p.m. news. Sometimes a task force is appointed to study the situation and 'make recommendations' in a report which will later be stored away to gather dust with the previous reports.

Caught in the jaws of a primal crocodile death roll, Mr Wilson 'Amush' Amunga, husband, father, distiller, dreamer, survivor, man has learned to take the blows and he does so to shield his loved ones from ghastly forces that have moved in to occupy the spaces in his life vacated by the Kenyan state. He lives; he has found some sense of peace. There is a steady line of hope in him. Listening to him as he imagines a better future for his wife and children, I am assailed by worry for him. Hope, bloody hope has betrayed Amunga before.

Here is Atlas.

Here is Sisyphus.

Here is an Old World father, one of those who still vow to their children that tomorrow will be a better day.

But a terrible undercurrent runs deep through the valley. It is a moaning thing. Ghoulish violence can and does erupt out of nowhere and at any time. It might be sparked by a look, the suspicion of 'wrong' political affiliation – it is always worse during the Kenya election blood-hunt season – links with politicians who have honed the arcane art of dividing people by exploiting differences; it could be the suggestion of transformation, of unexpected bounty, fear that one of those in the death roll might have slipped away, leaving others – the bitter, the resentful, the self-entitled – behind. And so we shall later hear that an older, stronger, troublesome man, a known bully addicted to Amunga's brew, had been heckling and hounding Amunga, accusing him of benefitting financially from the visit of strangers. The creature demanded his share of Amunga's proceeds. A few nights later, a little past midnight, he showed up with a machete, screaming and threatening Amunga's family. And Wilson Amunga gave in to the howl that lurked within his chest. He stepped out of his shack and launched himself on the bully. He beat him to a barely living pulp until neighbours had to intervene. Amunga, family sentinel, 'the Chef', gardener, tree-planter, water-carrier, father, husband, man, had to be pulled off and dragged away from the fool he was prepared to kill.

Amunga tries, how he tries, to keep a bright light shining for his own. He minds his own business, yet roaming phantoms still seek him out. He will try to hold them at bay, attempt to ignore them, until they make the serious mistake of reading his preference for silence as weakness.

It has been stated by others before, it bears repeating again. The valley is not what reveals itself at first encounter. It is *not* 'a problem'; it is a black scrying mirror inside which churns a potent, wounded, angry river. No human being is immune from its portents. Not one. ∎

Wilson Amunga, at home.

Small breweries producing liquor along the Mathare River. Distillers often burn rubber sandals and rubbish to save money on firewood.

Sweet steam makes its way out of the barrels.

Wilson Amunga returns home.

Coming home means returning to a one-room shanty. Neighbours have helped after rioters burned Amunga's old house during the 2017 general elections.

© DIETER GENSCHOW
Cairo, Egypt, 1954

THE GUESTS

Hisham Matar

I am not sure why it is that certain dreams vanish from memory while others remain, and remain not only vividly but are then recalled by certain indefinable occurrences in the waking hours. Ten years ago I had one such dream. Edward Said is sitting on the floor, on the blue carpet that I remember so well, in our old dining room. It's night-time. His back is resting against the cabinet that housed the plates and the glasses and the coffee cups, but in the dream it is instead filled with books. Edward Said here is in his mid-thirties; about the age I was when I had the dream. The pile of books on the floor beside him stood as high as his chest. He has one volume open in his lap; I had no idea what it was. In fact, I couldn't tell what any of the books in the stack were, but they didn't seem to be his in the dream. They seemed very much mine. And his expression of being at once grateful to have these books, their burden and pleasure, and somewhat daunted by them wasn't his expression either.

The dining room in the dream was from the apartment we had in Cairo after my family escaped the dictatorship in our country, Libya. Our situation was not unusual, of course; Cairo, like London, was a city to which many Arab exiles went. Thirty years before my family arrived there, Edward Said's family had also settled in the Egyptian capital. They had been expelled from Jerusalem, the city where Said was born and spent his formative years, when the family members were made into refugees in 1948. Even though my family's temporary exile stretched into a lifetime, we did in those days in Cairo, and for a long time after, retain the realistic hope of returning to Libya in a year or two to resume our life in Tripoli. But I suspect the situation for Said's family was different. Theirs was a bigger tragedy, one that involved a foreign occupation, which together with common colonial practices of appropriation of land and theft of resources included a third element, a theological claim to the land, and therefore had no implied end in sight and therefore must have seemed, even to the young Edward of those years, a long-term proposition. I picture Edward the boy thinking, in the still hours of his solitude, in his old bedroom in Jerusalem, occupied now by strangers, and the bedrooms of his parents and siblings, and those of the neighbouring houses of the relatives and friends he had grown up among: a map of stolen homes. I imagine him perceiving, in that quiet and unsolicited way in which some acts of dispossession are discerned, that his country and with it his own self were undergoing a very particular kind of violence, an assault that had the intention of erasure.

During those early years of my family's new life in Egypt, I would stand on our street very early each weekday morning waiting for my American school bus to arrive. Every time it appeared, large and yellow and out of scale, it seemed once again utterly implausible. The school was in the suburb district of Maadi. With its wide avenues and tall eucalyptus trees and villas wrapped inside gardens, this was where American and British expats preferred to live. Most of my fellow pupils were the daughters and sons of American diplomats, agents and military personnel. They were peculiarly uninterested in Cairo, Egypt or anything Arab. It was as if they were simply holding their breath till they could return to the United States. Even the bread for our daily sandwiches was shipped in from America. Whereas my school wanted to turn me into an American, Edwards Said's wanted to make an Englishman of him. Victoria College, which is also in Maadi and only a short walk from my school, was then, in Said's words, 'in effect created to educate those ruling-class Arabs and Levantines who were going to take over after the British left.' From the earliest moment, Said's life and education placed him at the fault line between the reality of Western dominance of Arab lands and the dream of Arab independence and sovereignty.

From that American school in Cairo, I came to Britain for school and then university in London. It was here that years later, in 2009, a few months after I had that dream of Said, I received an invitation to give a lecture at Columbia University, the very place where – having earned his PhD, the subject of which, incidentally, was Joseph Conrad – Edward Said secured a position in the English and Comparative Literature Department where he spent his entire academic career, from 1963 to his untimely death in 2003. I delivered my talk and a year later accepted a position at Barnard College – the liberal arts women's college of Columbia University – where I continue to teach, spending the autumn of each year in Manhattan. And so I see that dream as at once being part of a private conversation I was having back then about my relationship to my work, and at the same time a portent forecasting the semesterly life I was to have in Edward Said's university: a life of reading and learning and teaching.

Perhaps it wasn't an accident that my imagination or subconscious or whatever it is that authors our dreams had chosen Edward Said as the protagonist of that dream. I was, at that moment in my life, seeking liberty. I yearned for a sense of expansiveness. And Said represented to me then, as he continues to do today, a thinker with an unusually broad repertoire. Growing up in a contested time, when the culture I had come from and the one where I was living were frequently talked about in terms of an opposition or a clash – sentiments that I don't find to be true, interesting or useful – Said's work offered an analysis of this malaise as well as an open invitation to a broader spectrum. He showed how one's preoccupations and curiosities might be determined not by preordained cultural affiliations but rather by the private passions and compassion of a humanist. His intelligence and appetites gave me great confidence. He, along with other thinkers, poets and artists, helped convince me that the entire history of art and ideas was in very real and direct ways mine. His approach stood in constant praise for the spirit of imaginative enquiry and was therefore a direct affront to the limitations of incuriosity and prejudice.

I recall very clearly the first time I read *Orientalism*. The effect it had on me was more psychological than intellectual. It brought to the surface the complex web of tactics employed by one culture in order to dominate another, and how myths were integral to this project, those shadowy ghosts that seemed, to the young man I was then, impossible to grasp, and that any inexact attempt risked accusations of madness or superstition or, far worse, exaggeration. Said exposed a regime that relied on an intricate system of distortions and he did this with such relentless persistence and clarity that it left me deeply agitated. It literally made my heart race.

I was still at university and only occasionally then read writers like Said. I had, in the same section of my small bookcase, Aristotle and Ibn Rushd, Schopenhauer and Spinoza and Kierkegaard. And sometimes I would get the *London Review of Books* – to which Said was a regular contributor. But what I read mostly and more naturally was poetry and novels. Those were the places where I felt that inexplicable recognition of sensing myself to be remembered, where I came upon fragments of my own experiences, echoes of my consciousness. Poetry and fiction represented a mentality, a place for feeling and thinking. They had to do with my personal cognitive will.

One such writer who powerfully sustained my interest then, and to whom I have continued to return, was Joseph Conrad. His fascination with misaligned fates, the ineluctable force of human desires, the absence of an authoritative account, the inconsistencies between reality and the human mind, the nature of betrayal, the need for atonement and, perhaps most poignantly of all – and this is not so much a theme as a Conradian attitude – the searching anxiety of language, which is to be felt only in the subterranean depths of Conrad's prose and is, I believe, a symptom of his need to catch in words the most fleeting and fluent of adjustments, an impermanent realisation, the daily delicacies of a lived life.

Strangely, it was Joseph Conrad who introduced me to Edward Said and not the other way around. My passion for Conrad led me to those who had fallen under his spell, and Said, of course, suffered an unshakeable interest in Conrad's work. That PhD, which focused on a study of Conrad's letters and short stories, became Said's first book, entitled, *Joseph Conrad and the Fiction of Autobiography*. Over the following four decades the Palestinian scholar never really stopped writing about Conrad. Even Said's late memoir, *Out of Place*, obliquely implicates him deeper into the novelist's life and work and that ambiguous distance between fiction and autobiography. To Said, Conrad was the bass note, his cantus firmus as he liked to describe it, the melodic structure of a symphony. 'No one,' Said observed, 'could represent the fate of lostness and disorientation better than [Conrad] did'. Conrad had offered Said a secret agent or a secret sharer with whom he could have the sort of conversation that he could have with no one else. The biographies of the two men shared several characteristics: occupied homeland, exile from the mother tongue, exceptional success in their adopted countries that nonetheless did not altogether protect or cure them from estrangement and dislocation. They also shared something much more private: mischievous trajectories that are too complicated to account for quickly to a new acquaintance, lives that make it difficult to be brief about oneself, and therefore it is forever tempting to altogether avoid the subject. Take, for example, my life. I have probably already confused you about where I am from exactly or the places that I have lived. And if I were to commit to brevity and try my best to explain myself – if I were, for example, to tell you that I was born in New York City and at the age of three moved back with my family to Libya and at nine to Kenya and then Egypt and at fifteen to Britain and that for the past eight years I have been spending my autumns in Manhattan – I would probably provoke more questions about the causes behind such an itinerary. It would, in other words, take us a bit longer before we could reach the business at hand. And even once we do reach the business at hand, I would remain oddly fragmented, or impermanent, in the ways that I suspect Conrad and Said, and for different reasons, have experienced their place in the world to be.

V.S. Naipaul wasn't entirely wrong when he described Conrad as 'a writer who is missing a society', that his 'experience was too scattered' to make him an expert on any particular place. The same, of course, could be said of Edward Said. The difference, though, is that if not a society, Said had a people and a noble cause – virtues that could help a thinker and lend moral power to his or her work, but are not necessarily useful or even beneficial to an artist. If anything, Conrad's evocations of disorientation and estrangement were made more poignant by his lack of confidence in the solidity of any place or position.

To Said, orientalism the idea, that library of prescribed notions one culture holds about another, is a theatre, a space for performance, what he called 'an imaginative geography'. These weren't concerns that Joseph Conrad was unfamiliar with. One senses the disquiet in his pages, which often have a near-manic appetite for comprehension and comprehensiveness. Conrad was worried about being misunderstood, or not understood at all. He recognised the dangers involved in leaving things out. Leaving things out, of course, is the privilege of the insider. If you and I belong to the same circle we don't need to say much to be understood by one another: 'Quite', 'Certainly', 'Indeed'; these might be some of our most frequent sentences. Something about this state in which one cannot afford to assume much makes one both wary of and fascinated by becoming 'an enchanted man', as Conrad calls Axel Heyst, the protagonist of his late novel *Victory*. Being enchanted must surely involve being able to presume a lot of things, as indeed Heyst does. Both Conrad and Said believed that language contains evidence and culture; they seemed to agree with Freud that one of the purposes of language is to expose us, to get us to say a little bit more than what we believe we are saying, and that assumptions and presumptions invariably reveal more about the speaker than they do about the subject.

When Said writes that the chief role of the critic is comprehension and that Conrad's gift lay in his ability to fully expose his soul to 'the vast panorama of existence', he is recognising the contradiction that lies between critic and artist. Conrad, it seems, was condemned to progress without the prerequisite of comprehension. Like most artists, he journeyed without the full conscious command of his itinerary. Whereas Said, like most critics, had to carefully read the map and retrace the paths taken, illuminating their orientation. *Orientalism* was a study of a specific historical pattern, but also a desire for orientation and perhaps reorientation, of how to navigate the contested historical place the Arab world was at in the latter half of the twentieth century. The two figures, Conrad and Said, novelist and critic, were moving in opposite directions. They met at the most curious places. Looking at them from this vantage point, one cannot help but regard them as sharers of a tradition, honourable vagabonds – wary of fixed professions and identities – men determined, whether by nature or by the inconsolable gaps between their origins and where they found themselves, to remain forever guests.

Whenever I think of Conrad I do not think of the sea or the Congo or Siam but London, the city I have made my home ever since arriving there alone as a teenager. I remember that first day well. I went hunting for a place to live. I had limited time. I was seventeen and about to start university. It was late summer and the sun was out. I proceeded to do something I had never done before. Walking down the Bayswater Road I pulled out my shirt and began to unbutton it all the way down until I was bare-chested, the fabric winged behind me. Something about the city's acceptance and indifference, its many secrets tucked away into the folds of its streets, its promises of possibility, made me feel reckless and bold. It was the mid-1980s. London was a centre of Arab intellectual life. This was where poets and novelists fled when life became impossibly restrictive or dangerous at home, and this was also where Arab journalism had flourished free of censorship and with minimal personal risk. A couple of Arab journalists had been assassinated here, but it remained a rare and unlikely event. Therefore Conrad, to my seventeen-year-old mind, was just another writer who had found refuge here, and who had also recognised that London was a city of confidences, a city interested in privacy and discretion, a city with a taste for the variances and subtleties found in spoken and unspoken codes, a city of insiders and therefore careful about who is included and who is kept out of the script. London has been like this for a very long time. It must have seemed so back in the 1880s, a century before I arrived, when the young Polish seaman Joseph Conrad had first entered the capital. He too fell under its spell. It gained his trust. It seemed to him to be strangely aligned to his temperament, which leaned towards the implied, the half-suggested gesture. He was in his mid-twenties and already unenthusiastic about naked assertions or, perhaps, assertions of any kind. A lot had happened to him by then. He had lost his father to the cause of Polish independence, was cut off from his homeland, had spent several years at sea and had, at least once, tried to take his own life. He had acquired, besides Russian and his native Polish, at least two other languages: French and English. All this had happened by the time he was walking into London, a city that had seemed to him, after all that wandering, as he would come to write later:

> a monstrous town [that was] in its man-made might as if indifferent to heaven's frowns and smiles . . . There was room enough there to place any story, depth enough there for any passion, variety enough there for any setting, darkness enough to bury five millions of lives.

London was a good place to hide, or so it seemed to the young Conrad and his ghosts – for we must remember that he had arrived bearing his ghosts: those of his father and mother, the dream of national sovereignty as well as all of his former selves – the Polish aristocrat, the French and then English merchant marine seaman, the smuggler, the respectable captain who was known for his skill and honourable character.

By the time he reached his mid-thirties, Conrad had given up the sea and devoted himself to literature. He set only one novel in London, *The Secret Agent*, but lived in close proximity to the city, writing in his country home in Kent, till the end of his days. His output was remarkable. Judging from the set of complete works I have on my shelf, which stretches to some twenty-four volumes, Conrad averaged about one page of finished prose fiction every day of the week, minus Sundays. Together with his non-fiction and numerous letters, it would appear he wrote between 1,000 and 2,000 words a day.

Edward Said had a similar daily word count, but unlike the novelist, he never seriously suffered, as he once claimed in an interview, from three ailments: writer's block, doubt or depression. It is ironic that Said should have chosen those three in particular, for they were the demons that had most consistently bedevilled Joseph Conrad throughout his life and more vehemently so during his three decades of writing. But perhaps both men kept to such a demanding schedule out of a similar sense of restlessness. One gets the feeling that they both operated from a reverberating centre, and that that had to do in some way with how they could not lay claim to the language or the places where they had decided to settle.

It is no secret to anyone who has lived in England and tried to make it home, as I have now been doing for the past three decades, that it is impossible to become English. The impossibility is both cruel and appealing, particularly, I imagine, to Conrad's sensibility. I suspect there were times when it infuriated him. Here he could live, take up the nationality, alter the literature and yet never be assimilated. And yet I can also imagine it seeming a facility, a unique sort of freedom, to remain forever unobliged by a place.

Towards the latter stages of working on the manuscript that was to become his most ambitious novel, *Nostromo*, Conrad wrote, on the same exceedingly thin paper he liked to use for his fiction, a letter to a Polish acquaintance. He wrote it in English, explaining some of the details of his upbringing, his brief Polish life, his nautical days and then transformation into an English novelist. 'Both at sea and on land,' he explained, 'my point of view is English, from which the conclusion should not be drawn that I have become an Englishman. That is not the case. *Homo duplex* has in my case more than one meaning.'

Doubleness and duplicity concerned Conrad. He wrote as if believing he could locate absence all in one place. In *The Secret Agent*, his London novel, Adolf Verloc, the spy and protagonist of the story, has his cover blown. He can no longer keep the truth from his wife Winnie. She, confronted with her husband's true identity and the tragic consequences of his actions, is inconsolable. She does not ask him questions though. She neither rebukes nor enquires. She knows that such responses have in them the consolation of engagement and the hope of resolution. Instead, she refuses to engage. She becomes as impenetrable as stone, as ungiving as a blank page, and it torments Verloc. He does not know what to do. His biggest mistake, he thinks, this man who had lived most of his days a double life, is that he had allowed himself to believe that he could be loved for himself. What does one have to do to be loved for oneself? What are the impediments? And what happens when one is not loved for oneself? What are the appropriate things one ought to be loved for? What sort of love can we live with? These questions of desire and duplicity, of home and estrangement, hover over *The Secret Agent*. They return in the short story 'Amy Foster', what Said deemed to be 'the most desolate of [Conrad's] stories.'

'Amy Foster' is about an East European stowaway who, while making his way to a new life in America, is shipwrecked off the southern coast of England. He appears to be the lone survivor. He lands – tired, bearded, long-haired and without the English language – in a Kentish village. The locals are suspicious and hostile. Eventually, though, he shaves and learns a few English words and they begin to tolerate him. He even finds love, marrying the plain Amy Foster, the local farmer's daughter. They have a son, towards whom the foreigner is a little more affectionate than is usual in these lands, but such excesses are also tolerated. One day he falls terribly ill. A violent fever overtakes him. He begins babbling in his mother tongue. Amy

Foster cannot bear these unfathomable hallucinations. She wonders if her foreign husband has been possessed by the devil. 'There was nothing in her now but the maternal instinct and that unaccountable fear,' Conrad tells us just before Amy Foster grabs hold of the boy and abandons the sick immigrant who, like Adolf Verloc in *The Secret Agent*, had made the mistake of believing he might be loved for himself. It is a tale of a man who cannot make himself understood, and must remain in constant need of translation, vulnerable to its variable tools, which are inevitably approximate. The things he says in these feverish last hours are never translated to us. Conrad never tells us what the man was trying to say, as though we are meant to understand that contained in every stowaway's mouth are all of the unuttered words, all of the absences in one place.

This story profoundly affected Edward Said. It made him think, he wrote, 'that Conrad must have feared dying a similar death, inconsolable, alone, talking away in a language no one could understand'. And it makes me wonder if similar fears occupied Said too. He often lamented how the story of his family's dispossession and expulsion from Palestine, which is also the story of Palestine, was not a stable one; that he had to keep on retelling it, for part of the Israeli project was and remains to be the wilful act to demolish the narrative structure that supports the people and history of Palestine. Whereas other peoples' and nations' stories could rely on certain presumptions, the Palestinian one was, particularly in America then, a contested account. That, in other words, Palestinians cannot expect to be loved or valued for themselves, that their national predicament of living under occupation means that they are liable to not be believed. Just by their mere existence they are captured inside a contested ground.

Another author who was moved by Conrad's work and, in particular, by the short story 'Amy Foster', was the British philosopher Bertrand Russell. Russell began a correspondence with the mysterious novelist living in the depths of Kent, in fact, very much near where 'Amy Foster' is set, and soon after they began writing to one another Russell boarded a train from London to visit Conrad. When they met Russell was taken aback by the fact that the man who wrote some of the most eloquent English prose spoke in a thick Eastern European accent. According to some accounts, Conrad's accent grew thicker and more knotted the longer he remained in Britain, as though with time he needed to signal his strangeness or else out of his longing – for although he never writes about it, it is impossible to believe he did not occasionally yearn for his mother tongue. He grew up in a literary home. His father had translated Dickens and Shakespeare into Polish. But beyond this first impression, the whole encounter marked Russell. He wrote about it with a certain tone of ecstasy, and did so immediately on leaving Conrad and boarding the train back to London, in a letter to his lover Lady Ottoline Morrell. The literary hostess and patron of the arts had, in fact, introduced the two men. 'Here I am on my way back from Conrad,' Russell begins his letter. 'It was wonderful. I loved him & I think he liked me. He talked a great deal about his work & life & aims, & about other writers.' This was 1913; Conrad was fifty-five and Russell forty-one. Both men felt shy and awkward. Then Conrad took his guest on a walk and in the silences, Russell felt a great intimacy develop between them. He writes:

> I plucked up courage to tell him what I find in his work – the boring down into things to get to the very bottom below the apparent facts. He seemed to feel I had understood him; then I stopped & we just looked into each other's eyes for some time, & then he said he had grown to wish he could live on the surface and write differently, that he had grown frightened. His eyes at the moment expressed the inward pain & terror that one feels him always fighting. Then he said he was weary of writing & felt he had done enough, but had to go on & say it again.

Here something odd happens. Conrad began to speak to Russell of a subject that he rarely broached in conversation or in his work. He began to tell this Englishman whom he hardly knew of the silent subject: Poland. And once he started he couldn't stop. He reminisced and did so fondly and vividly. Perhaps he wished by some magic he could take his new friend there, bring him to the places from where he had first set off. When they returned from their walk, Conrad was still on the subject. He pulled out an old album of family photographs from the 1860s of life in Warsaw before his family was shattered by political violence, death and exile. Seated on the train and firmly within his country, Russell wrote that Conrad spoke to him about 'how dream-like all that seemed, & how he sometimes feels he ought not to have had any children, because they have no roots or traditions or relations'.

Conrad's wish that he could live on the surface is painful and ironic. As an outsider, he remained somewhat on the surface while his work plunged into the depths. Perhaps what he had confided in Russell during that rare moment of nakedness was the wish that his character had been different, that like Jean Rhys, that other displaced writer, or perhaps like any reasonable person, if he had to choose he would have rather been happy than write. Eleven years later, he died in his home with his wife and only son beside him. When Virginia Woolf received the news, she wrote an obituary. It opened with the lines: 'Suddenly, without giving us time to arrange our thoughts or prepare our phrases, our guest has left us; and his withdrawal without farewell or ceremony is in keeping with his mysterious arrival, long years ago, to take up his lodging in this country.' Woolf here illustrates that peculiar and stubborn impediment of the English, whereby a man can live with them for four decades, write some of the most luminous English prose ever written and still remain a lodging guest. But despite her snobbishness – which revealed itself in other instances when she wrote about non-English writers such as James Joyce, for example – Woolf had astutely noted something true about Conrad. He was oddly determined to remain a guest. Perhaps his choice of England as a home, and the English 'point of view' that he wrote of in his letter to his Polish friend, was in part due to a reluctance to fully assimilate or join the club. It is also revealing that Woolf evoked the question of timing – 'without giving us time to arrange our thoughts' – for one of the characteristics of being a guest is that, no matter how hard one tries, one rarely succeeds in arriving or departing on time. As a guest one remains in tangible ways subject to the host. And like his worsening accent, Conrad's prose too stands out. It is a language haunted by subjectivity. It is English but not from England. It is odd. His sentences are strange. They come from Conrad country, which is no country at all of course. Part of what we admire about Conrad, and what would have interested Virginia Woolf, is that without 'ceremony' he accomplished extraordinary things from within his strangeness, remaining in that unresolved and possibly unresolvable territory where the past is scattered in old family photographs, communicable only through half-recalled reminiscences that are probably meaningless to those around him, and where the future is an uncertain and rootless country. To be a guest is to feel oneself held in between what has happened, which is now distant and forever in need of translation, and the desolation ahead, days that will require further acts of relinquishing, where life risks being a project to be defined and fashioned rather than lived.

Guests believe themselves to be alone, that they are on the brink of something, that there is no one else who could possibly be like them. 'Exile is a jealous state,' Edward Said wrote. 'What you achieve is precisely what you have no wish to share . . .' There was no other Pole who had gone to England and turned novelist with whom Conrad could exchange notes. Said was a writer whose very existence contradicted the claim, made by the Israeli prime minister Golda Meir in 1969, when Said was thirty-three, that there was 'no such thing as Palestinians', a declaration that was paralleled by a policy of assassinations that targeted Palestinian voices, including writers. The novelist Ghassan Kanafani's car was blown up with him and his young niece in it. A year later, Israeli Special Forces also killed the poet Kamal Nasser. Such actions attracted little controversy in New

York, where Said lived and wrote. Palestinians seemed not only to be guested and ghosted at home, but also on the world stage.

A guest's place is at the threshold. They stand at the border. They stand at the point of conversion, a vertiginous and dizzying place where it is easy to lose one's way. Razumov, the character in Conrad's novel *Under Western Eyes*, becomes interested in the possibility of his own transformation. He is 'fascinated by its approach, by its overpowering logic', believing that 'a train of thought is never false . . . [that] falsehood lies deep in the necessities of existence, in secret fears and half-formed ambitions, in the secret confidence combined with a secret mistrust of ourselves, in the love of hope and in the dread of uncertain days'. Perhaps to be a guest is to be constantly susceptible to conversion.

As with Conrad's accent, Said too seemed to sound more Arabic the longer he remained in America. The places where both men settled played a role in the trajectory of their writing. Had Conrad gone to America, for example, where the wrecked ship of the unlucky stowaway of 'Amy Foster' was heading, he would have written different books in part because one could imagine Conrad relinquishing his displacement in, say, San Francisco, writing books, yes, about the sea and so forth, but also books about America. I cannot, for example, imagine him writing *Heart of Darkness* from California. And I think that says as much about Conrad and *Heart of Darkness* as it does about England, the place with the slippery surface, where it is exceedingly difficult for a new arrival to find traction. In a similar way, it is hard to imagine the Edward Said who might have gone to teach at, say, Cambridge, where Bertrand Russell taught for many years. I can imagine him writing his book on Conrad from there or the wonderful *Beginnings*, the book of literary criticism that examines the early lines of a work of prose and the determinate implications of those half-conscious gestures. I can even imagine him writing his memoir, *Out of Place*, which of course would be a different book, given the English life Said would have had. But it is hard to picture him writing *Orientalism* or that excellent forensic study of causal distortions and their political and cultural consequences, *Covering Islam*, about the automatic coercive strategies the Western media often employs in its coverage of the Muslim world. In other words, my point is that the sentimental policy as well as the foreign policy strategies Edward Said faced in America and perhaps more ardently in New York – where, because of his criticism of Israeli international law and human rights violations, he suffered repeated death threats and once had his university office firebombed – helped sharpen and make more rigorous his desire to expose injustice and hypocrisy. Both Conrad and Said found an unlikely stimulus in the places where they had settled and which were, in different ways, indifferent or hostile to them.

And this I believe is at the heart of why Conrad and Said have remained vital. Each had a different kind of hope: Conrad in the possibilities of art, and Said in how the experience of exile and dislocation, the very condition of the guest, means that today's dispossessed will be better suited to future requirements, that the immigrant and exile who are condemned to daily acts of translation – of translating themselves into foreign customs, manners and language and who are therefore having to endlessly traverse that threshold between intention and expression, between the concealed sentiment and its outwardly shape – will tomorrow be advantaged by their burden. I would like to think this is true, but I am not certain. What is clear to me is that notwithstanding their different approaches and sensibilities, and the differences in their work, both Conrad and Said seem to speak directly to where we find ourselves today: the wars, the epic scale of the displacement and migration of people – and hostility to immigrants – and that quiet recognition that we live in times of great fragmentation, as though we are witnessing the surface of things crack open. The pieces that will form the future remain unclear and unreliable. It is this unreliability that permeates everything Conrad and Said wrote. And it seems, to this grateful reader at least, that it is one of history's more mischievous turns to have those two men, Joseph Conrad and Edward Said, born in different cultures and times, meet not only in the English language but also in their private moments. ∎

ARVON

Creative writing courses & retreats 2019

Workshops, one-to-one tutorials, time and space to write

Tutors include:
Kamila Shamsie, Liz Berry, Simon Armitage, Mark Haddon, Vahni Capildeo

Genres include:
Fiction, Poetry, Starting to Write, Children & YA, Non-Fiction, Playwriting, Screenwriting

Grants are available to help with course fees

Book now at arvon.org

Arvon: A Clear Space

You've needed this trip, you've committed
you're in the room and you feel guilt, guilt and fear;
this clear space is a gift you gave yourself.

Your window opens into the fields and trees,
your phone has no signal, (that's a good thing).
Empty your too full brain to make space for yourself.

These walks amongst the Sequoias
nervous squirrels at their root, with your boots
caked in mud watching static cows in the distance.

Your lungs expand, you've lost the wheeze of ash.
The birds are singing loudly and the grass is wet;
Your body adopts a different rhythm despite yourself.

The bell rings out for food and you'll talk to others
who are on this journey of clearing
and you'll bond to your temporary tribe.

At night the wine will flow with feelings
and in conversations with strangers
a poem will start blooming

rising up your spine; filling your head,
and a story like burgundy will spill
on to the white sheet of your page.

And as you take your taxi away down narrow lanes
your work will always help you remember
this time you gave yourself; space to be.

—*Roger Robinson, poet and Arvon tutor*

Supported using public funding by
LOTTERY FUNDED
ARTS COUNCIL ENGLAND

Fabián Martínez Siccardi, age seven, at his grandparents' sheep station, Lake Cardiel, Argentina, 1971
Courtesy of the author

FEELING SOUTHERN: A PATAGONIAN STORY

Fabián Martínez Siccardi

Reyes's hands, veiny and brown, would mix flour and water to make *tortas fritas* with the same gentleness they stuck a knife into a lamb's throat. From Chiloé he'd brought a way of talking that dropped letters in many words; and memories of his father carving a canoe out of a tree trunk, of a stone mill turning wheat into flour, of circles of women spinning wool and singing: images from a faraway fertile land that, in the dry steppe where he lived now, seemed to him like fantasy. Not for me fishing and canoeing, hooks and nets, he used to say. But if you paid enough attention, you could tell from what he didn't say that a part of him wanted to go back.

Reyes worked for my grandparents at their sheep station by Lake Cardiel in southern Patagonia. He arrived alone in the 1950s, and died alone some fifty years later. His coffin sits in our family vault in Piedrabuena, next to Grandpa Eladio and Grandma Angelina. He called himself a *chilote*, and so did everybody else, a euphemism whose meaning I didn't know back then. He told me of a dinosaur skeleton hidden in a cave. He told me of a cave painting of a one-horned bison on a rock wall as tall as a mountain. He told me of a lady named Margot whom he had fallen in love with in Punta Arenas. Reyes was old enough to be my grandfather. I have no recollection of my mother's father. I vaguely remember Grandpa Eladio. But I remember Reyes as if he were still right here, offering me a maté.

My grandparents' sheep station is one of seven that surround Lake Cardiel. On a map they look like rectangular petals springing out of a blue daisy. In contrast to the Patagonian postcard pictures of snow-capped mountains and lush forests, it sits on the *meseta*: a tableland of low thorny bushes and grasses with yellow tips and dark roots. It is a desert of sorts, an expansive terrain that entrances the mind and always brings on a calmness in me.

Originally an open territory where the Tehuelche and Mapuche indigenous people roamed freely, hunting guanacos and rheas, moving their tents day after day following the rhythm of a nomadic life, it was subdivided by the Argentinian government in the early 1900s, once the occupation of southern Patagonia was complete. The best land went early on into the hands of the Braun-Menéndez tycoons and other powerful landlords, mostly British. The remaining acreage was subdivided into lots large enough to support a few hundred sheep and a household, and sold at favourable rates or simply assigned to families or men willing to put up fences, build houses and barns, and work hard to reap the fruits of the land: mutton and wool. At about the same time, the roaming lands of the Tehuelche and the Mapuche were reduced to a few small reservations, one of them about fifty kilometres from the Lake Cardiel shore called Reserva Lote 6.

My grandparents Eladio and Angelina purchased the estancia in 1946 from the first white man to hold title there, a Spaniard like my grandfather, a thin guy with bulging eyes who lived alone until he got himself a Tehuelche woman. The woman died on the farm and her grave lies beside the road leading to the house, a rectangular structure of iron bars that looks like a pen for a small animal. At the head of the grave is a cross engraved with her name: TERESA BARROS. As a child, that grave scared me like nothing else on the farm, but it was also alluring, like the bottom of a well can be.

On a gravel road not far from the estancia, my eight-year-old brother Roni, a dark-haired boy, died in a car crash. I was two when it happened. Five years later my father, his eyes as blue as the lake, died in another car crash. By then my mother had separated from him and moved me and my siblings 2,000 kilometres away, so time and distance plotted against our going to the funeral. Six months later Grandpa Eladio passed away, from cancer and sorrow over the death of his eldest son, and the option of going to his funeral was not even on the table. By the age of eight, I was surrounded by death, living at close quarters with the ghosts of the three older men of the family, though I had never seen a coffin or attended a service. The grave of the Tehuelche woman – those iron bars rusted by rain and wind – was my first palpable image of mortality, and I projected all the others onto it, as if the death of Teresa Barros had been the original one, and all the rest had sprung from it. I knew nothing then about the ugly details of the conquest of Patagonia and the genocide of native peoples that opened the way for settlers. Nonetheless, her grave was preparing me to recognise historical truths.

B arrientos was younger than Reyes by more than twenty years. He wore dark shirts with a white kerchief around his neck, and *bombacha* trousers with a knife in the waistband. His cheeks and nose were reddish, his eyes black and sombre. As a memento of an old fight, one of his front teeth was missing. He liked telling the story of that fight. You could tell he liked it by how he lowered his voice and threw punches in the air. He spoke like an Argentine, but where he came from was never mentioned. Some people called him *paisano*, another word that hid something I didn't discover until much later.

As Reyes grew older, Barrientos took over the butchering. His knife had a silver pommel with engraved flowers and traces of blue paint on the petals. I kept him company while he slaughtered. He showed me how to hang the carcass upside down so the blood would drip from the hole in the throat. He taught me to dress the carcass by sliding the knife between the flesh and the inner lining of the skin.

Once he asked me to slip the knife in above the belly and work my way down slowly. He helped me haul the guts out – our hands covered in hot blood – and we threw them to the dogs. The lungs were red. The stomach, green. The dogs growled at each other over the feast.

The first day of every summer visit to the farm, Grandma Angelina sent me to the *despensa* to pick a pair of espadrilles. The *despensa* was a large room separate from the house where cans of peaches and pineapples with blue and yellow labels were stacked on shelves, next to bags of flour and rice, maté and sugar piled on wooden pallets. There were also tins of condensed milk and motor oil, cans of corned beef and *pâté de foie*, cartons of matches, jars of tomato sauce and pears in syrup and every other imaginable provision.

Sliding my feet into the espadrilles, feeling the hard hemp soles and the soft denim, transformed me. I turned into a rougher version of myself: a gaucho, a true Patagonian, a real man. At the time I was attending an all-male Salesian school where playing the guitar, reading books and shying away from fights was met with insults and beatings. My stepfather, echoing my classmates, called me *maricón* as a constant reminder of how little of a man I was. So those espadrilles, in my mind, turned me into an equal of Reyes and Barrientos and the other hands, men tougher than my stepfather and rougher than the roughest of my classmates. And believing I was like the peons for a while let me forget what people back home told me I was.

It wasn't just Reyes and Barrientos I spent time with. During the shearing, which went on for almost a week, the farm was invaded by a crew of long-haired men with baleful stares who travelled like gypsies from farm to farm turning fleece into wool bales. Many shearers came from northern Argentina, where the shearing season started, and worked their way southwards through the summer. There were more than twenty men who lived on mutton, bread and maté; rolled their cigarettes with one hand; sang folk songs accompanied on a beaten-up guitar; and, when night came, stretched out in the corners of the barn and faded into silence. Their hands and faces were brown, like Reyes's. I still remember the guttural and whimsical language they spoke among themselves, which sounded like music.

As a young teenager, I sat with them silently at their breaks. I shared their maté, smoked their dark tobacco. One late evening, they passed around a girlie magazine – nude women looking into the camera with a stare that was as arousing as it was frightening. They looked at the photos and whispered to each other. I could hear their quiet laughter, and I laughed too.

Ismael came with the shearing crew the summer I turned eleven. He was an antsy young man with long skinny fingers that moved like a concert pianist's. He was the oiler, responsible for the smooth running of the motor that, through a mechanism of arms and gears, kept all the clippers swaying in unison, creating a hypnotic beat that gradually regulated the pace of every other movement in the barn – from the shearer to the fleece-sorters, from the bale-presser to me sweeping the floor.

Many years later I saw a photo of the young Kafka that reminded me of Ismael. He spent his short breaks cutting jumping jacks out of used oil tins. He painted smiley faces on them that looked like evil clowns, and put them together with a meticulousness that meant they barely needed a pull of the string to start moving. He gave me one with a crooked smile and a half-closed eye. I kept it for a few days and then I threw it away. It was too frightening to look at.

By the mid-1800s, the original settlers of southern Patagonia – the indigenous nations that had lived there for centuries – were faced with the relentless arrival of new settlers. These were mostly fair-skinned men with long beards; men with no children, no estate and no reputation to look after, social outcasts from every corner of Europe and North America. These were people willing to journey to the other end of the world to make a quick buck hunting whales, wolves or nutrias. Some came looking for gold, after newspapers reported in 1883 that sparkling nuggets had been found on the muddy coastline of Tierra del Fuego. These men considered the world inherently hostile and unfair, and didn't see much difference between shooting a guanaco and an indigenous person. After the few years it took to exhaust all gold reserves, most of the Selk'nam population lay underground with a deadly bullet from a gold prospector; while the rest were being deported to the Salesian mission on Dawson Island to die a slow death of isolation and sadness.

By the dawn of the twentieth century, the territory taken from the indigenous peoples had been subdivided and was in the hands of assorted landlords. The prospect of work attracted European field hands like my great-grandfather, who crossed an ocean for wages two or three times higher than back home – men looking for a new Jerusalem in which to grow the next branches of their family trees. But most of the hands they'd work alongside were Tehuelche or Mapuche, tough men cheated out of their land and language; scorned men hiding behind words like *chilote* or *paisano*; men sentenced to a life without wife or children: the last branches of their family trees.

I visited Grandma Angelina shortly before she died. My aunt Ursula had called me. It can happen any time, she said. So I went. Grandma was eighty-six, and still washed clothes on the cement washboard, gave me jars of sour cherry and *calafate* jam to take home, and went fishing with me on the lake. She passed away three months later of a weak heart, and I returned for the funeral. Her face in the coffin was unrecognisable. The flowers of the wreath I ordered on the phone were plastic.

After that trip, distance and her absence from the farm discouraged me from going back – until an idea for a novel made it indispensable. The novel would be called *Los hombres más altos*, the first of a trilogy about southern Patagonia told through the lives of the Tehuelche people, the field hands and my family. Twenty years had passed and there were many memories I needed to reclaim: the redcurrants, round and shiny as pearls, I picked under the Lombardy poplars; the dry smell of corn cracking inside the grinding mill; the wind howling through the willows. I wanted to see again how the *cañadones* turned yellow and orange at sunset, how the blues of the lake danced to the movement of the clouds. I wanted to lie down on a haystack, bury my nose in the fleece of a fat sheep, see light until midnight in the endless summer days.

By the time I returned to the farm, I was living in Buenos Aires, a city of millions. There I disappeared under clouds of smog coughed up by forty-year-old trucks, tripped on the broken sidewalks and shared the narrow bike lanes with carts of indigent dumpster-divers who were part of my daily routine – features of a so-called 'peripheral' country that used to upset me when I was younger, but had begun to comfort me. Through the chaos and the frustrations, I recognised an unruly humanity that I would miss in the orderly subdivisions of Washington, or on the manicured boulevards of European capitals.

As a man of fifty who had lived in the US and Europe for over a decade, I considered myself almost cured of the fascination with the North that most Argentines seem to be born with. A line joining South Africa, Argentina and Australia made more sense as the centre of my world – southern hemisphere countries that share similar colonial histories, vast and mythical inner territories (Patagonia, Outback and Karoo), and the singularity of celebrating New Year covered in sweat and wearing bermudas and short sleeves. Countries with troubled histories of genocide and dispossession, children of colonial parents who need to talk to each other without the mediation of the north.

I was harbouring a southern feeling, a deep connection with the South of this real world, where I was born and will probably die. A unique world – in the words of J.M. Coetzee – with its unique skies and its unique heavenly constellations, where the winds blow in a certain way and the leaves fall in a certain way and the sun beats down in a certain way that is instantly recognisable from one part of the South to another.

As I researched my novel about the Tehuelche I uncovered the horrors of the Argentine occupation of Patagonia – the killings, the concentration camps, the invisibilisation of thousands of people under a veil of lies and oblivion that most Argentines are still happy to accept. As I dismantled one by one the official narratives of what is still called 'the Conquest of a Desert' and replaced them with the reality – a blatant invasion of a foreign territory half the size of the original Argentina, inhabited for centuries by indigenous nations with complex lives and interrelations more humane than the Spanish and Portuguese ex-colonies ever had – it became clear that Argentina, infected by the colonial disease of the North it had fought so bravely to free itself from, had turned into an even crueller coloniser. I began to discern new norths and new souths.

On the flight to Lake Cardiel, as I looked out at the endless plains that cut off Patagonia from the rest of the continent, it occurred to me that there was not only a south, but also a south of the south – and that was where I was heading.

I was driving Aunt Ursula's truck when the blue waters of Lake Cardiel appeared in the middle distance. I prefer for men to drive, she said before taking the passenger seat. Ursula is my uncle Muñeco's widow, a short lady with an easy laugh who recently retired as a school principal. While we skirted the edge of the lake, she told me how most sheep stations in the area had been abandoned. Persistent droughts, the meagre price of wool and the ashes of a Chilean volcano that killed half a million sheep in the early 1990s were the last blows to a system in agony – a failed colonisation project. My aunt and my cousins, however, are set to defy the trend. Our grandparents' farm, which they now run, is one of the few still in operation in the area.

The deserted sheep stations, once inhabited by people I knew and cared for, were not the only changes. Ursula warned me about her 'improvements' to the house, but it was still shocking to see Grandma's square kitchen turned rectangular, her pastel-green walls painted a hideous beige, the white enamel wood stove replaced by a black iron one. Outside the house, among the four acres sheltered by willows and poplars planted by my grandparents, the vegetable garden had vanished. The crisp lettuce that Grandma harvested right before lunch, the crunchy radishes and the juicy potatoes, had been replaced by produce bought in the supermarket before we left town – wilting already in the back of the truck. You can't find anybody to take care of a vegetable garden around here any more, Ursula apologised. And too much bending is not good at my age, you know.

The house of the peons had also been upgraded. There was a new tin roof and a larger bathroom, but I could still recognise the green bench where I used to sit and talk to Reyes, the oval table where we played cards with Barrientos. I knocked and walked in like I used to. A stocky man, wearing a black beret and a red waistband, was seated by the wood stove listening to the radio. His name was Tito. We shook hands and I grabbed a chair. I didn't seem to need the magic of the espadrilles – as soon as I started talking, my accent changed and I knew what to ask. We started off discussing the national rodeo competition, then I asked about his dogs (two furry mongrels I had seen outside the door), and then his horse (which I hadn't seen yet). He fixed a maté and told me about his last visit to town, how he lost his second horse betting on dice. It wasn't a very good horse, he said. We were both feeling increasingly comfortable. He talked about his brother, how he was killed by a truck while walking along the road on a moonless night. He was very drunk, Tito said. There was also a story of a brothel, a new black Dominican girl everybody fancied. Tito's stories were painfully similar to those I used to hear from other peons thirty years before, men trapped in cycles of isolation on the farms, relieved by occasional days in town splashing all their wages on cheap liquor and worn-out women. In a place where many things are changing, the fate of the peons remained unaltered.

At some point, I asked Tito where he was from. He told me he grew up in Reserva Lote 6, that he was a Tehuelche. I looked at his narrow eyes, at the whiskers growing on his chin. I looked at his hand as he passed me the maté gourd, the nail of his middle finger turning purple. My heart raced. I was lost for words for a moment, and then all I was able to talk about was the novel I was writing, the research I'd been doing about the Tehuelche. I explained to Tito their rituals and hunting methods. He smiled and said nothing. Then I ranted against the Patagonian invasion, against Argentina freeing itself from the metropolis only to turn around and kill, displace and subjugate tens of thousands of indigenous people. Tito kept smiling, but I was not sure he understood why I was telling him all this. I didn't know how to go on. Should I talk about Tehuelche students in Salesian schools, made to kneel on corn kernels as punishment for speaking their native tongue? About the children abducted from their mothers to be whitened in state institutions, as late as the 1980s? Should I admit that I cried watching a documentary about 85-year-old Dora Manchado, the last living speaker of their language – Dora, who recalled how she hid her indigenous background to avoid being treated like dirt? Tito's silence told me to shut up. He went back to the topic of the rodeo, we drank a couple more matés and I left.

Back in the house, Ursula was baking bread. The aroma coming from the oven was different from Grandma's in ways I couldn't explain. I asked her about Reyes and Barrientos, but I already knew the answer. Most peons in our family's sheep station have been indigenous, she says matter-of-factly, but we never called them *that*. Clouds drifted sluggishly over the lake. Tito's dogs were howling in the distance. It was almost sunset, and the blues of the waters, the ochres and oranges of the *cañadones*, the browns of the *meseta* were getting brighter and brighter.

My gaze wandered through the window, towards everything and nothing, while I thought of the hands – the hands that helped me up onto a towering horse, the hands that taught me how to shuffle a deck of cards, the hands that scythed the alfalfa and sheared a sheep – the work, the habits, the repetition of care. Hands that helped me see myself differently from what my stepfather and the school bullies told me I was – and I was grateful for that. It may have been the same white-European-male system that hurt us all, a system that conceived and built just one world, with little room for different strands of humanity and less for indigenous people. And yet to think of that only highlights my privileged position: the one barely grazed by shrapnel being tended by the heavily wounded. ∎

Lake Cardiel, Argentina, 2017
Courtesy of the author

PICKING UP NATHAN FROM THE AIRPORT

Benjamin Markovits

When Nathan's flight was cancelled (the whole Eastern seaboard was about to be buried in snow), Jean persuaded him to make an earlier plane to Charlotte out of T.F. Green. At least that got them out of the cold front. From there they could fly to Dallas, it put them in the ballpark, and even though they were landing too late to catch the shuttle to Austin, she offered to pick them up – which meant six hours in the car for her, there and back. His kids would be exhausted, his wife wanted to stay in Boston anyway, but Jean bullied her brother into it because Henrik was coming after Christmas, and she wanted Nathan to meet him.

It's a boring drive to Dallas/Fort Worth Airport, you just take I-35 the whole way. The radio was broken in her parents' Volvo, and the tape player had swallowed its last cassette. All you could listen to was whatever was on that tape, an early Billy Bragg, which belonged to her brother in grad school: *Talking with the Taxman About Poetry*, not his best. But Jean put it on anyway and knew the words well enough to sing along. In her jet-lagged state, it helped her to stay awake. Something about the tinny guitar, the cheap acoustics, reminded her of Nathan's old room at Holywell Manor, Balliol's graduate student housing, just opposite the law faculty. Jean had visited him there during her final year at Yale, over spring break. His English accent was terrible, but he liked to sing along: *whoops, there goes another year, whoops, there goes another pint of beer* – and the world it opened up to her again, of his goofiness and happy ambition, before the success kicked in, almost brought tears to her eyes.

When she was young, eight or nine years old, starting to read for herself, to want to follow adult conversation, Nathan was her point of access: a high-school kid, dark-skinned and wild-haired, with an unshaved mustache, too clever for his teachers and quick enough to pick fights with his parents, too. He could always see the principles at stake in any situation, no matter how small or petty they seemed, and could push you into positions you didn't know you occupied, until you found yourself defending stuff you didn't want to defend. So you gave in or gave up and let it go. She used to practise copying his handwriting, one of those facts about the depth of her child-devotion she only mentioned to him fifteen years later. 'Huh,' he said; he didn't know what to say. Sometimes she wondered whether she had failed Susan somehow, by not directing more of her imitation-flattery toward her big sister, and whether this failure involved a more general kind of failure, to grow into a normal woman – to go through not just the rites of passage, but the ordinary feelings you're supposed to have, about boys and sex and motherhood. So that now she was stuck at the age of thirty-two trying to make up for lost ground.

Her other brother Paul once said to her, when she first told him about Henrik, 'There's plenty of time to make your own life with someone.' As if she were trying to steal someone else's. She got mad at him, but it's not always easy to tell, especially in the heat of the moment, if you're pissed off because someone's right about you or because they're wrong. And she knew that what she was doing, the reason she was thinking these thoughts through, was to prepare herself for a long conversation with Nathan. Sometimes it's easier to talk late at night, in the dark, when you're both staring at something else, like the road in front of you. Of course, for the first part, his kids would be awake, his wife would probably sit between them in the back. But then they'd fall asleep (after ten hours in transit, it was even later East Coast time), and the noise of the road was loud enough to make it hard to hear in the back. The Volvo was an old car – there was no sound protection. Even the background warmth of sleeping kids contributes to the sense of intimacy. Well, it doesn't matter. You never have the conversations you want to anyway; almost never. Something always comes up, other people get in the way. But still she prepared herself, she wanted to get her story straight, even in her own head.

When Henrik was first diagnosed, she thought, *that's it*. Her initial reaction was selfish: *that's it for me*, he'll go back to his wife. When shit like this happens, people don't walk out on fifteen-year marriages. One morning he woke up with an ache in his – 'balls area', this is how he put it. The truth is, he had felt something before, a sort of numbness, like you get when someone kicks a football into your . . . between your . . . legs. But when you're forty-seven, forty-eight, a lot of things hurt, especially when you get up in the morning. And if you pay attention to everything that hurts . . . But he was also coming down with a cold, something was going around the kids' school, everybody back after the long summer holiday, the temperature had dropped, leaves were falling, real life had begun again.

He called Jean to tell her that he wasn't coming in – an easy call to make, because she worked at the company and needed to know. In other words, one of those conversations he didn't have to conceal or disguise. Monica was almost out the door, dragging the kids to school. Emil and Freya still needed to be walked (Sasha had left earlier for her cello lesson), and he had come down in his dressing gown to make himself coffee and wave them off, before going back up to bed. For some reason it gave him pleasure to be able to speak openly to Jean in front of his wife. Later, around eleven o'clock, he called again, just to pass the time; he was feeling sorry for himself. 'I think I found something on my . . . I think I felt something . . . on one of my testicles. It hurts a little, too.'

'Have you talked to somebody about this? Does Monica know?'

'It's fine, I'm sure it's . . . I'm just lying here and feeling bored and sorry for myself.'

'Go see someone,' Jean said. 'Go see someone today.'

'I don't feel well, remember. That's why I'm in bed.'

'I don't care,' Jean said.

He knew she would react this way. Like many practical and competent people, she treated complaints as problems to be solved, but she also had a nervous tendency, she took everything seriously and had a habit of thinking in terms of worst-case scenarios. Maybe this is what he wanted from her, and he was using her anxieties as a kind of test, to see if he should be worried or not.

'I'll do it,' he said. 'I'll go see someone, but not today. This is nothing new.' He meant, the feeling of numbness or the slight ache. 'I can go tomorrow, when I don't feel like shit. I can go next week.'

Ten minutes later Jean called back to say she had booked him an appointment with his GP – for three o'clock. (She had worked as his assistant for several years; it felt natural for her to take charge in this way.) So he went.

Among the various things she blamed herself for, Jean sometimes added this to the list: that she had somehow made the cancer happen to him, either because it was a kind of accretion of his guilt, something his kidneys couldn't process or whatever . . . or because she had made him go to the doctor and it was only because the doctor had found something that it was actually there. He had to wait three weeks to see a specialist at the clinic in UCL and then another week for the results. In other words, almost a month of keeping the lid on her anxieties, which is more or less what it felt like. She was conscious of a kind of rattle in her manner, an almost audible low-level and constant need to release internal pressure. They were carefully polite to each other, both at work and afterward, in their moments of manufactured alone-time – sharing a taxi, for example, to a screening at Soho House. Jean couldn't tell if he was distancing himself from her, for understandable reasons, in preparation for the necessary break, or just hunkering down, or if in fact she herself was pushing him away. Selflessly or selfishly, who knows.

Still waiting for results, Monica rented a cottage in Somerset for half-term and he drove down with her and the kids one Saturday morning. Jean's envy felt like a kind of poison, which makes you unrecognizable to yourself. One night he called her from his cell phone – their first contact in almost a week. The cottage had no reception so he had to walk about ten minutes along a B-road to the nearest pub, where there was free Wi-Fi. ('I told Monica I wanted to check my email.') It was about six o'clock, the sun was setting, he would have to walk back in the dark. Already the pub was filling up, she couldn't hear him clearly, background noise of people and music, the signal quality was poor, so he stepped outside and she could feel the change in atmosphere like a shift in weather – he was standing outside in the mild evening cold.

The clinic had called, while they were having lunch at Coleridge Cottage, in Nether Stowey. What he had was a stage 3 embryonal carcinoma. It had spread to his lungs, and maybe elsewhere – he needed more tests. The good news was . . . it was . . . he wasn't very good at the terminology, yet – seminomatous, which is typical of . . . older patients. He laughed. Most of the time it's very treatable. Jean was still in the office, about to go out for the evening – she was meeting a few girlfriends at the Curzon on Shaftesbury Avenue, and took her cell phone into the bathroom, so she could listen in peace and talk to him without being overheard. Or break down if she wanted to. He said, 'It's what Lance Armstrong had. But not as bad.'

'Okay,' she told him, as clearly as she could. 'What do you want me to do?'

'Look,' he said, 'I've been thinking about it all day. I can't live like this and make them care for me.' No, thought Jean, you can't, and knew what was coming next. But then he said, 'I think we should move in together. I want to tell her.'

'That's a terrible thing to do to somebody,' Jean said.

Even in the bathroom she kept her voice low. The floor was tiled (a strand of wet toilet paper lay by the loo) and everything echoed. There was a smell of running drains and disinfectant. She leaned against the door, with her back against it.

'I think it's better in the long run. It is already terrible, what we're doing. But I have to . . . I have to live a life I want to live. I want to live it with you.'

'What about the kids?'

'We need to get an apartment together. They can't come and visit you – in that room. You are not saying anything now. I don't know if this is something you want.'

'Yes,' Jean said. 'I'll do whatever you want me to. I love you.'

'Okay, good. Me, too. Okay,' he said. 'I should go back now – it's dinner time. I'll see you Monday. We can work everything out.'

When the phone went dead in her ear, she didn't move for a moment. It was like lying in bed and thinking, I should get up. The pressure of conflicting feelings . . . a kind of stand-off . . . but she also thought, if my life has an emotional center, a moment on which all the different forces converge, it's this, and I'm going through it now. But maybe this is just a kind of self-importance, which means you haven't digested or thought through what's actually going on. Not yet anyway. When she came out of the bathroom, she sat down at her computer again and typed 'Lance Armstrong's cancer' into Google and followed the various threads until it was time for her to meet her friends at the cinema, about a fifteen-minute walk away – across New Oxford Street, busy with buses, the lights coming on and people going home – into Soho.

For the next few days, until he came back, apart from everything else that she was worried about (and she spent much of her spare time online, looking up his diagnosis, coming to grips with the various terms, trying to understand the treatment options, and following the science and evidence-based research behind recent developments), she also worried that he would change his mind. Maybe it was just the heat of the moment. He was stuck in Somerset with the kids. But his explanation when he saw her again sounded perfectly reasonable.

'I knew as soon as I heard from the clinic that I had to tell Monica. I mean, about us. You can't ask someone to care for you on this basis.'

They were having lunch at one of these *bibimbap* places you find on the backstreets by the British Museum, among the second-hand bookshops and expensive ceramic stores, the tartan outlets. Hot-sauce bottles sticky on the plastic table; a strangely provincial air of quiet and neglect. The staff seemed to live downstairs, where the kitchens were – there was only one other group of customers, four men, sitting in the back by the restroom door. Henrik and Jean had at least a little natural light, such as it was – falling between tall gray buildings.

'I expect there will be . . . a certain amount of drama . . . in the next year,' he said. 'Even if it is mostly very boring. And I won't ask her to feel whatever she will feel about that . . . we have not had such feelings for each other in many years . . . without telling her about you. And as soon as I tell her, our marriage will be over. I don't expect anything else.'

But even then, as she lay in bed that night, too excited to sleep (not happy exactly but deeply agitated, and debating whether she should call someone – Paul, Nathan, Susie, Liesel? anyone but her father), she remembered what he had said and wondered if it left room for doubt. As if it were still up to Monica in the end. But she never found out if that's what he meant, because it didn't matter: Henrik was right. Monica kicked him out. And for a week he stayed either on the sofa bed in the office (which they sometimes offered to 'friends' in the business, other directors and producers, visiting London) or at her room in Brondesbury, while she looked for an apartment. For years she had lived, more or less, in student squalor – either in Oxford, in a shared house on Marlborough Road, near the Head of the River pub; or lodging in various rooms in north-west London. Her landladies were mostly divorced mothers whose children had become adults and moved out. But now she was looking for her own first grown-up flat – and they needed three bedrooms, so that Henrik's kids could stay on weekends, once all that was sorted out.

The fact is, she was having fun, and she felt guilty about that, too. And not just fun – she knew that whatever else she was doing, she was living more importantly than she had been living before. Spending more money, living on a grander scale, with bigger things at stake. They looked around Kensal Green Station, because the rents were still borderline affordable and they could catch the Overground train to Euston and walk from there into Bloomsbury. It was like shopping for an imaginary life, which you then pay for, and live. Here's where I'll sit and have my coffee, here's what I'll look out on from my bed. A city life – with a commuter train to catch each morning, and a home with somebody to come back to at the end of the day.

And that's more or less what happened; they moved in together. The walk between residential streets to their apartment, the top half of a bay-windowed Victorian on Buchanan Gardens, wasn't always totally scare-free; but she got used to that, and most of the time she walked home with Henrik. As the year wore on his kids began to stay over, and their Saturdays were taken up with homework and trips to swimming pools. Something else she felt guilty about, nervous, clumsily on edge, but also secretly . . . not secretly . . . but with her deeper emotions very near the surface, ready to do their duty, the work that you have them for. Emotions like love and fear, expressed among other things by trying to remember your seventh-grade math.

She had to figure out what they liked to eat, and to learn how to cook it so that they didn't complain. Like every other second wife – part of what you realize is how many there are around. It's like buying a car, you begin to spot them everywhere: at the Tesco Express, and on the bus, and outside the school gate, picking up the kids with a purse full of crisps and chocolate. Even this was part of being alive, and belonging to a demographic, or whatever you want to call it – one of the types.

Not that she was quite yet a second wife. Also, you never stop forgetting, these aren't my kids. Part of the guilt is that you sometimes think, this isn't my problem, and then on Sunday night, after you hand them over, it isn't any more.

The first time she saw Monica after the . . . they didn't have a word for it, the announcement, after Henrik had told his wife what was going on, Jean was sitting in a Zipcar van outside their house in Acton. (When he first moved out, all he took with him was a duffel bag full of clothes and shoes, and a backpack with his laptop and a couple of books.) Henrik had an office in the house, with an exercise bike and a bench press – his response to middle age, as he put it, was low-key but traditional. Anyway, Monica wanted them gone. She needed the room for a lodger, a friend of hers, who could also help with the kids. 'I don't care what you do with them,' she said. 'Just get rid of them.'

'This is expensive equipment. I have nowhere . . . at least not yet,' he began to say.

'Get them out! Get them out! Get them out!'

Jean heard about it all later. And now she sat in the van, in the driver's seat, not quite daring to go in. *You're a coward,* she told herself. You're a bad human being. But still she didn't move.

Their house had four or five steps to the front door; the ground floor was slightly raised up, with the kitchen in the basement, and Jean could see the entrance hall and Henrik backing out with the exercise bike in his hands. It was a heavy machine; he couldn't carry it himself, and Monica had taken the other end. Jean immediately got out of the van and moved quickly, that half-scuttle, to indicate hurry. But since Henrik was first, she started to take the weight off his hands, until Monica said, 'I need a little help here, I need to put it down.' So they put it down – Jean squeezed past (the front garden was narrow, and unevenly flagged; she had to push against the recycling and garbage bins) and reached out awkwardly to grab a pedal, but by that point the work was mostly done. Monica stood up to arch her back and rub the blood back into her hands. Jean, half crouching, stood up, too; they looked at each other.

'I think you can take it the rest of the way,' Monica said.

They had known each other a little, inevitably; Monica had always been friendly to her, if slightly condescending. She used to try to set her up on dates, and sometimes called her last minute if they were having a dinner party and needed an extra woman. Monica liked to complain about Henrik to her – not complain exactly, but to include Jean in her wifely frustrations. 'He always says yes yes I'll do it and he never does it, he isn't even listening . . .' That kind of thing; as if Jean would know what she meant. Jean used to resent these appeals, slightly; she didn't like being lumped in with the sisterhood of female patience. Although in fact Monica herself was a busy and competent woman – she worked in PR for a film distribution company.

'I can get the other stuff, too,' Jean said.

'That's fine,' Monica told her, un-angrily. And then, matter-of-factly: 'I don't want you in the house. I don't want the kids seeing you.'

She had passed Waco (in the dark) and was coming up to the turn off for 35E. Some of the streetlights weren't working. Even thinking about that interaction made the blood concentrate in her face. Sometimes you find yourself taking sides and you don't exactly like the side you happen to be on. Driving through the dark like this . . . she wouldn't be back until one in the morning, at the earliest. All of this looked even now like a kind of penance. The road at night went inward, too, and the landscape you were traveling through looked a lot like . . . nothing much . . . a few gas stations . . . a few half-built developments . . . tractors or cement mixers or some kind of paving machine, standing on dirt, with those bright rolls of temporary fencing, curled over and lying on the ground. And the cars kept coming at you. From time to time, you had to get out of the middle lane, move around a truck or to let someone pass. What did she want to say to Nathan about all this? What was she trying to prove? She could talk about Henrik's kids but even the thought of them, of telling Nathan about the way she had learned to . . . brought out in her own mind a tone of voice, the tone she would use, and which she wouldn't like. Anyway, he doesn't care, that's not what he cares about.

Henrik had surgery the week before Thanksgiving. Even by then Monica had relented a little. Henrik wanted the kids to visit him, he wanted Jean's company, he wanted 'all of this to start now'. He meant, an acceptance of the new arrangement. He also thought, I can make use of my weakened condition, and everybody's sympathy, to force them to get along. For Emil's sake, he pretended to be a monster. He was hooked up to all these wires, there was a stent in the veins above his wrist, he looked very white. *Ooh ooh,* he said, lifting his arms, like a zombie – and the graphs on his readout flared. You could see the tangle of wires, running through his sleeve and from around his waist, to the monitor, which was connected to the wall by a mechanical arm. Emil said, 'Stop it, I don't like it.' Sasha, the oldest, politely laughed.

They took out his testicle and used keyhole surgery to remove the lesions on his lungs. For the next two months he went in for weekly chemo sessions, followed by a six-week recovery, which was followed by two more months of chemo, another recovery period, and then another round of chemo, which brought them roughly into summer, into the school holidays. He lost his hair but he didn't have much hair to begin with and there were times, when one of the kids had a cold, for example, that he wasn't supposed to be in contact, and even on his weekends to see them, they didn't come. This kind of thing had to be worked out with Monica – Jean often ended up being responsible for the arrangements. On the whole, Henrik was a good patient. He was relatively unafraid of dying (it's hard to measure these things, as he said himself) and he had a high tolerance for physical discomfort. Boredom upset him; he didn't like not working, and when she could, Jean made it possible for him to work at home, doing what could be usefully done by computer. During his recovery periods, and at the beginning of each treatment cycle, he also went into the office, although Jean worried a lot about what he might pick up on the train. Part of what sustained him, what sustained both of them, was that this period of his life also coincided with the open and honest committed beginning of their relationship – they were living together, playing house, could meet friends and go to the movies (when he was up for it) without any pretense or surge of guilt, and it turned out that the pleasure of living naturally more than made up for the excitement of what they had been doing before.

Henrik also got to see Jean at her best – competent, loving and selfless. And he got to see her with his kids.

Her relationship with Emil was the simplest, he was an easy boy, very like his father, square-jawed, silent, he did what he wanted but generally didn't cause much trouble because he wanted harmless things. He played with Lego for hours – they set up a corner in their new kitchen where the box of Lego lived, so they could cook and talk and eat while he was occupied. And he could also be suddenly and surprisingly physically affectionate. Sometimes, when Jean was standing with her back to him, or sitting on the sofa, watching TV, he would throw himself at her – holding on to what he could, her neck if she was sitting down, her waist, and not let go. The fact that she had taken his father away didn't mean much to him; he was still too small. And also, as the youngest child, he seemed to have been born with an assurance that everybody loved him . . . one more person didn't matter.

And Sasha, the oldest, seemed to like her, too. There was a kind of pleasure she took in having this extremely adult relationship with a woman who was not her mother. She had just started secondary school, at Henrietta Barnett, a grammar in north London, which meant getting a train and then a bus every morning by herself – over an hour each way. She was still at the stage where independence pleased her; you could almost see her consciously adopting what she considered to be adult poses and attitudes. Of course she was also sometimes very tired and stressed, and Jean tried to imagine her real thoughts, the thoughts of a twelve-year-old girl, getting on a train and then a bus with everyone else, the other commuters, keeping to herself, clutching her backpack on her lap if she could find a seat, and taking the same journey back at the end of the day to a home radically altered from the home she had been living in just a few months before. That's a lot of adulthood at once, Jean once said to Henrik, and she made a point of reading some of the books that Sasha was reading, not just John Green, but *Lord of the Flies* and *The Canterbury Tales*, which is what they were studying at school. So they could talk about them on the weekends.

Only Freya was difficult, resentful and misbehaving. If a kid wants to act up, there really isn't much you can do about it. You can threaten and you can plead, but game theory isn't on your side (as Nathan put it to her, when she complained to him over the phone), especially for someone in your position. 'What do you mean, my position?' she said, but she knew what he meant. She just wanted to hear how he was going to put it. Well, you're in a setup where what the kid actually wants is a breakdown of law and order. She didn't eat Jean's cooking. Jean could ask her, what do you want to eat tonight, what's your favorite thing, and she would make it, and Freya would suddenly pretend not to be hungry. If you pushed her, she'd explain, almost sweetly, I don't like it the way you make it, which was maybe even true. Well, what do you want to eat then, and the whole thing began again. She made a mess at the table, picking the middle out of a baguette, for example, rolling it around between her fingers into a ball, and flicking it at Sasha, until Sasha complained. If you told her to clean up after herself, she looked at you like, make me. And you couldn't make her. Henrik sometimes lost his temper, which made everything worse. 'I hate coming here, I don't want to come . . .' and so on. All of which Jean sympathized with.

In spite of all this, it gave Jean pleasure to be in the middle of a family again, in the middle of all that, the way she used to be, as a kid – caught in all the webs of intimacy, even if in her case she was the least involved and could remove herself when she wanted to. But she was good at family life, too. She had spent eighteen years training for it, living at home with parents and siblings, and then, when they kick you out and send you to college, and later expect you to make a life on your own, all of these skills have nothing to do. And she was using them again. The density of her life had increased. And she felt also a new proximity to the big beasts, the monsters of childhood, which loom so large and seem so vivid and terrifying, until you hit your twenties and turn everything into a kind of domesticated pet: a job, a love life, somewhere to live – these are the things you think about, and not death, and what it means to Freya, an eight-year-old girl, to find out that your father isn't your father anymore, but somebody else, who sleeps in a bed with somebody you don't know.

By this point, she had merged onto the north fork of I-35 and was counting the exit signs for the turn off to 121. There were actual neighborhoods, with trees and front yards and quiet streets, peeling away below her – she had entered again into conurbation, and could see the skyline of Fort Worth ahead of her, something to shoot for. Waves of sleepiness had been coming and going for the past half-hour, but paying attention was good for her, and she felt like she'd emerged again, come up from under, and now lay beached and dry – not rested exactly, but out of danger. An incident in the road meant a build-up of yellow lights, the tow truck was just arriving as she passed by, but at this time of night, two days before Christmas, the slowdown in the remaining lanes was just a case of rubbernecking: a Mazda hatchback and some kind of throwback pickup sat parked or slewed at awkward angles to each other. There was glass in the road, glinting in the headlights, and the weird wobbly but silent rotation of the sirens, which fattened and thinned out like a swinging water balloon. Everybody looked okay though; a woman in a man's coat sat on the barrier talking on her cell phone, she looked like she'd been there a while, and Jean kept going (the traffic flowed again) away from other people's problems.

Part of what you want to prove, part of what you want to show people (people like Nathan), is that this is now something you know how to do – to look after kids. Only she didn't have the kids around to show it with. She missed them, especially Emil, who had started climbing into their bed with a book on Sunday mornings. Jean, even if she didn't feel like it, would sit up and read to him, though her audience, as she knew full well, was also Henrik, who lay with his face in the pillow and left her to it. Sometimes you can read without even really waking up. She needed to concentrate now; there were signs for the airport, among dozens of other signs, and the highways were starting to metastasize as they approached the city, entangling and disentangling, it wasn't always clear what lane to be in. Cars thickened around her, and she felt the mass of people, like a kind of contraction, after driving at night through the empty country; this was different and you felt it in your head. Joining a queue for the toll, she opened her window – and the cold December air came in, flavored by exhaust, the wide continuous noise of cars, like a fact of life, and she had to shift her butt to get her wallet out and find the change. Even two nights before Christmas it was somebody's job to sit in a booth and take her money. On an eight-hour shift how many cars went by? Then you drive home.

Right from the first his doctors were optimistic. One of them said to him, 'This is a good time to get this kind of cancer. Even five years ago, you'd be looking at a very different set of outcomes.' And Henrik believed in professional expertise. If the people you paid to be good at something told you something, you believed them, that's what you paid them for. Jean was more skeptical, she spent too much time online. It's like I'm having an affair with his worst-case scenarios, she said to Nathan. I can't tell him about it, but this is what I do when he's not around. Henrik went through ups and downs, but they were mostly physical. When your white blood cell count declines, you feel small, you shrink, and in fact he also lost a lot of weight, your presence changes, people change around you, but even at his lowest he assumed this phase would pass, and wanted to make plans for when it did.

About the divorce, for example; if possible he hoped to arrange things so that Monica could keep the house. Really so the kids could keep their childhood home. But he also needed to get some money out of it, if they were ever going to buy a place themselves. Jean had always made it a point of pride to get by without her parents' money – except for flights home. 'You have to pay to see me,' she told her mother. But the money was there, and Henrik wanted to have a reasonable conversation about what kind of apartment they could afford.

By the end of the summer, when his final round of chemo ended, he looked like a different person. The shape of his face had changed;

he looked almost younger. He had always been a square, strong, competent Danish-sailor type, with a little fat on him, but not too much – a solid citizen. And now even the way he moved in his clothes seemed to suggest a kind of nervous energy or restlessness, you could see the shape of his skull, his face looked naked, the egg of his bald head looked like it would crack if you tapped it with a spoon. But he was very happy; they were very happy together, and the habit of the past six months had made him feel dependent and affectionate, he wanted to sit next to Jean at parties, he smiled more, and the fact was, the roles in which they had gotten to know each other, when he was married and her boss, had shifted, too.

At his three-month checkup, when the doctors gave him the all-clear, they went for a drink afterward at the Russell Hotel. He asked Jean to marry him, when the divorce came through, and she joked: 'I think you're feeling emotional now because you've had good news.'

'Does that mean you don't want to?'

The tone of the conversation had suddenly changed – it was like a change in temperature. 'I want to, but you haven't even met my parents.'

'You think they will change my mind?' Then, smiling: 'You think they will change your mind?'

And she said, 'I want you to meet them.'

So he agreed to come to Texas that year, after spending Christmas with his kids.

There were traffic cops working the access road to the terminal, and she joined the queue of cars and taxis and tried to keep an eye out on the side of the road for somewhere to pull in. But you could only pull in if your passengers had arrived. What a day. Henrik was almost certainly asleep – it was four o'clock in the morning in London, and she still had at least another three hours to drive. All these people looking for cabs and rides, college students, flying home for Christmas; young parents, crying kids. But the cops wouldn't let you linger, they kept waving everybody along. Then you went through the whole business again, pulled out of the queue and onto the freeway, heading out again, into the night, into the wide country, before you doubled back. But on her second time around she saw them: Nathan, in his travel suit, by the side of the road, handsome and fidgety, after sitting on flights, waiting in airports – he was walking up and down, a big restless well-dressed man. His hair was even wilder than usual, he looked tired. His wife sat on a bench with one of the kids; the other lay on a couple of suitcases pushed together, fast asleep.

'Hey,' Jean said, pulling over, lowering her window. 'You made it.' ∎

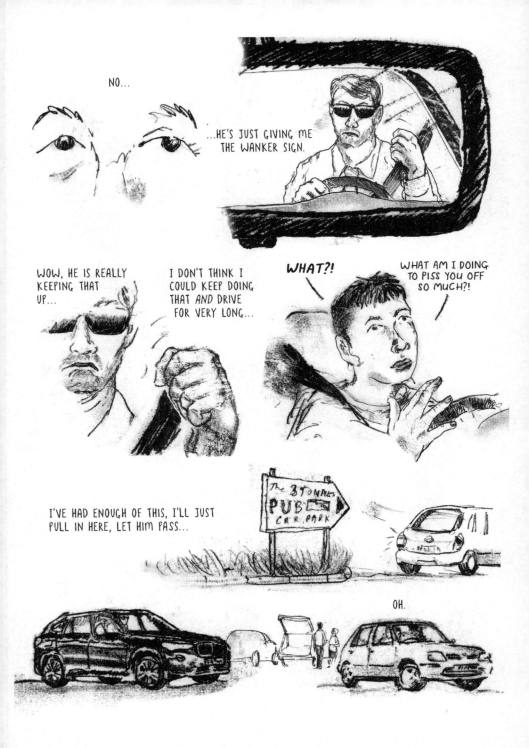

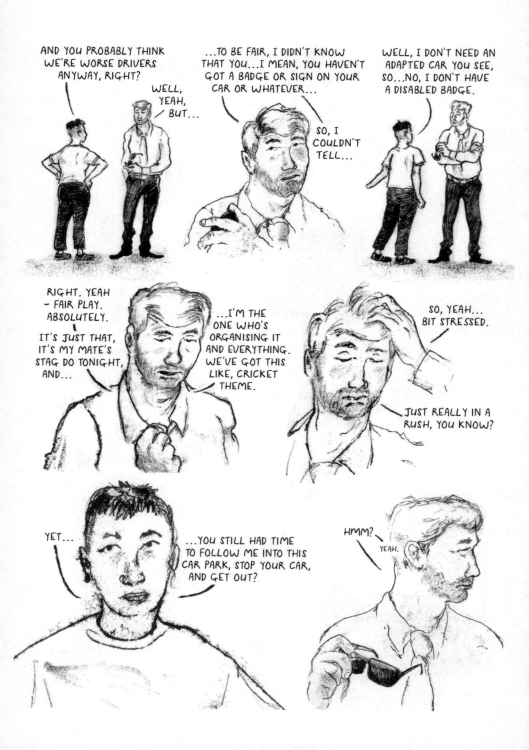

Tweets
13.2K

Following
5

Followers
56.3K

Likes
15.2K

Jacques Derrida
@JacquesDerrida

Philosopher and Writer

📍 Paris, France

🗓 Joined Oct 2000

⟲ You Retweeted

David Baddiel ✓
@Baddiel · Aug 18

Replying to @revkollektiv @meralhece

That isn't what she means: if so, she would not be frightened of being accused of a/s. Plus she has just been furious about a video in which a Jewish person has talked about a/s making her feel in need of a safe haven. I make this clear in a separate tweet, this one.

> **David Baddiel** ✓ @Baddiel · 3h
> Replying to @Gonzoking
> It is of course reasonable to examine the history of Jewish persecution, the reasons for which are always to do with Christian scapegoating and with all majority cultures psychotic need to have an alien hate object. That isn't what she means.

💬 1   ⟲ 2   ♡

⟲ You Retweeted

David Baddiel ✓
@Baddiel · Aug 18

Jerry thinks Corbynistas are my tribe. He thinks I have a tribe. How hilarious.

> **Jerry Taylor** ▨▨▨**#FBPE #LibDem** @JerryTaylor
> Replying to @Baddiel
> Yes you just wanted to smear the Lib Dems. It's a crying shame you can't let go of your narrow tribalism even for such an important issue.

💬 19   ⟲ 3   ♡ 72

#TEAMBADDIEL VS #TEAMBABEL

LOSING THE GAME OF MEANING
ON SOCIAL MEDIA

David Baddiel

L et's just do the most recent one. There will be another by the time you're reading this. There will probably be another one by the time I've finished writing it.

On 11 August 2018, in response to a video entitled 'I Am a Zionist', Baroness Jenny Tonge, a peer in the House of Lords, wrote this on her Facebook page:

 Jenny Tonge shared The Israel Institute of New Zealand's video. •••
11 August · 🌐

This is excruciating to listen to. Self justification, complacency, manipulation of 'history'. Just sickening.
We would all like a safe haven to run to when the going gets tough, but we stay on and ask why it is getting tough. Why have the Jewish people been persecuted over and over again throughout history. Why? I never get an answer. If we discussed this we would be accused of anti Semitism, so better not, and so it goes on!

A few days later, my attention having been called to it by one of my Twitter followers, I wrote:

David Baddiel ✓
@Baddiel

Follow ⌄

And meanwhile I'd like to know why Jenny Tonge, a Lib Dem peer in the House of Lords - the Lib Dems btw, have always had their fair share of anti-Jewish racists - can say this and retain her seat there, as the implication of her question *is* just straightforward Nazism.

Jenny Tonge shared The Israel Institute of New Zealand's video. •••
11 August · 🌐

This is excruciating to listen to. Self justification, complacency, manipulation of 'history'. Just sickening.
We would all like a safe haven to run to when the going gets tough, but we stay on and ask why it is getting tough. Why have the Jewish people been persecuted over and over again throughout history. Why? I never get an answer. If we discussed this we would be accused of anti Semitism, so better not, and so it goes on!

Sorry – before we go any further – about the screenshots. Sorry, in fact, about the first of what will be many 'X posted this, so I posted this, and then Y posted this', but this is what social media, particularly Twitter, is. It's a conversation: a much more aggressive and polarising conversation than most that take place through speech – although I get the sense, from anger I have seen on the streets recently, that the aggression on Twitter is bleeding out into what one can still just about call 'The Real World'. Very little is said on social media that isn't a response to something else, and thus it's the final proof of – I'm in *Granta*, a safe space, I assume, to say this – the post-structuralist idea that utterance only has meaning in relation to a continuum – a network – of other utterances. Actually, I have no idea if that is a post-structuralist idea – I haven't been in academia for a while – but it sounds like it. Which would be enough for Jacques Derrida.

Derrida would also be down with the idea that the meaning of an utterance, as soon it's out there and being refracted through other utterances, starts to slip and slide. He'd be overjoyed, for example, to discover that my post contained errors. Tonge, I was immediately told by various people, is no longer a Liberal Democrat. So I posted this:

David Baddiel @Baddiel · Aug 18
OK, apparently she was expelled from the Lib Dems, but her time as a Lib Dem MP still got her a seat in the House of Lords where she now sits as an independent peer. Apologies for error but that is almost *more* fucked up, as means she can't be removed whatever she says.

David Baddiel @Baddiel
And meanwhile I'd like to know why Jenny Tonge, a Lib Dem peer in the House of Lords - the Lib Dems btw, have always had their fair share of anti-Jewish racists - can say this and retain her seat there, as the implication of her...

25 30 124

But then that turned out to be wrong too, as @NobodyNorman then told me. So I retweeted his tweet:

You Retweeted
Nobody Norman Esq. @NobodyNorman · 3h
Replying to @barnyskinner @Baddiel
Wrong. She resigned. Lib Dems suspended her, but did not "kick her out." She will always be the anti-Semite in the Lords put there by the @LibDems AFTER many years of antisemitic attacks.

1 4 14

Despite all this refining of detail, people continued to tell me that Tonge was not a Lib Dem along with other information about her political history that you might have thought those three tweets would have cleared up. That is because – for anyone who doesn't do Twitter, and I suspect the exhausting opening to this piece will not feel like an invitation in – most people will only see one of these tweets and react to it immediately without bothering to check my timeline. Which is why, in Ricky Gervais's words, posting on Twitter can feel like fucking Groundhog Day.

In fact, here is one such example:

Jerry Taylor ❄ **#FBPE #LibDem #londependence** @JerryTaylor · Aug 18 ⌄
And you say that makes it OK for Labour to be antisemitic then.

As it happens Jenny Tonge left the Liberal Democrat's in 2012 as I am sure you know perfectly well.

💬 2   ⟲   ♡   ✉

To which I replied:

David Baddiel ✓
@Baddiel   ⌄

Replying to @JerryTaylor

A. I didn't know that as my TL makes clear if you read it.
B. I'm not saying that you idiot.
C. Bye.

12:40 PM - 18 Aug 2018

16 Likes   🤪😠😡😋

To which Jerry replied (before I'd had a chance to mute him, which was the point of C, above):

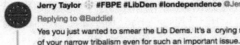

Jerry Taylor #FBPE #LibDem #londependence @JerryTaylor · Aug 18

Replying to @Baddiel

Yes you just wanted to smear the Lib Dems. It's a crying shame you can't let go of your narrow tribalism even for such an important issue.

○ 6   ⊔ 1   ♡   ✉

To which I replied:

David Baddiel ✓ @Baddiel · Aug 18

Jerry thinks Corbynistas are my tribe. He thinks I have a tribe. How hilarious.

Jerry Taylor #FBPE #LibDem #londependence @JerryTaylor

Replying to @Baddiel

Yes you just wanted to smear the Lib Dems. It's a crying shame you can't let go of your narrow tribalism even for such an important issue.

○ 19   ⊔ 3   ♡ 75   ıl|

There are other elements you need to know to understand the context of my reply here – Twitter cognoscenti will see that I've quoted Jerry's tweet here, in order to bring it to the attention of a wider audience, and Twitter cognoscenti will also know that I am regularly bombarded with hate tweets from the lovely new Labour Left – but I think we should leave it there, although we will have to come back to Jerry's central point, about tribes.

By 'it', I mean the digression. The more eagle-eyed among you may have noticed that I've so far failed to talk about the issue at the centre of this piece: the implicit anti-Semitism within Tonge's original post. That's because I think all this backstory, all these addenda, help to understand the complexity of what you might call right and wrong in 2018. I tried to highlight a wrong in Tonge's post. But then very quickly got drawn into a series of battles over a different, failed wrong, which distracted from the far greater wrong inherent in the not-any-more-Lib-Dem's message. One possibility would be to ignore those diversions, but I find this difficult, I reflexively want to answer everyone who writes to me on Twitter. This is a bad urge, as disregarding about 90 per cent of what comes in in response to tweets, especially tweets on the subject of Jews, can definitely be a good option. However in this case, dealing with the digressions felt right. Because if someone is saying something deeply wrong, deeply untrue, then, in calling them out, it's your responsibility to get everything right, to hold your utterance to a higher standard of truth.

So let's try and do that. Tonge's implication in her question about Jews – 'Why have the Jewish people been persecuted over and over again throughout history. Why?' – is that there must be some reason for this, and that the fault lies with the Jews. It's what we now call victim-blaming, although that isn't a term that, say, Adolf Hitler would have been familiar with when he claimed, in *Mein Kampf,* that the Jew 'was only and always a parasite in the body of other peoples'. (To find this quote I went to a random chapter of *Mein Kampf* – available, of course, freely on the internet – and put 'always' into the search engine because the one thing I know about anti-Semitism is that the anti-Semite believes the Jew never changes, which is the reason they might have been persecuted throughout history.)

I knew in advance, because Twitter has conditioned me to second-guess people's responses, what the challenges to my tweet about Tonge's post would be. I knew some people would tell me that Tonge's post – which has a silence at its heart – does not say that Jews are responsible for their own persecution. It simply puts forth a question about why:

Luke McDonough @Gonzoking · Aug 18

Isn't it reasonable to ask the question of why they have been persecuted, even though the answers maybe jealousy of success and superior intellect 😕 doubt this lovely lady would agree with that statement though.

💬 3   🔁 1   ♡ 2   ✉

This was the first tweet of that nature that came in, and is carefully worded so as to put some distance between Luke and anti-Semitism. He does this in two ways, first by the implication that Jews are naturally clever and successful – ironised nicely by the smiling emoji – and secondly by suggesting that Tonge – 'that lovely lady' – would not agree with that explanation. By doing this, Luke is positioning himself as a philo-Semite. I replied:

Luke McDonough @Gonzoking · Aug 18
Isn't it reasonable to ask the question of why they have been persecuted, even though the answers maybe jealousy of success and superior intellect 😃 doubt this lovely lady would agree with that statement though.
3 1 2

David Baddiel
@Baddiel

Replying to @Gonzoking

It is of course reasonable to examine the history of Jewish persecution, the reasons for which are always to do with Christian scapegoating and with all majority cultures psychotic need to have an alien hate object. That isn't what she means.

12:20 PM - 18 Aug 2018

1 Retweet 81 Likes

13 1 81

I wrote this reply because I am not a philo-Semite and I think that assuming that the reasons for Jewish persecution lie with Jews, even if those reasons are 'good ones' associated with a perception of

Jewish success, is wrong and dangerous. Luke, although clearly not a bedfellow, joins hands with Tonge when he imagines that there must be a Jewish reason for Jewish persecution.

Another tweeter agreed that the reasons lie outside and are imposed on Jews, but didn't necessarily assume that Tonge couldn't have meant this:

Revelation Kollektiv
@revkollektiv

Follow

Replying to @meralhece @Baddiel

In a way @Baddiel you illustrate Tonge's point bc I read her statement to mean 'why has antisemitism endured for so long, what structures perpetuate it &who are its enablers?' The same question and implication for antiblack racism, btw. But your response closes down this convo.

5:16 am - 18 Aug 2018

◯ 2   ⇄   ♡

This tweeter is a person of colour, or at least presenting as such – remember, all online utterance is deceptive. That's interesting as the idea of blaming people of colour for their own persecution, by ascribing to them eternal and unchanging negative traits, would of course be anathema to anyone, such as a Lib Dem (sorry, ex-Lib Dem) with progressive politics.

I replied, quote-tweeting my previous reply:

David Baddiel ✔
@Baddiel

(Follow) ⌄

Replying to @revkollektiv @meralhece

That isn't what she means: if so, she would not be frightened of being accused of a/s. Plus she has just been furious about a video in which a Jewish person has talked about a/s making her feel in need of a safe haven. I make this clear in a separate tweet, this one.

> **David Baddiel** ✔ @Baddiel · 3h   ⌄
>
> Replying to @Gonzoking
>
> It is of course reasonable to examine the history of Jewish persecution, the reasons for which are always to do with Christian scapegoating and with all majority cultures psychotic need to have an alien hate object. That isn't what she means.
>
> ◯ 7 ⇄ 1 ♡ 46 ılı

7:22 am - 18 Aug 2018

◯ 1   ⇄   ♡

You may notice that I repeated the phrase 'that isn't what she means' in my reply. How do I know that? That the question Tonge says she'd like answered is not one about the psychosocial power structures that perpetuate racism against Jews but: *what is that the Jews do – always, eternally, throughout history – to make themselves so eminently persecutable?*

How do I know – to ask a rhetorical question – that Tonge's question is rhetorical? That this answer she so desperately claims to want is in fact one she has absolutely at the ready?

Well, part of it is gut feeling. I saw her words and knew straight away, before thought intruded, that this was what she was insinuating. It's years and years of being aware of these tropes, in particular that the Jews are secretly in control, secretly behind all global ills, that makes me know reflexively that Tonge's post is inviting a discussion not of the racism that leads to these tropes, but just how these tropes are true. And – apologies for anyone who's heard me say this before – that Jews have these high-status reasons to hate them in conjunction with the usual low-status reasons that racists apply to any ethnic minority: that they are filthy, dirty, repulsive, stinking, et cetera, et cetera. Through a particular doublethink, Jews are accorded this special wall-to-ceiling negativity, both as rats and heads of SPECTRE.

You can feel both hates – or rather the one double-sided hate – coming through in Tonge's post. It's worth watching the video, even though I assume there are readers of *Granta* that cannot, when faced with the words 'I Am a Zionist', click play. It's an ultra-reasonable New Zealand Jewish woman, fully aware, as most Jews now are, of how reflexively bad a thing a Zionist is assumed to be, explaining why she nonetheless is one. I'm not a Zionist – as I and others have said many times, this is something that Jews have to state when talking about all this, a calling card that says 'and so I have acceptable un-agenda'ed opinions on the subject' – but I was not sickened by it. I didn't agree with it. I was not sickened by it. And I have repeated the word sickened enough times now to make my point, I hope, clear: Tonge's response was, to use a word the anti-Zionists use a lot, disproportionate.

It is visceral, it is physical, her response: the video makes her feel sick. The primary feeling I get from the whole post is disgust. Disgust with Jews, for both manipulating history (high status) and for snivellingly wanting a safe haven to run away to (low status), for so failing to be the tough that get going when the going gets tough (like, y'know, when you're being herded naked at gunpoint with your children into a self-dug mass grave). This disgust is what drives Tonge into the silence, the silence at the heart of the post. I mean, she had me at the disgust, but for anyone still in any doubt, her frustration at not being allowed to speak truth to Jewish power, as she would see it, is where, to quote Bono, she gives herself away. Because if what lay behind her silence was not anti-Semitic, she needn't feel frustrated at not being allowed to give voice to the question: why are majority cultures always in need of a minority to fear and loathe? What is it in the psychosis of the mainstream that requires Emmanuel Goldstein and his Two Minutes Hate? It can only be anti-Semitic to ask the other question which is not a question but just a statement of hate: what is it about the Jews that makes them so hateful?

And then, just to confirm that this is what Tonge means, I got this tweet:

Riza Hariati ▬
@rizahariati

(Follow) ∨

Replying to @Baddiel

But that is a fair question!! Why? You always brings nazi everytime the questiom arise. You even bring Nazi while killing Palestine. Why? The next generation will think Holocaust is a scam by Zionist. Better make more Evil Nazi movies fast!

6:43 am - 18 Aug 2018

♡ 11   ⟲   ♡

Again, it's difficult to know who Riza is. She presents as a person of colour, and a Muslim, I think from Indonesia, but it's entirely possible that her real name is Sergei.

Let's assume for the moment she's 'real'. It's hard to deconstruct her tweet, because, obviously, she doesn't quite speak English, and, obviously, she doesn't quite speak Logic. But she is doing something that aids *my* logic, which is drawing out the not-so-latent racism in Tonge's post. She did this most effectively in her continued conversations with others (it's always worth remembering these are onstage conversations, there's an audience-participating audience):

Riza Hariati ▪▪ @rizahariati · Aug 18
You haven't answer the question tho

ALTER EGO @Ego9Alter · Aug 18
It's because some people are racist towards Jewish people Riza. Simply question. Simple answer.

Riza Hariati ▪▪
@rizahariati

Follow

Replying to @Ego9Alter @Baddiel

PWAHAHAHAHAHAHHAHAHAHAHAHAHAH AHAHAHAHAHAHAHAHAHAHAHAHAHAHA HAHAHAHAHAHAHAAHHA

3:49 PM - 18 Aug 2018

Riza, you see, isn't so bothered as Tonge with discretion, and therefore with silence. She doesn't need to worry about being accused of anti-Semitism, and therefore is happy just to laugh in the face of an accusation of it. More profoundly, she just thinks the idea that Jews might suffer racism is itself laughable. Which again is useful, as it can be spooled back to fill Tonge's silence: the sense that Jews are powerful and in control and therefore oppressors, which means that discrimination against them can't be taken seriously – at some level, isn't even possible.

To come back to Jerry's point a hundred years ago about tribes: the central reason why meaning slips and slides in Derrida-ish ways on social media – why it is continually *contaminated* – is that so many people on there *are* either in tribes or working from an assumption that you are. Early on in Twitter, the hashtag #Team appeared. I think I first saw it when Angelina Jolie and Brad Pitt got together and then it was #TeamJennifer vs #TeamAngelina. This may seem like nothing, but the discursive structure it provides remains in place for much more serious debate. As we know, Twitter is not really about debate. It is much more, as all our world is now, about identity. Social media has allowed everyone in the world to raise their own little flag of self, and much that is said on social media is really about the waving of that flag. Many things may be being said on the surface, but fundamentally what is being said is: 'I am on #TeamX: this is who I am.' It provides huge comfort to the confusing abstraction that identity actually is for billions of people.

Which is complicated for me, as I like my identity to be a confusing abstraction; because that's what identity is and also because it means, as regards incoming news, that I have to think on my feet. Politically, I consider myself no wing. When stuff happens in the world now, I try to react to it in as individual a way as possible, rather than imposing on it a prearranged ideological map. This may involve having opinions that do not match up politically, or that are non-linear, or apparently contradictory. That's fine. I play – in my mind at least – only for #TeamBaddiel.

But yourself, and your own truth, particularly if that truth is complex, are a hard team to play for these days. There is something I don't understand about professional trolls, the ones paid by the Kremlin. I get that Putin wants to destabilise the EU, or get his man into the White House. But why pay trolls to spread conspiracy theories about vaccinations, as apparently was the case, or, as is clearly the case, about Jews? What is the geopolitical benefit to Russia of anti-Semitism? I have asked this question on Twitter, and people in the know have talked about Adam Curtis's *HyperNormalisation*, a documentary which looks at, among other things, a provocateur close to Putin who (the documentary claims) has led him to believe that confusion and uncertainty – never quite knowing what the truth is about anything – is the state you want your enemy in. Confusion and uncertainty are enough, because when people start to question everything, they don't believe anything, including their leaders, and from there – presumably – you get to take over the world. And the many conspiracy theories that swirl around anti-Semitism are just part of the general undermining of truth and escalation of paranoia that follows.

I don't know – of course – whether that is true (or if Putin just personally is an anti-Semite, and so wants that doctrine spread far and wide). But I do know that this piece has perhaps demonstrated something. Which is that to decode the meaning of just one social media post takes a lot of time and effort. By 'decode' I don't mean 'find out what the person who wrote it was trying to say', although that is part of it: I mean root out all the possible meanings played, as they will be, against others in the conversation while the world turns and changes the meaning in time anyway. Since I began writing this, eleven Jews have been killed in Pittsburgh by a man who truly believes that Jews control the world. Jenny Tonge posted instantly about that, another racist statement implying – despite the gunman's clear expressed hatred of Jews for, in his mind, promoting multiculturalism, for aiding Muslim refugees in America, and therefore nothing to do with the Middle East – that the responsibility lies with Israeli treatment of Palestine. It is all part of the same tapestry, but it is a tapestry that keeps expanding, into newer and more difficult-to-untangle corners.

On-screen meaning will continue, endlessly, to slip. Others on social media will take what they want from my interaction with Tonge's post and plug it into their #Team thinking. Some years ago, I did a show about fame, in which I quoted Erica Jong's maxim that 'Fame means millions of people will have the wrong idea of who you are'. Fame has always meant misrepresentation, but before now it was only the famous who experienced the full blast of what misrepresentation meant: the confusion and disorientation of self that came with seeing things you said being misquoted or misattributed, or simply misunderstood, on a large scale. Now, that happens all the time, to everyone. Anyone can now experience, in seconds, the downside of fame.

Being familiar with it doesn't make it any better. When people ask me, 'How does it make you feel, when you're on Twitter, and people are saying stuff about you, or responding angrily to something you've said, or sending you rows of crying laughing emojis?' It makes me feel many things, but mainly, misrepresented. Mainly, it's the frustration of thinking, to quote T.S. Eliot – an anti-Semite of course, but someone I feel comfortable quoting in *Granta* – 'That is not it at all, That is not what I meant, at all.' ■

Eva and Chloe Aridjis ready for a night out, Mexico City, 1989
Courtesy of the author

THE TENSION OF TRANSIENCE

Chloe Aridjis

D id we feel safe at the time? I no longer remember. My father had read in a newspaper that El Nueve was dangerous, so whenever we went there, which was often, my sister and I would say we were going somewhere else.

At the age of seventeen one drama swiftly supplanted the next, just as one obsession drove out another, yet I shall never forget the events of Friday 19 April 1989. At first it seemed like simply another night out, another nocturnal reply to the daylight hours, yet two details had already set it apart. At school I'd received an admissions letter from Harvard: in other words, that autumn I would be leaving home, and Mexico, possibly forever. I also recall it was a full moon; there are at least twelve full moons a year and most of the time I wouldn't attribute much importance to them, but that night it felt as though the moon was exerting an unusual pull.

As was the custom, a male friend – in this case, Yoshua – came to pick us up. As was also the custom, my father saw us into the car, checking with Yoshua that he indeed intended to keep his promise and deliver us home by our curfew. On some nights two thirty seemed generous; on others, cruelly early.

Located halfway down Calle Londres in downtown Zona Rosa, El Nueve had been opened in 1978 by Frenchman Henri Donnadieu as an alternative to the more mainstream synthetic nightlife that dominated the city at the time. It was a place that championed tolerance and creativity, and a gay haven that hosted underground gigs, drag shows and magazine launches. Donnadieu envisioned night itself as a cultural enterprise in which everyone could take part, and its *noches bugas*, or straight nights, attracted younger folk like us, lured above all by the music: goth, post-punk and industrial. At the entrance beckoned the sign ELLAS NO PAGAN (women don't pay) and, even more enticingly, another sign, farther in: BARRA LIBRE, free drinks all night, although it was widely believed that ether was added to the ice to curb the drinking.

Upon arriving that April night my sister and I encountered some of the regulars. There was Adán the Aviator, in his bomber jacket, goggles and motorcycle boots, aviator cap with earflaps; he always seemed about to lift off but in reality never left the dance floor. Standing against a wall wrapped in his melancholic aura was El Sauce Llorón, the weeping willow, a magazine editor by day and drama queen by night. Tall with a Roman nose, he was often in tears over insurmountable crises, real and imagined, his long black hair framing his face like a shroud. There, too, were El Nueve's cross-dressers, presiding over the rooms like rare nocturnal flowers. And finally, Los Ultravox, a group of young men in gray raincoats. These were their night selves; I had no idea what most of them did during the day – some must've held down humdrum jobs, others may have been students – and any further knowledge would have dented the enchantment.

The dance floor officially opened at midnight, announced by a clap of thunder and the appearance of the fog machine. Each week it was the same: the DJ would put on 'Carmina Burana' and the chanting would build in volume, like the re-enactment of something medieval, bombastic, portentous, that came rolling in from a distant century. After a few minutes its dramaturgy would segue into the beats of the Sisters of Mercy's 'Lucretia, My Reflection', the modulations driven by the throb of the drum machine. The downfall of empires or a battle cry: whatever the music evoked, it felt empowering, and the dance floor grew ever busier, its figures enveloped in the thick emissions of the fog machine. Its plumes were redolent of a metallic vanilla; unlike the heavily contaminated air of our city, one had the urge to inhale deeply before they dissolved.

Looking back, nearly everything about the scene felt ephemeral. A baroque ephemeral. The Swiss art historian Heinrich Wölfflin once described the baroque as an expression above all of the 'tension of transience' – one shouldn't expect perfection or fulfillment from the baroque, he claimed, nor the static calm of being. Only the unrest of change. Wölfflin was attempting to describe the baroque line in art – restless and liberated and succumbing to an upward urge – yet I've often found that his words encompass many facets of Mexican culture. And not only Mexican culture, but adolescence itself, driven as it is by a sense of the fugitive, and a spilling over of emotions that constantly threaten to destabilize the present.

Adolescence is an encounter, indeed an ongoing negotiation, with a self in transformation. Yet there's something undeniably alluring about unrest and, equally, about anything mutable and ephemeral and hard to pin down. Any fine experience is that more thrilling in the knowledge that at any moment it may well slip through our fingers, send us back to the mundane. Permanence doesn't inspire the same intoxication as does the fugitive, and somehow the atmosphere within El Nueve brought the tension of transience into relief. For the gay community it provided an inspiring space in which to enact extravagant dreams and simply feel free – not to mention that a few years earlier Aids had arrived, exposing a deep-rooted homophobia within Mexican society – and for us teens, it was the site where our urges for nihilism and abandon could be lent a certain theater.

In Mexico, three hundred years of colonial rule produced an art that was exuberant and excessive, in which emotionality seemed to triumph, every time, over restraint. El Nueve's aesthetic was similarly fed by a syncretism of European and Mexican cultures (and subcultures) – though of course without the tense backdrop of conquest and subjugation. In my memory I have always thought of it as a gay goth club. Was it truly goth? Perhaps not, apart from our *noches bugas*, which certainly were a *danse macabre* of skull rings and funereal garb. But my memory prefers to envision a space haunted by a spirit of mystery and concealment, emotions worn freely under a collective pall, silver crosses against a sky of black. Goth culture itself owes more than a little to the baroque – a love of contrasts and extremes, of monsters and hybrids, a celebration of the strange and marvelous, even an element of the carnivalesque. And, of course, the sense that any pleasure in life is stalked by the shadow of death.

Wearing black required little explanation: it stood for an internal weather, predominantly overcast, a heavy tilt toward melancholy that channeled a nineteenth-century Romanticism. Moonlight landscapes by Caspar David Friedrich, cues from Victorian mourning dress. Much of my own penumbral wardrobe came from Garage Union, a vast shop set up in a car park in West Berlin that sold clothes by the kilo. During the two summers our family spent in the city my sister and I would drop by weekly to scour the racks. Yet most of the clothes were dyed, and each time we washed them the water would run black, the garments slowly rinsed of their duskier shades. Much more permanent were the tattoos we got a few years later. We'd presented a copy of Edgar Allan Poe stories illustrated by the little-known German artist Wilfried Sätty, who often made montages inspired by the occult, and asked the tattooist to take the face of Roderick Usher and attach wings. The result was an androgynous angel, a curious marriage of goth and baroque, which has outlasted all the black.

That April night I remember looking around at the various characters on the dance floor, imagining how they would carry on with the same theater long after I'd left to study abroad, and how these nights out, so charged with sorcery, would soon end. I had just kissed the Scottish DJ, a fully fledged goth from overseas, when our friend Jair cut his hand on a white metal trash can on the side of the dance floor. At first no one paid much attention – until it started gushing blood. Seeing that the matter required more light than what was on offer, a handful of us repaired to the Denny's diner on the corner. As we sat in a booth pressing napkins to Jair's hand, an elderly cross-dresser with painted eyebrows approached and, after seeing what was wrong, suggested rubbing cigarette ash in his wound. The man was charming and convincing, why not try, but Jair winced as soon as the ash came into contact with his wound. We hurriedly rinsed his hand in the bathroom and bandaged it up as best we could and, impatient to resume the night, returned to El Nueve.

A scuffle had erupted while we'd been gone. Two men were pushing each other threateningly, other men soon joined in and before long the scuffle exploded into a fury that threatened to swallow us all. Someone pulled out a gun. A bartender yelled out. Now, in the face of real death, all the young vampires went scurrying to find cover. Yoshua grabbed our hands and we flew down the stairs, past the bouncer at the entrance tensing up in anticipation of a fight, and into the parking lot across the street. We were about to climb into Yoshua's white car when one of the men came rolling down the ramp and before we knew it the brawl continued there. My sister and I quickly hid under the car, heads spinning, nausea on the rise. Bullets began crossing overhead. With our faces pressed against the damp cement, we breathed in the petrol and tried to block out the shouts and gunfire. When the fight moved into a corner of the parking lot we made a dash for it, jumped into the car and sped off.

We were already in our neighborhood and had just turned off Reforma when, overcome by vertigo, I asked Yoshua to stop the car and let me out. I stumbled over to a tree and was breathing in some night air when all of a sudden two men came running out of the building in front of us, which we now realised was a bank, a bank that was being robbed. An alarm started sounding. My sister and Yoshua yelled for me to get back into the car and off we sped a second time, as the moon, gazing down, shook her head.

Nights like these seem tame compared to now. Those had been small-scale criminals, most likely, or local drug dealers, and in the late eighties the main blight on our nights out were Los Anticristos, a gang with inverted crucifixes tattooed on their temples. Their leader would carry a sword sheathed in his cane and his sidekicks had chain belts they could remove in combat; they listened to the same music we did and often turned up at our haunts to pick fights on the dance floor. Yet overall there reigned a sense of solidarity, particularly after the disastrous earthquake of 1985, and our then-president's gross mishandling of the catastrophe. This led to a massive social mobilization, and civilians of all ages had quickly teamed up to assist in the search for survivors.

That autumn Rockotitlán, the first large venue for live music, had opened, followed by places like Tutti Frutti and the L.U.C.C. The alternative Mexican bands at the time – Caifanes, La Maldita Vecindad, Santa Sabina, Café Tacuba – reflected the ideals of young civil society and the social movements to come, and most musicians became fervent supporters of the Zapatistas.

I once described the music of my youth as a twilight always waiting to unfurl, but now that darkness has dramatically deepened in tone. In the years after I left Mexico, drug cartel violence spun out of control and journalists began being gunned down on streets across the country. The turbulent nineties saw the Zapatista uprising, NAFTA (Mexico thrown open to global trade and influence), the weakening of the PRI Party, economic collapse and a series of high-profile political assassinations. Gruesome stories and their images have been a daily presence in the papers ever since.

The spectacle of El Nueve was indeed like a *danse macabre*, but while the *danse macabre* of medieval Europe was a cultural assimilation of the horrors of the Black Death, in our culture it prefigured the horror rather than assimilated it. In the late eighties macabre iconography resided above all in our mood and our music and, more ancestrally, in the pre-Hispanic gods of stone in the Museum of Anthropology. But over the past few decades the trope of death has taken on a new dimension thanks to the spectacle of violence of the drug cartels.

H ow unusual that April night had been, yet how normal it had seemed at the time: a gunfight, an aging cross-dresser professing shamanic powers, a bank being robbed before our eyes – everything veering into the carnivalesque, the Dionysian tinged by barbarity and hyperbolized emotion . . . When I returned home I knocked on my parents' door to let them know we were back and then lay down and tried to sleep, aware that soon these outings would come to an end. What I didn't know at the time was how bleak things would become, and how the aesthetic of our cultural choices somehow foreshadowed the events to unfold – still unfolding – in our country. In Mexico skulls no longer conjure up goth-y anthems from the eighties or the metaphysics of pre-Hispanic times; they now appear in mass graves, or as decapitated heads tossed onto a dance floor. ∎

AUTHOR'S NOTE: El Nueve closed a few months after I left Mexico, in December 1989. On a recent visit home, I returned to the site. The building is now boarded up; its last incarnation was a bar called Ghost.

Courtesy of the author

HOW I BECAME AN SJW

Anouchka Grose

I could never hit my little sister quite hard enough. No matter how far back I drew my fist, how purposefully I launched it at her, the punch never did what I wanted it to. On impact, my arm seemed to buckle and flap, and there she'd be, still standing. Once I pushed her and she hit her head on the corner of a bookshelf, but that didn't feel right either. She bled, which was unexpected, and it felt uncontrolled and accidental.

Fights with my sister could erupt out of nowhere. I can't remember the subject of a single one. All I remember is the overpowering sense of hate and rage and the desperate urge to act on it. I suppose you could describe it as 'murderous', and that's often the way it felt, which makes me wonder why I never took the opportunity to kill her in her sleep. Perhaps I knew that forethought made violence unacceptable. It was only ever justifiable in real time, in response to a live provocation. These could, of course, be easily engineered; I could make my toys speak in ways that would cause her to lash out, and then I could strike back, even if it was always disappointing. Unfortunately, our mum worked out the trick, so I had to stop.

My hatred for my sister was standard-issue, prelinguistic stuff. She is eighteen months younger. I hated her before I knew what hate was. She was simply an outrage, an intrusion. She screamed, snotted and ate mashed banana. She was also an impossible Dad-thief. When I was five and had mumps, she went on a long holiday with our dad to visit our grandparents. Apparently it was the best holiday either of them, or anyone else, had ever been on. The sun shone every day, the parrots flocked to the garden where they were staying, my sister learned adorable new tricks, like swimming and being the perfect granddaughter. I stayed in bed feeling envious while my mum went out and bought me a 4B pencil – so soft! – and expected me to be delighted.

Over time, eighteen months becomes a smaller and smaller gap. Pretty soon you end up the same size. One day – we must have been eleven and twelve – my sister chased me into the bathroom. I remember feeling genuinely frightened. It seemed clear that this wasn't going to go well for me, but the shame of losing a fight to my baby sister would have been too great.

'I'm a pacifist,' I told her.

'You're what?'

'You can hit me if you like. I don't care. I won't hit you back.'

She looked peeved, but it had slowed her down. If she hit me now she'd look bad, but she was easily smart enough to know that something wasn't right.

'But *you* just hit *me* back there in the bedroom?' she said.

It was true. I had become a pacifist in the time it took to run between the bedroom and the bathroom of a London flat. And the amazing thing is that I stayed one. I don't remember us ever getting into another physical fight. Not long afterwards, I became a vegetarian, then vegan. I started to go on marches. I joined the Amnesty International letter-writing club at school. If anyone was disadvantaged or downtrodden, I wanted to be on their side. All this didn't translate into having a better relationship with my sister, although it probably made us both physically safer. I could keep thinking she was nasty, while getting on with trying to be 'nice' to everyone, and everything, else.

O r maybe the whole SJW thing isn't only to do with my sororicidal tendencies; there's also the fact of my dad's Pete Seeger records, and his boundless love for Louisiana bluesmen. I have never overcome my father's idea of what's 'good'. One night, after a party, my dad fell asleep drunk in the living room leaving a scratched Lead Belly record playing all night. It didn't sound 'good' to me at the time, in fact it sounded terrible. My sister and I were kept awake, frightened by the repetitive, jangled rasping, but unable to go in and switch it off. Still, it was as if, in our paralysis, we understood that it was one of the happiest nights of his life. The 'goodness' of Lead Belly had to be respected, even when it ruined your sleep.

Kent joined our primary school in the middle of the second-to-last year. Our headmistress, Miss Calloway, was obsessed with multiculturalism. She collected children from as many different races, ethnicities and nationalities as possible. My sister and I lived slightly outside the catchment area, but since the school didn't have any Australians, we were welcome. Kent was a black American who'd just moved to London from New York. There were no other Americans around, so he was in. To a child in 1979, New York seemed the most frightening and exciting place. We'd seen it on the news. If you walked a few metres down just about any street, you could get shot. If Kent had made it to the age of nine he deserved our respect.

Our classroom was divided into five large tables, each with six children around it. We had never asked ourselves about the meaning of the seating arrangements. Within a couple of weeks Kent had worked out that we'd all been ranked according to academic ability. As he put it, 'We're the brainiacs, those are the tutti-fruttis and the others are just floatin' around in the middle.' We felt lucky to be on his table; he was endlessly entertaining. He also wore the rattiest, most threadbare plimsolls we had ever seen.

'Plimsolls?! What the hell, you guys?' he'd say. 'Is that Shakespearean? They're called *sneakers*. Jeez!'

American things were modern and correct, while British things were *stoopid*. Although it could be annoying to be pulled up on details the whole time, we basically agreed with him. The first McDonald's had just opened in our neighbourhood, plus a Dayvilles ice-cream parlour with thirty-two flavours. With their arrival, we now knew that of course America was better. We thought his sneakers were cool.

Kent's mum was cool too. She was a street performer who wore colourful clothes with grimy puppets strapped to the outside. Although everyone at our school had been chosen for their 'difference', she was more different than most. If you didn't know her as Kent's mum you might have thought she looked nuts, but when you heard her talk she was really friendly, with a sweet, gentle voice. She and Kent lived in temporary accommodation somewhere near the school. We asked all sorts of questions about it, and about Kent's dad, who wasn't around. We needed to know every detail of his amazing life. I didn't know which was more brilliant, his Americanness, his cleverness, his blackness or his poverty. He was practically Lead Belly. I must have registered unconsciously that my dad would surely love me if I loved Kent. He might even start to love me more than my sister, and possibly even take me on a paradise holiday. So loving Kent must be the right thing to do. In fact it seemed so obviously the right thing that I imagined everyone else must feel the same way. Everybody loves Kent! I perceived a kind of permanent group euphoria around him. It never occurred to me that he might notice and wonder what the hell was going on.

One lunch break, a year later, my friends and I were playing tag in the playground and needed to choose somebody to be 'it'.

'Eenie, meenie, miney, moe, catch a nigger by the toe . . .' chanted someone, maybe Sahara.

'You're not serious,' said Kent.

'What is it this time?' we all wondered.

'That's, like, totally racist,' he said. 'I can't believe you're all so backward over here.'

It was the first we'd heard of it, so we had to ask him to explain. His answer seemed head-twistingly weird, but also revelatory. In spite of Miss Calloway's cultural lepidoptery, we still had a copy of *Little*

Black Sambo in the library. And I'm sure I wasn't alone in owning a golliwog. When I was growing up in the 1970s it was still seen as only slightly strange that my grandmother would walk into Biba and ask the black sales assistant for a pair of nigger-brown shoes. No one had ever run through it with us.

One side effect of all this was that Kent began to seem more wise and futuristic than ever. It felt like you could hardly get enough of him. Being chased by him during tag was an honour. Having him sigh and spell stuff out for you was a treat.

'One day my mum's going to come to the school and buy you all doughnuts,' he announced. 'With jam.'

The prospect was almost too brilliant. We waited and he mentioned it a few more times, but the doughnuts didn't appear. Still, if Kent was bluffing, that was OK.

'No, she really is going to do it,' he insisted.

We got on with admiring him, goading him to be interesting and letting him continue to patronise us in the ways we so obviously deserved. Then one day Kent's mum appeared at the end of the school day and cornered the top-table people in the coats area. ('Then one day' was an expression we had been told emphatically to avoid in our writing.) She was holding a pile of doughnuts, each in its own paper bag. She picked us off, one by one, calling us by our names.

'Nicole? With the beautiful curls? There you go, sweetie. Sacha? Here's the one without jam . . .' And so on, until everyone had exited the cloakroom and it was just Kent's mum and me.

'Anouchka?' she said. 'You need to go easy on Kent.' I didn't know what she meant. 'Could you just be a bit gentler with him? You know?' She handed me the doughnut in a not unkind way and I wasn't sure whether to cry. It had never crossed my mind that the way I was dealing with Kent was causing him distress; I was enjoying my side of it too much. And why had she singled me out? We all loved Kent, didn't we? What had I done to him that had made his mum press me in this way?

While it was impossible for my nine-year-old brain to grasp it cognitively, I think I must have registered that my love for Kent was somehow toxic. My passionate misrecognition was freaking him out.

Fifteen years later, reading Frantz Fanon on a postgraduate course, I finally saw the problem. My dad and I had both been bound up in a massive cultural delusion that placed Kent and Lead Belly in the unbearable role of the abject-sublime; they had been 'cast out' in a way that made them irresistibly beautiful to certain white people. It was pretty eye-opening. Despite this, it still appears not to been have fully, consciously graspable. I was also taking a module on Hegel with a wonderful black, male lecturer. I must have loved him too much too; when the head of department assigned him to be my dissertation tutor, he refused to speak to me and ran out of the room. I had to find myself a new tutor, but didn't quite know how to explain to them what had happened. At the time, I couldn't explain it to myself. Once the course was over he asked me on a date, but I was already going out with an acquaintance of his. I am so glad for my lecturer that something – a white man, non-coincidentally – came between us. I dread to think what I might have done to him otherwise.

And I'm still not 'cured': a year ago I found myself at a party of PhD students where I attributed an idea of Fanon's to James Baldwin. Whenever I think of it, the shame is so great that I almost double over in pain. And now I double over at the ridiculousness of admitting such shame. Will there ever be any escape?

Not long after the doughnut incident, Kent left our school and we never saw him again, although I spotted his mum on the tube a few years later. Her shoes were made from cardboard and strips of shredded fabric. I didn't dare speak to her, although I desperately wanted to. I can't believe she spent all that money on junk food just so she could ask me, so exquisitely politely, to back off Kent a little with my disturbing, racist love.

I often feel that I don't know how to be kind to people, to love them in a way that's good for them. Sometimes it can almost seem easier to hate people; at least then you don't feel you're trying to lure them in with false promises. Having said that, I've also noticed that hate doesn't work very well as a social bond.

After O levels, my secondary school gave up on me. I'd had a scoliosis operation and fluffed my exams, plus my haircuts had become increasingly evil. One day the deputy head hid me in a back room till home time so the little kids wouldn't see. I then spent a few years post-school doing weird things that didn't add up so I wasn't feeling too clever. I worked full-time in a basement making lampshades with a tiny male boss who said things like, 'When I take a woman out to dinner I always make sure she gets her desserts.' I don't think I'd ever heard a man be so chauvinistic outside of a *Carry On* film, which may have had something to do with the fact that my dad was friends with Andrea Dworkin. After that I got a job in a call centre, which was nice in that it was full of people with various 'unsightly' bodies: freaky, pierced-up clubbers, trans men and women, and those who might be considered conventionally ugly. Still, the work itself was terrifyingly boring and there was another totally cunty thin, English, white male boss who fussed about us taking toilet breaks. He seemed to think that the fact we were all otherwise unemployable meant he could mistreat us with impunity.

When the job became too unbearable, I started busking, but was put off when someone shouted, 'Can I pay you to shut up?' It seemed that the world of work wasn't exactly welcoming. But what to do instead? Getting onto one of the least prestigious art foundation courses in the country finally gave me a sense of direction and purpose.

I moved out of my vegan, LGBT, dole-claiming houseshare and moved in with some regular students. For some reason I had thought it would be good for me. Perhaps I had begun to worry that I was existing too far outside the general run of things and didn't want to self-marginalise forever. I didn't feel I could tell these new people that I was attracted to girls, nor did I want them to know that I was largely uneducated. I felt I had somehow slipped off the face of the Earth and this was my chance to get back on. I did whatever I could to fit in, although always with the sense that it was only really working up to a point.

There were six of us in the house: Anja, Sophie, Diann, Paul, Elise and me. Throughout the year our friendships strengthened, weakened or stayed the same, but not in a neat way. We didn't form tribes. Sophie and I never spoke, but it didn't seem unfriendly. She and Paul would go clubbing together. Diann liked clubbing, but not with those two. Anja worked in her room a lot, and she and I often shared meals. Elise, Sophie and Paul played in the same orchestra. Diann, Paul and I sometimes liked to smoke spliffs together first thing in the morning.

Still, out of this snarl of interactions one thing gradually became clear – you wouldn't have a very nice time if you got stuck in the living room with Elise. Her complaints about life would bring you down. Diann, Paul, Anja and I all had conversations about it at different moments, ripping our flatmate apart on the grounds of her endless unhappiness. Why did she think it was OK to tell us about it at such great length? Disliking Elise helped us all to get along. The more we got along, the less we gave a fuck about her very evident suffering. She almost stopped seeming human. Although you can read about things like this in psychology, sociology and history textbooks, it's hard to believe you could actually perpetuate it. Even now I can hardly bear to think about how it all worked. Add to that the more slippery individual stuff that weaves its way in; Elise was like a little sister to me. She ate horrible food and cried a lot, therefore she must die. It almost makes *too much* sense.

One of Elise's biggest ongoing complaints centred on a boy called Damien, with whom she was in love. He was shy and jumpy and she couldn't tell whether he liked her back. This provided endless situations in which to feel confused and dejected, which could then be discussed ad infinitum with anyone who appeared in the living room.

I was curious about Damien. I'd been hearing about him for years from various people. The main thing I knew about him was that his parents lived on one side of a hill in the middle of nowhere, and my parents lived on the other. I very much hoped to meet him one day.

Somehow it started to seem like a good idea to go and visit my parents during the Easter break, with Elise and Anja in tow. From there we could walk around to the other side of the hill and pay Damien a surprise visit. The thing I hadn't expected was to instantly develop a massive crush on him. I hadn't fancied a boy for years, and Damien was a particularly inconvenient one. I knew at once that he had to be mine. The problem was that I wasn't actually wicked enough to try to steal him immediately; I had to wait for an opportunity. This arrived a few weeks later when Elise told us that the situation had been reversed; Damien was now madly in love with *her*, but she didn't like him any more. I waited a day or so before cycling over to his house and claiming him.

So what was my instant and unquestionable attraction *really* made out of? It seems unlikely that he and I had a biological compatibility such that I took one sniff and knew we had to breed. What seems much more likely is that, through him, I could triumph over a surrogate little sister at the same time as demonstrating my socially acceptable heterosexuality, not to mention giving my housemates a pleasurable shot of schadenfreude.

The last few weeks of our houseshare were hell. Elise and I no longer spoke. Paul and Anja had to listen to a constant barrage of complaints about me. I felt totally sanctimonious about it – Elise had said she didn't like him any more, and anyhow you couldn't argue with the fact that our parents lived on the same hill. Her pain meant nothing to me. Damien and I stayed together for four years, until I destroyed the relationship by suddenly marrying someone else. Still, it's amazing that a partnership with such inauspicious beginnings could hang together for so long.

A decade after that, an old orchestra friend of Elise's spotted me in a cafe. He told me she was just next door and was due to come out for her tea break. I felt sick but didn't let on. Whatever pathetic self-justifications I'd used while we were housesharing had stopped working. As I waited for the confrontation, her pain rushed in on me. I felt it, saw it, understood it and was completely horrified. How could I face her knowing what I'd done? Luckily everyone had a mobile phone by then; he must have tipped her off because she never appeared.

If anyone ever chose to point out that my concern for other people was insincere, for show, I wouldn't argue; of course it's true. Like any SJW, I'm an easy target. When I go on marches, buy organic, sign petitions, forgo plastic, I'm doomed to feel endlessly inauthentic. What is all this shit-for-show? Wouldn't it be better to actually be a nice person, directly, to other people? But then again, what if I didn't feel like such an irredeemable fucker the whole time? Would I just sit back on my sofa, being 'nice' and eating corporate burgers? These questions flip around, literally driving me crazy, but meanwhile I can try to do my bit to save the world.

Perhaps, like all humans (you tell me), I will never, can never, be as good as planned. I try, I fail, I try, I fail, I try, I fail. Still, if you repeat something often enough, perhaps you can find a kind of peace in it. My SJW-ness certainly doesn't make me better than anyone else, but neither does it make me any worse. I feel myself permanently caught between the bedroom and the bathroom of my family home, confused, afraid, and endlessly running, trying to make sure no one gets hurt. ∎

Chatham House, the Royal Institute of International Affairs, is a world-renowned independent policy institute. Based in London, our mission is to help build a sustainably secure, prosperous and just world.

The World Today magazine is Chatham House's bi-monthly publication. It presents authoritative analysis and commentary on current topics providing a vital resource for governments, businesses, academics and those curious about the world we live in.

The World Today

Subscribe at chathamhouse.org

AMERICAN ORCHARD

Diana Matar

Introduction by Max Houghton

'But a man is a part of nature, and his war against nature is inevitably a war against himself.' – Rachel Carson

Invoking Edmund Spenser's *The Faerie Queene*, the poet and Kentucky farmer Wendell Berry links 'the natural principles of fecundity and order' with the principle of justice. Berry's thought, as laid down in his collection of essays, *Home Economics*, is freighted with centuries of nature writing and its insistent bedfellow, activism. Travelling through America last year, photographic artist Diana Matar sensed a profound sense of disorder in society, which, she observed, was replicated in the natural world, as though the trees were losing the fight for environmental justice.

America's earliest folk hero, John Chapman, aka Johnny Appleseed, influenced by the religious philosophies of Emanuel Swedenborg, dedicated his life to planting apple trees along the expanding western frontier. His belief in the essential harmony of nature outlawed grafting as harmful to living things, so he sowed seeds instead. It was in this spirit of expansion and industrialisation that the American orchard flourished, and, with it, an enduring vein of intellectual, cultural and sensory life, connected to the land.

In a way, Matar was looking closely at the soil of America when she travelled around California, Texas, Colorado, New Mexico and Oklahoma, documenting sites where law enforcement officers had killed citizens. The level of violence is exceptionally high in the US; 1,093 members of the public were killed by law enforcement officers in 2016.

The photographic images she made for her 2017 series *My America* – remnants of desert, pieces of sky – became a kind of memorial to lives obliterated, and to the American dream turned sour. Yet while she was looking in one direction, she was also summoned irresistibly elsewhere; seeing with more than her eyes. In the country of her birth, something was happening; difficult to define, yet perceptible. It felt like the very foundations of democracy might be shifting underfoot. And the orchards were dying.

To create the images that would become *American Orchard*, Matar followed her unconscious instinct with her camera-eye, harnessing a series of half-remembered moments, forgotten dreams, liminal images that drift around the outer edges of our consciousness. She captures delicate flora, a sudden eddy, the protrusion of a gnarly burl, a symptom that appears when a tree is undergoing a form of stress. A screen grab of James Comey, former head of the FBI, pictures him sightless, blind to his actions, or their consequences, as he tries to serve the interests of justice. A classical statue rises skyward, itself tree-like; a reminder of how it was once hoped 'the days of Greece may be revived in the woods of America', as Barack Obama put it not long ago. Instead, this unsettling imagery points to a dereliction of civic duty – politically, sexually, environmentally, democratically.

Henry David Thoreau famously went to the woods, where he wrote the definitive transcendentalist work *Walden*, because he 'wished to live deliberately, to front only the essential facts of life'. Those 'essential facts' are now in flux in the new political landscapes in which we dwell, but Thoreau believed his life depended on being able to draw such facts 'from the perpetual instilling and drenching of the reality that surrounds us'. In this form of photographic discourse, where seemingly disparate images are united in the visual register, certain questions are made manifest: what is visible? What remains unseen? What is hidden in plain sight? Such a meditation on the very nature of reality is purposefully disquieting. Who ya gonna believe, me or your own eyes?

Photography is frequently derided for its superficiality and inability to depict the invisible, yet Matar employs the medium resolutely otherwise. She grants the viewer access to an 'optical unconscious', as defined by Walter Benjamin, writing in the 1930s as fascism spread across Europe. Working with a camera-eye, Matar bypasses straightforward representation, granting access directly to the unconscious. In this realm, instinct is king . . . and (faerie) queen. Its oneiric images are worthy of our acute attention.

Neuroscience has confirmed that we are more than passive perceivers; that we generate the world as much from the inside out as vice versa. The camera, in Matar's hands, becomes a powerful tool with which to witness the restless journey from the interiority of emotion to the outside world of reason. *American Orchard* is a photographic augury borne of an instinctive knowledge that nature itself is out of order. Lady Justice, blindfolded, cannot see the dying trees, though she might feel their suffering, or hear their howl from within the earth. For all their quiet beauty, these are photographs of protest; a call to loving arms. ■

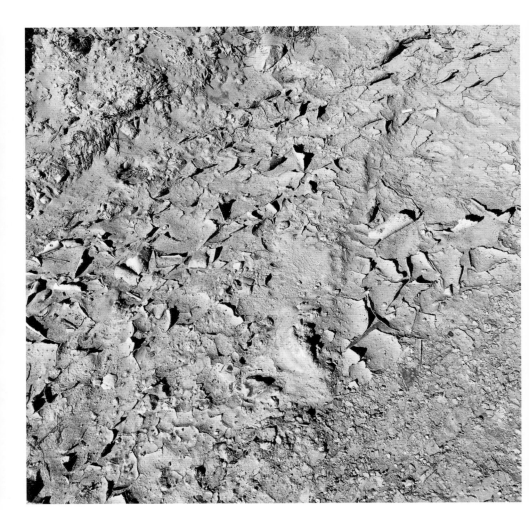

PHOTO
HISTORY
PHOTO
FUTURE
PHOTO
FAIR

PHOTO
LONDON

16–19 MAY 2019 | SOMERSET HOUSE

In association with
FT Weekend

Supporter of the public programme:
LUMA FOUNDATION

Candlestar ❖ PICTET

photolondon.org
#PhotoLondonFair19

POPULISM AND HUMOUR

William Davies

Amid the shocks, upsets and outrages that have characterised politics in the West over the past three years, it is easy to focus on a single basket of 'negative' emotions as the driving force of historical change. Anger, resentment, envy, fear and aggression have all palpably played an important role in populism and the return of authoritarian nationalism, which have heaped scorn and hatred upon 'liberal elites' who are accused of being 'smug' or 'cold'. I think we can assume that these sentiments were not suddenly triggered circa 2016, but had been lying in wait for many years, shut out of 'mainstream' public institutions until a combination of brash celebrity populists and social media allowed them to all come flooding in.

But there is another affective state that has circled around populism, its figureheads and media for many years, which is far more politically ambiguous: laughter. Among the senses that are mobilised by many contemporary political movements, especially online, is a sense of humour. Reflecting on the social, cultural and physiological aspects of laughter and humour is crucial if we're to get a fuller grasp of how populism and nationalism work on our emotions and feelings.

It is scarcely news that racism, sexism and nationalism have often achieved an everyday normality via the medium of jokes. Growing up in 1980s London, many of the first jokes I ever heard were at the expense of 'the Irishman'. The white heterosexual male has distinguished himself from virtually every other possible set of identities on the planet via the telling of some joke or other. Many of the chesty laughs that have greeted these jokes over the years, ricocheting around pubs and clubs, are as much an affirmation of shared white heterosexual English male experience as they are about the quality of the joke or the comedic talent of its teller. And when someone with any other identity wanders into earshot and objects, there is the perennial get-out that they need to 'get a sense of humour'.

Many of the earliest controversies over 'political correctness', the notion that now triggers such hostility on the right, were over the freedom to tell racist, ableist, sexist or homophobic jokes – the freedom that the 'alternative comedy' scene of the 1980s renounced and which has been progressively curtailed in the mainstream media ever since. 'Alternative comedy' referred to a cluster of young, left-wing stand-ups, such as Alexei Sayle and Ben Elton, who challenged the often conservative clichés of so much 1970s comedy. Long before campuses were afflicted by 'free speech' wars, the BBC was getting embroiled in controversies over the limits of acceptable comedy. Yet to understand our present cultural and political moment, we need to see that the terms of engagement and conflict have shifted in a number of subtle ways.

First of all, there is the role that men such as Nigel Farage, Boris Johnson and Donald Trump played *before* their political breakthroughs, at a time when it felt as if the power of liberal technocrats could last forever. Each was – and in some ways remains – a figure of fun whose appearance and behaviour was held up to ridicule. In Britain, *Have I Got News for You* played a significant role in making Johnson, and to a lesser extent Farage, an attention-grabbing joke in the eyes of the cosmopolitan middle class. In the United States, Trump was notoriously ridiculed for his haircut and presidential ambitions by Barack Obama at the 2011 White House Correspondents' dinner. In the long build-up to the Trump presidency, American liberals relied on *The Daily Show* brand of knowing satire to vent their rising disbelief with the direction that conservative politics was taking. The Dutch populist Geert Wilders is also instantly recognisable for his extraordinary haircut, while Beppe Grillo, founder of the Italian Five Star movement, was originally a professional comedian.

The fact that these men attracted laughter and mockery from educated liberals, and did not shy away from it, no doubt played a crucial role in building their appeal in the eyes of those who felt belittled and sneered at by 'elites'. The somewhat comical nature of their haircuts and outfits unlocked something politically. After all, Ian Hislop or Jon Stewart would never publicly laugh at someone for their accent or class, but didn't hold back when the target was another white man with money. The feeling of being laughed at became routed vicariously through these pantomime figures, who seemed brave enough to withstand the ridicule.

Even since the electoral shocks of 2016 in Britain and the United States, some of this dynamic is still being played out. While it is often expressed along with a tinge of dread, even fear, one of the recurring political sentiments of the past few years has been 'Oh my God, is this actually *real*?' This may not be the same thing as laughter, but we shouldn't ignore the fact that it nevertheless delivers a form of stunned enjoyment. Given the mastery that men such as Trump and Johnson exercise within the 'attention economy', drawing on all their experience in reality television and the media, it should scarcely be any surprise that they can make us feel light-hearted as well as afraid. It would be comforting to say that 'there is nothing funny about President Trump', but I'm not sure that's true.

The constant churn of scandal and exposés that accompany these political figures adds to the grotesque spectacle of it all. Trump's White House spews out gossip of a sort that is putrid and absurd in equal measure. Lying has become some sort of spectator sport, in which the contestants aim for ever-more audacious manoeuvres. 'When I said would, I meant wouldn't.' What is there left to do, other than laugh? But as reality has grown more absurd, the job of satirists has grown harder. The tone of *Have I Got News for You* and *The Daily Show* now seems stuck in a pre-2016 time warp.

But surely it is the prominent role of humour in our digital political activities that makes this new epoch unprecedented. Recent work by cultural and media studies scholars, such as Whitney Phillips and Angela Nagle, has cast new light on the bizarre logic and mentality of troll culture. As Phillips emphasises, the quest for 'lulz' (humorous entertainment) has been the abiding purpose of trolling for many years on message boards and chat forums, certainly for far longer than the rest of us have been using social media. This can tip into mischievous and malevolent interventions, whose only justification is that other trolls might find them funny. Nagle's analysis demonstrates how politically dangerous – and advantageous to the far right – this culture can be when it is used to undermine the possibility of any public solidarity or faith in institutional norms.

One doesn't have to paddle into the darker waters of the alt-right in order to sense that humour has a greater political salience in the age of social media. Memes (pieces of photographic and textual content that can be instantly shared from one social media user to another) have become mainstream ways of spreading political messages that even the Conservative Party has strived to master. A successful meme has to hit a particular affective target by being instantly familiar, instantly different and – usually – funny. What's more troubling about meme culture is what it holds in common with traditional racist jokes, namely the promise of instant community among the laughers, and instant alterity for those who don't, or won't, 'get it'. As bandwidth and connectivity has grown, online humour has become evermore esoteric in order to facilitate feelings of community.

This is the dark side of the lacing of politics with humour that is not in itself new, but which has combined with new weaponry, importing the logic of the battlefield into democracy. The ultimate intent of the troll or the meme is to achieve a form of encryption, to send messages between allies that cannot be intercepted by enemies because they are designed with a particular recipient in mind. A sense of humour, combined with familiarity with previous jokes and conflicts, becomes the affective equipment through which the signal can be extracted from the noise. When politicians use this kind of tactic, it's known as a 'dog whistle'. The immediacy and embodiment of laughter, meanwhile, represent a goal that cuts out the slow work of consensus-building and understanding and puts instant sensory recognition in its place. Enjoyable, of course, but also a reminder of other affective states rooted in survival instincts and fear which operate via similarly psychosomatic channels, but where the final outcome can be far more fatal. ■

Bosworth Farm, Transvaal, South Africa, 1970s (year unknown)
Courtesy of the author

HARMFLESH

Margie Orford

(White) Girl 1972

The car is hot, the sticky back seat crowded with the three of us. Two days we have been driving. It might as well be forever. A sign flashes past. Johannesburg. My father says we don't go that far. Two hundred miles. My mother says we're nearly there. My father says keep an eye on the electricity pylons, eagles sometimes build nests in them. I fold my arms on the open car window and rest my chin on them. The wind roaring in my ears silences the voices in the car. I count the pylons that march like giants across the veld.

The car bumps off the tar road and onto the gravel. I slit my eyes against the red dust that plumes behind us as my mother counts off the landmarks that signal the last ten miles of this journey. The bend in the road near the dry riverbed. The big stand of blue gum trees where a barn owl nests. The mielie fields. Shabalala's place. Three silver windmills. The russet Sussex cattle studding the veld. The metal sign points its black finger at the whitewashed gates. J.L. ORFORD, BOSWORTH FARM. We turn down the avenue lined with pine trees. The farmhouse is at the end.

Falling out of the hot car and dashing ahead of the others. My grandmother – we're each other's favourites, that's long been agreed

– opens her arms wide for me – the oldest – to fly into. Then I hug my grandad, then the dogs, then it's time to check that nothing has changed in the house.

The fly-screen door slams behind me. It's cool in the little sitting room. The phone on its table, next to it the upright blue armchair where my grandmother sits, my grandad's rocking chair, the heads of two lions he shot long ago when he was young and didn't know better. They fix me with their dusty dead eyes. Greet me with silent yellow-fanged snarls. Francis of Assisi stands on the mantelpiece below them. He has his right hand uplifted and there are doves at his wooden feet. Next to the saint is the horse I covet – fashioned from a piece of golden wood that Grandad swapped for a tin of bully beef in Florence. These are the things he brought back from the war that took him away from the farm for five years. I run illicit fingers over both of them.

And rush on. Past the bathroom with its peeling wallpaper. Past the guest room where my parents sleep. Down the dim passage where the paintings list. Open the door and through the dining room where Christmas things are gathering. Into the nursery where I always sleep. I stop in the middle of the room, breath held, checking that my bed with the headboard is in its corner. My brother's and sister's beds – without headboards – are next to each other against the opposite walls. I scan the shelf high above the picture rail. The carved elephant, the tin soldiers, the Russian doll with half her insides missing that have all been here since my father and his brothers shared this room are in the same places. I climb onto the bed and stand on my tiptoes but I still can't reach them. The relief. I can breathe out. I might be a little taller, I might have gone to a new school, but nothing else has changed.

It's time to make tea. I follow my grandmother in the kitchen. She puts the kettle on and I check the tea trolley. The servants have gone home – they'll be back tonight to turn down the beds and serve dinner – but they've left biscuits that are laid out on a silver platter. I lick the finger I've dipped into the dusting of sugar. Two plastic mugs.

One for my brother, one for my sister. I count the teacups. For the first time there are five. Four for the grown-ups and one for me. I set a tiny silver spoon to rest on each saucer.

'Will you check if Jackson filled the dogs' water bowls?' asks my grandmother.

I open the back door and run down the steps. The bowls under the pomegranate tree are brimming and Jackson is trimming the lawn. He looks up at me and smiles and says, 'Hello, Miss Margie.' I go over to him. I greet him but I don't know what to say after I've said hello and how are you, so I just stand there. He says my bike's in the garage. That he checked the tyres. No punctures. 'Thank you,' I say, but I don't know what to say to him after that either. So I just keep standing there, the sun burning my bare shoulders until he turns back to his task. Cutting the grass with an old pair of shears. I kneel beside him and gather the clippings into the sack.

We work together in silence. His sleeves are rolled up and each time he closes the blade in his hand the tendons flex. I know those strong arms. I love them. They carried me when I was as small as my brother is now and, last Christmas, they steadied me on my new bicycle. After everyone else lost patience with my clumsiness and tears, it was Jackson who taught me to ride, loping along beside me, one arm pressed against my back, the other to my side as he held the handlebars of my impossible bicycle, up and down the long driveway. When I found my balance for the first time he cheered me as I took off. Not falling, pedalling faster and faster.

My grandmother is calling teatime, teatime. I dart around the house. She's already pouring but I'm in time to hand out the biscuits. We drink our tea. My mother says a hot drink cools you but I don't think so.

'You children need some water to play in.' My grandmother turns on the tap.

The sprinkler starts. Slowly at first, but when it goes fast the sun turns the spray into water diamonds and scatters them across the lawn. My mother undresses my brother but my sister and I have already pulled off our sundresses and our panties. We drop them and run through the water. Back and forth, back and forth. They are heaven, these jets of icy water splashing my legs, my belly, my back. We catch the water in our mouths and spit at each other.

The dogs pant in the shade. The grown-ups pour more tea and watch us and smile. The sun glides a little closer to the trees.

A movement in the corner of my eye. Jackson. A sack in one hand, clippers in the other. He's watching us play. I wave. He waves back before pulling his hat low over his forehead and kneeling to cut the unruly grass on the edge of the drive. Click, click, click.

'Margie.'

Something's wrong. My grandmother's command makes my heart go faster. A cobra slithered out of the rockery once and Jackson cut its head off. One chop with his spade. But nothing's there but my brother and sister. They stare at me. I've done something. I turn the other way. My grandmother is stepping off the shaded verandah, striding towards us. She's wearing dark glasses. Her hands fasten onto my wet shoulders. 'Put on a costume.'

I'm slick as an otter so I wriggle free and do another cartwheel.

'You can't be bare.'

That stops me in my tracks. 'Why not?'

'Because the boys are working in the garden and you're a big girl now.' Her hands are back on my shoulders. I can't move. Anger rises in my throat as hot and sudden as vomit. I've seen girls just a few years older than I am – knowing looks in their eyes, their lips pursed – sitting with their idle mothers on verandahs. I don't want to be like them.

'I won't.'

'Don't be silly. You're a big girl now.' She does not raise her voice but her thumbs press into my collarbone and her fingers with their long orange nails reach all the way down my back to my wing bones. Everyone on the stoep is watching. It's as if her hands on my shoulders are speaking to my skin on behalf of all of them. This separation – me from them – is frightening. It's exciting too. I persist. 'Why?'

'Because Jackson's here,' she says, 'and it's not fair on him.'

Not fair. To Jackson. I turn my head. He's still there of course, kneeling in the dust, edging the lawn. How am I unfair to him? I am afraid of the answer so I swallow the question. 'I don't want to,' I say.

'Wearing a costume will do no harm.' There is the scrape of steel in her voice.

Harm. I did harm. I did not know it. Everyone knows it. Everyone except me. What is it that I do not know? I search my grandmother's face for an answer but her eyes are hidden by her dark glasses and all I find is myself reflected tiny and doubled. Naked. Nipples like two bullseyes on the target of my chest, hands creeping up to cover the cleft between my legs. This burning girl that I am with skin stretched white hot across unfair flesh. Harmflesh.

Click, click, click go the shears in the hot afternoon air.

'Jackson.' My grandmother's sharp voice stops the cutting.

'Yes, madam.' He stands up, the shears in his hand.

Her hard hands on my shoulders shield him from me. 'That's enough for today,' she says. 'Go home.'

'Yes, madam.' Jackson picks up his bag of cuttings and disappears around the house. I put on the costume my grandmother hands me.

'That looks lovely, darling,' says my mother. I don't like how it feels.

My sister squats down next to me but I don't talk. 'Come play with us,' she says, but I shake my head. My brother calls her and she runs back into the water.

I slink onto the verandah. I sit where no one can touch me but I'm given a special-occasion Coca-Cola. My parents and grandparents sip gin and tonic. They say it's hard to know with the natives these days. They talk about the drought and what it's done to the price of cattle. They say they hope 1973 will be better but what with the petrol going up, food prices too. They say we'll do the tree tomorrow or the next day.

I listen, my chest tight, to the ice cubes tinkle.

(Black) Boy 1973

Two days after New Year and we're in the car before the sun is up. The gravel road is deserted. My parents' voices go back and forth across the front of the car.

'No rain yet,' says my father. 'Look how dry the veld is.'

'The river will be too low for waterskiing,' says my mother.

'They've started farming pigs,' says my father. 'A tough business.'

'They've done well,' says my mother.

We stop for breakfast. A concrete table under a tree beside the road. Cheese sandwiches and oranges. Leftover Christmas cake. My task is to throw away the peels. There are bullet holes in the drum that's filled with the waste of those who picnicked before us.

Back in the car. My mother says we've visited here before but I don't remember.

We get to the farm at eleven. The gate is closed but as we slow down three boys in dirty white shirts race over to open it. My father gives me coins to give them. Ten cents. Five cents. For sweets. I open the window. The boy who is the same size as me holds out his hand. I place the money in his open palm. It is hard to the touch.

We drive in past a treeless huddle of huts where children play with cars made from twists of wire. They watch us skirt the milking sheds and the outbuildings where the tractors are parked.

Ghost gums spread their pale shade over the stables. Behind them, a man in overalls faded to the colour of the sky rests on a bench. He jumps up when he sees us, dips his brush into his bucket and paints creosote onto the wooden fence. Our car makes the turn towards the river and there's a grey mare and her foal standing in the dappled light.

There's the farmhouse surrounded by oak trees. A red roof, whitewashed walls, columns guarding the front of the deep verandah. A man and a thin woman, three girls and a boy my age wait for us on the lawn.

We get out of the car. The girls all wear matching dresses. The boy has a graze on his cheek. The woman hugs me. She's my mother's friend from before any of us were born, from before my father even. I'm saying hello and shaking the man's hand. He is big and red. Bigger and redder than my father. He bellows. Someone's name. I hook my arm around my father's solid leg. A maid dressed in a starched black-and-white uniform appears and takes our bags.

We go into the house. The interior is as cool and silent as a museum. There's not a speck of dust. The mother of the house says that the flowers are all from the garden. They stand to attention as if they have been stabbed into the cut-glass vases.

There is cold beer for my father and the man. The mothers disappear to catch up. It's been years. The boy vanishes. The daughters don't want to play but there's time for a swim before lunch.

I put on my swimming costume. It's red with a white ruffle that goes over my bottom and dips down in the front like a stiff little skirt.

The pool is a rectangle of blue, as if a piece of sky had been cut out and stuck into the earth. I know how to slip in without splashing. How to swim dolphin-silent below the surface. I know I won't drown but it's forbidden to go in if there are no grown-ups. I sit by the water and wait for one.

No one comes.

The water glitters when I swirl my feet in it.

I don't hear the boy until he's right next to me. He picks the scab on his cheek and flicks it into the water. It bobs on the surface.

A bell rings inside the house.

Lunch is sliced tomatoes and ham arranged like bloody wagon wheels on a silver platter. Then there's pumpkin and sugary carrots, a mountain of beans, roast lamb, the fat congealing on my plate. Vanilla ice cream and chocolate sauce, because I do eat up, and then it's time for an afternoon sleep. 'Everyone deserves it.'

I lie on my back and watch the blades of a ceiling fan hack at the heat. I'm listening to the horse whinnying from the stables. She's calling her new foal. She's calling to me. I get up and look into my parents' room. They're asleep. My sister, wedged between them on the bed, is too. My brother sleeps on the floor, his thumb in his mouth. I'm the only person awake. There's an apple on the table. It just fits into the pocket of my yellow shorts. When I slip out, I'm nothing more than a shadow on the verandah.

I get to the far end of the house before I make a break for it, racing across the emerald sea of lawn, arriving at the sanctuary of the trees. I flit from one oak to the next. A rustling grove of bamboo keeps the bush at bay. I push my way in but the leaves are sharp and they slice my skin. The horse neighs. Another summons. I make my arms into swords, cross them in front of my face, plunge through and escape the garden.

No shade here. A narrow path snakes between the acacia scrub in the direction of the stables. My bare feet burn on the stony ground. It's better to run despite the thorns.

The stables, the smell of fresh creosote heavy in the quiet air. The foal is testing his rickety legs. His mother whinnies and I extend my hand. She lips the apple off my palm and is quiet. I rest my face against her warm neck and breathe her in.

Voices are raised. A man and a woman. The mare lifts her head, ears pricked. Then she's gone, her hooves ringing on the hard ground.

I listen to the shouting as I creep along the sticky wooden fence. There's a gap. There are the rustling ghost gums. There is the bench. There is a woman pressing her hands against her breast. '*Nee, baas,*' she whispers.

The man from the house has her boy in his grip. He's pushing the silent boy down the bench. He ties his thin wrists to one end, ankles to the other. I cannot move.

He picks up a sjambok. '*Asseblief, baas,*' says the boy's mother, 'Please, boss'. '*Asseblief.*'

The man only has eyes for the boy's quivering back. The boy raises his head and looks straight at me. I feel his palm in my fingertips. This morning he opened the gate. I cannot look away and he does not blink.

The man runs the whip through his hands. It's as limber and quick as a snake.

The mother puts her hands over her mouth.

The man hisses his whip and brings it down on the boy's back, splitting his white shirt open.

His mother screams but the sound is trapped in her hands.

The man raises his whip arm again. Cracks it on the boy's back. The boy does not let my eyes go. The man brings the whip down again. The boy's eyes are as hard as stones. He will not make the sound that will stop the man. He will not cry while I'm watching. So I must make it stop.

I step through the gap in the fence.

The man sees me. He looks me in the eye and he cracks the whip above his head. A fifth time, a sixth time, a seventh, the whip whistles through the air and is silenced on the boy's wet skin. When the boy's torn white shirt is red the man stops and climbs into his truck and drives away.

The mother unties her son. When she cradles him he lifts his arm to strike her, but she grabs his hand and presses it to her mouth. I burn. Other women, other children materialise, gathering around the bench, their backs to me. I turn and run back past the horses, down the stony path, through the lacerating bamboo, under the trees, over the lawn and back to the silent farmhouse to tell my parents.

They sleep on. I know it's not right to wake sleeping people. That it's not right to tell tales but I must tell them and that it's my fault. It must be my fault because I tried to stop it but I could not, I could not. Why could I not? I must have said something because my parents are looking at each other. They're looking at me.

'You must talk to the man,' I get these words out. 'You must tell him it's wrong.'

My mother hugs me. 'Poor girlie,' she says.

But it wasn't me that was beaten, I want to say, it was the boy. But my shame at my failure to help him crushes my words. The words I don't have to make them hear a whip whistle through the air like a bullet. To make them smell the iron tang of blood in the sun. To show them the man's face twisting with pleasure. That I saw a boy's eyes turn into stone.

'It's never a good thing to go off by yourself like that,' says my mother.

'Maybe the boy stole something,' says my father.

'No,' I say.

'I'm sure there are reasons,' says my mother.

'No,' I shout. 'No.'

My father's shoulders hunch. I've hurt him. He doesn't like his children to suffer, my mother told me that.

There's a braai when it gets dark. There are chips for the children. 'Cokes for the good ones,' says the man. He gives me a bottle but I don't drink it. There's wine for the adults and they drink it fast. There is talking. My father and the man stand by the fire but the boy's ripped skin is not mentioned. The meat goes on. It sizzles and flames. The pork sausage done first. My father says he knows it's my favourite. He breaks off a piece, blows on it to cool it and brings it to me. I don't want to eat but I open my mouth. I chew. I swallow.

We leave the next day. There are only two ragged boys at the farm gate. They stop their game but the gate is already open so there's no need for coins to be dropped into palms. They watch us pass. They watch until a bend in the road shields us from view. 'I'm carsick,' I say.

'Shame, darling,' says my mother.

We stop. I get out. My stomach heaves. And again. Burning my throat.

Cicadas thrum. I wipe the bile off my feet.

Get back in the car. My father drives on.

My mother's tanned arm lies across the seat and she massages the back of his neck. He loves that.

I lean against the closed window. Watch dust devils shimmy on the horizon. See the man's whip arm falling, falling, falling. ∎

Alissa Quart

In Ballard

Aquarium abuts
hipsterium. My heart
beats fast – blame
Synthroid, that's uppers
without sin. Maybe
I'm breathless for
obelisks of lost feeling,
my love. Or at 6s
and 7s over
my ruinous profession,
reporting, that used
to pay for words.

Viewing tanks
next to the hot algae
chick, the ginger, tattoo-
anchored corner men.
The maritime condo
clatches, the watering holes
spitting out old sea
dogs or aging yoginis,
for whom breathing's
a career choice.
For nearly all: 'self-
employed' means
still alive. This
Census is eternal.

Marriage our collective
scar tissue webbing
over extreme emotion.
We name stuff and hope
that's proof. How
reporting works.

'Cities like this
are much married,'
I say, 'There's a pro–
bird ban on
drones. Against
voyeurs?' You check
your retweet.
Speak sockeye-
voiced, as if swimming
upstream, praising
The Family; the 'burb-
boisie. I remind that
the chinook arrive home
then DOA.

As water levels
are different
for each body
of water, the lock
evens them out,

while panic is always
in a body as well as
a head.
Beside ourselves:
upset but also
outside our 'I'.
Breathe fast:
algae robots;
sprinters with gills.
Tears a symptom yet
we are also sad.
Reporting equates
naming with truth.

Nearby artisanal
dives blink pink,
in neon announcing
that though we are far
from home we are
still somewhere.

NORMALNOST

Peter Pomerantsev

Ideas replaced with feelings. A radical relativism that implies truth is unknowable. Politicians who revel in lying openly, shamelessly, as if being caught out is the point of politics. The notion of *the people* and *the many* redefined ceaselessly, words unmoored from meaning, ideas of the future dissolving into nasty nostalgias with enemies everywhere, conspiracy replacing ideology, facts equated to fibs, discussion collapsing into mutual accusations, where every argument is just another smear campaign, all information warfare . . . and the sense that everything under one's feet is constantly moving, inherently unstable, liquid . . .

Almost a decade ago I left Russia because I was exhausted by living in a system where, to quote myself invoking Hannah Arendt, 'nothing is true and everything is possible'. Those were still relatively vegetarian days in Moscow – this was before the invasion of Ukraine – but it was already a world where terms like *liberal* or *democracy* were used to mean their opposite, where paranoia was increasingly replacing reasoned argument and where spectacle had pushed out sense. You were left with only gut feelings to lead your way through the fog of disinformation. I returned to London because, in the words of my naive self, I wanted to live in a world where 'words have meaning', where facts were not dismissed as 'just PR'. Russia seemed a country unable to come to terms with the loss of the Cold War, or with any of the traumas of the twentieth century. It was ultimately, I thought, a sideshow, a curio pickled in its own agonies. Russians stressed this themselves: in Western Europe, America, things are 'normalno' they would tell me. If you have the chance, that is where you send your wives, children, money . . . to 'normalnost'.

Back in England, however, I soon noticed things that reminded me of Moscow. A familiar triumphant cynicism was prevalent in the restaurants and offices of Mayfair, among the money and image launderers who served the newly-minted global rich. No one here was even pretending they were part of some great story of liberal democracy, of capitalism as a moral project, of that notion of 'freedom' which supposedly won the Cold War. 'Free markets, free people' went the mantra of the *Wall Street Journal*, which you found in marbled meeting rooms or at glistening black bars; but no one believed that any more.

Yet the refined anarchy of this world still seemed very aloof from the rest of the country. Television and newspapers looked no madder than usual. America had always had loony cable channels, but in my many trips to DC, politicians still talked more or less within the boundaries of reasoned argument.

Then came the revolutionary year of 2016, and things began to go topsy-turvy. Brexit, the US elections, the bombing to bits of Aleppo: 'normalnost', and with it many norms, went out the window. Since then there has been the emboldening of the conspiracy peddling by so-called populists throughout Europe; tsunamis of social media hysteria; fake news, post-truth, alternative facts and the sort of polarisation where people can't talk to each other any more without spitting. Sitting in upper-middle-class homes in New Jersey or Peterborough I would hear phrases that replicated almost word for word those I had heard throughout Russia: 'You can never know the truth about anything these days. There is just too much information and disinformation out there. I just have to follow my instincts, go with my emotions.'

Not only were attitudes I had witnessed in Russia uncannily prevalent in the West, but Russia itself was also headlining Western news all the time. Invading Ukraine, bombing Syria . . . Russia was definitely back among the big boys of politics. And then it transpired that President Putin was employing covert cyberhacks and leaks to discredit Western leaders, organising masked social media campaigns to 'subvert democracy' and influence elections, so that one began to suspect that behind every unusual Twitter or Facebook account there was a Kremlin troll spouting conspiracies.

Russia had gone from being a niche interest to being an agenda setter. President Putin smirked at me from news-stands and from the top of the *Ten O'Clock News*. 'You thought you could get away?' he seemed to be saying.

Despite all my efforts to leave Russia, it had followed me. Why? Are we suddenly living in a Russian-like world that Putin has created? Has his 'information war' really been so spectacularly effective?

Or is there another way to look at the Russianisation of reality?

What if I had been wrong during my years there? What if Russia was not an agonised curio on a historical blind alley, but was instead foreshadowing what was to come in the thing once known as the West?

With these questions in mind, I have found myself turning back towards Russia, to the end of the Cold War and the roots of the system I saw during my years in Moscow.

It was the artists who sensed it first. Even while the politicians, pundits and economists were still fantasising about Russia catching up with the West in five years' time (tops twenty), with the help of a few judicious reforms, the artists and poets of the Soviet Union in the late 1980s and Russia in the early 1990s were already sensing the oncoming collapse. This collapse was not just of the political system, but of a system of making sense of the world.

In *History Becomes Form*, the Russian art historian Boris Groys describes this process as the 'Big Tsimtsum', a term he borrows from the Jewish mystical tradition of the Kabbalah, an alternative version of creation where God first brings the word into being and then retreats from it. 'The withdrawal of Soviet power, or the Tsimtsum of Communism, created the infinite space of signs emptied of sense,' writes Groys. 'Soviet ideology knew nothing of chance . . . It saw itself as the necessary product of historical development as understood by dialectical materialism . . . In the early 1990s this ideology was suddenly gone – and the world became devoid of meaning . . . Soviet citizens found themselves in a sea of empty signifiers.' Many Soviet citizens may well have thought the USSR a sham long before its collapse, but they still constructed their world view around it, whether they supported, ignored or opposed it.

Artists found different ways to respond to this Tsimtsum. Lev Rubinstein delivered spoken-word performances where he stood with a stack of library catalogue cards, those little emblems of cultural order, on which he wrote cryptic stanzas, throwing them away as he read them. The sense of bemused disorientation is already there in 'Farther and Farther On' from 1984:

> Here, the sharpest bout of nostalgia grips you. How it comes about is unknown . . .
>
> Here, everything reminds you of something, points of something, refers to something.
>
> But as soon as you start to understand what's what, it's time to leave.

By 1993 the catalogue cards were even more disjointed, the author's 'I' submerged in a lack of sense before coming up for desperate air:

> Now, here I am!
> Could I have dreamed . . .
> Not even in a dream . . .
> . . . just yesterday . . .

(Repeat four times)

So . . .

So here I am! Hard to believe, and yet . . .

While Rubinstein used library cards to relate the collapse of coherence, Pavel Pepperstein toyed with the idea of rebuilding sense inside tiny bubbles. 'He invested his energy and ambition in the creation of micro-social groups that are bound together by a common personality,' writes Groys. Pepperstein described the end of the Soviet Union as a period where 'the sky opened up', akin to a psychedelic experience, 'when a rupture between systems brings anxiety as well as the promise of renewal'. He and his collaborators created what they termed 'Medical Hermeneutics'. 'The texts and images of Medical Hermeneutics always refer to other texts and images . . . [they] repeatedly reveal empty spaces, seemingly chance constellations of words and images that Medical Hermeneutics fills with meaning,' writes Groys. In Pepperstein's own words it meant 'investigating social consciousness and also applying gentle therapeutic measures to calm it down . . . [to] oppose collective psychosis with a conscious individual schizophrenia that seeks to cool any excessive fervor'. In a world of chaos, interpretation, however private, is sanity.

Yet another artistic response was to move away from language altogether into 'Actionism'. This form of physical performance, with its heightened emotion, seemed the only viable communication after words had become meaningless. The Actionist artist Oleg Kulik, for example, reinvented himself as a dog, down on all fours, growling at gallery visitors, a role he would maintain for weeks on end.

The reason I mention these artists is not merely because they reflected the drastic changes in society and anticipated its political future, but because many from this milieu went on to shape government. The coiner of the term 'Medical Hermeneutics' (Anton Nossik), the country's most famous modern art impresario (Marat Guelman) and one of its most famous poets (Timur Kibirov) all joined the Foundation for Effective Politics, a new public relations company set up by the founder of the Post Factum news agency, Gleb Pavlovsky, who directed President Yeltsin's campaign in 1996 and then Putin's in 2000. Pavlovsky was dealing with a country where most had lost faith not only in Communism, but also in the disastrous version of democratic capitalism that came in the early 1990s, during which millions died not just from destitution but from depression.

'The Communist ideocracy was sluggish, but it was an ideological entity, nonetheless,' Pavlovsky told me when I interviewed him over the phone, gently admonishing me every now and then to ask more precise questions. 'Even up to the end people could at least argue over the positives and negatives of Communism. Now a vacuum arose, requiring a new language. We were an absolutely blank canvas. We had, in a sense, to reinvent the principles of the political system as best as possible.'

The landscape was scattered with a plethora of micro-movements that made up their own terminology as they went along: National Bolsheviks and Neopagans, Liberal Democrats who were actually conspiratorial nationalists, Communists who were more Orthodox Monarchists with a dash of Social Democrat. When he polled the country Pavlovsky found Russians believed in a mishmash of contradictions that didn't fit into any of the old conceptions of left and right: most people believed in a strong state, as long as it didn't involve itself in their personal lives. Soviet demographic categories like 'workers', 'collective farmers' and 'intelligentsia' were useless for elections – like Rubinstein's defunct library catalogue cards, they were labels which indicated nothing.

Pavlovsky experimented with a different approach to assembling a winning electorate. Instead of focusing on one ideological argument, he took quite different, often conflicting, social groups and began to collect them like the parts of a Russian doll. It didn't matter what their opinions were, he just needed to gather enough of them.

'You collect them for a short period, literally for a moment, but so that they all vote together for one person. To do this, you need to build a fairy tale that will be common to all of them.'

That 'fairy tale' couldn't be a political ideology: the great ideas which had powered collective notions of progress were dead. The disparate groups needed to be unified around a central emotion, a feeling powerful enough to unite all of them yet vague enough to mean something to everyone. The 'fairy tale' that Pavlovsky wrote for the Yeltsin campaign played on the fear that the country might collapse into civil war if Yeltsin didn't win. Pavlovsky cultivated the image of Yeltsin as someone so reckless and dangerous he would be prepared to plunge the country into war if he lost. Survival was the story. The fear of losing everything the feeling.

At the same time, the Foundation for Effective Politics went about smearing the opposition Communist Party in an early echo of today's internet-powered 'fake news' campaigns, led by 'sock puppets'. Pavlovsky created posters that purported to be from the Communist Party, which claimed they would nationalise people's homes. He filmed actors posing as Communist Party members burning religious pamphlets. He hired astrologers who would go on TV and predict that electing the Communists would lead to nightmare scenarios – like war with Ukraine.

All the country's oligarchs got behind Yeltsin, lending him money and the support of their television channels in return for bargain-basement deals on lucrative state-owned companies. American image consultants gave Yeltsin a makeover and he danced onstage with pop groups, the first Russian entertainment candidate. He pulled off the most unlikely of victories.

Pavlovsky had conjured up a new notion of 'the majority', but as this was no more than an emotional trick with little political content it fell apart soon afterwards – and work immediately began on a new majority to support Yeltsin's successor. Pavlovsky polled incessantly – this was a new science in Russia. When it became clear that the candidate people most respected would be an 'intelligent spy', a Russian mix of M and Bond, Pavlovsky began to search for potential successors from the former KGB.

This might seem a strange place for someone like Pavlovsky to end up. He had, after all, started out as a dissident. As a schoolkid in

1970s Odessa he was pulling pranks by sticking sheets of paper to teachers' backs which read I VOTE FOR JOHN F KENNEDY – quite an act of anti-Soviet rebellion. As a student he proliferated samizdat copies of Solzhenitsyn's *The Gulag Archipelago*. When the KGB hauled him in he – to his own amazement – broke instantly and shopped one of his friends. Pavlovsky would later recant his testimony – which meant his friend only had to serve a small stint in a city psychiatric ward rather than in prison. In the early 1980s Pavlovsky went up to Moscow, edited one of the main dissident journals, *Searches*, was arrested again and to his surprise he broke again. This time he confessed that he was guilty of 'slandering the Soviet Union'. Being broken by the KGB was seen as shameful in a dissident culture which prized the sovereignty of the individual in the face of state pressure above all else: mental strength was a value in itself. In a book of conversations with Pavlovsky, the brilliant Bulgarian politician scientist Ivan Krastev points out that Pavlovsky would end up shifting the dissidents' stress on the sovereignty of the individual towards the idea of a strong state which could protect the individual. He believed a reformed, cosmopolitan USSR was a better vehicle for progress than an ahistorical, accidental, potentially racist Russian nationalism. He spent the years in internal exile that followed his arrest writing letters to the KGB, saying they should work together with dissidents for the good of the state. Now, as he worked to bring Putin to power, he had his chance.

'I first came up with the idea of the Putin majority – and then it appeared!' he told me.

This time the guiding principle was 'the Left Behind'. Pavlovsky identified all the groups who had lost out from the Yeltsin years. These were completely disparate segments of society who in Soviet times would have been on different sides of the barricades: teachers and secret-service types, academics and soldiers. Putin himself was cast as a sort of political extension of Actionism. When he arrived on the scene he offered photo ops of derring-do instead of ideological coherence – the emotional highs of 'Make Russia Great Again'. Over time his slogans became sublime in their emptiness: 'Putin's Plan is

Russia's Victory' ran one. To the question of what 'Russia's Victory' was, one could only really answer 'Putin's Plan'.

The technique developed for the Yeltsin campaign was perfected. In an age where all the old guiding ideologies have gone, where there is no coherent competition among political ideas for the future, then the aim becomes to lasso together disparate groups around a new notion of 'the people', bound around an amorphous but powerful emotion – the recovery from humiliation, for example – which each can interpret in their own way. This new majority is sealed together with phantoms of imaginary enemies who threaten to undermine that feeling. In Russia, the overarching aim was always to communicate the sense that the state was strong by making it seem that it was everywhere and could do anything – an illusion of omniscience that covered up its actual fragility.

During Putin's almost two decades in power since Pavlovsky first helped him become president, his party's idea of who 'the people' are has been reorganised over and over, but that idea always manages to unite utterly disparate groups around a rotating enemy: oligarchs at first, then metropolitan liberals, and more recently the outside world. Conspiracy theories, always prevalent, have become the dominant idiom. They are not so much a means of supporting any one single belief, but act more as a world view in themselves: all the world is full of unfathomable conspiracies, so the nation needs a strong hand to guide it through the murk. 'Conspiracy is what happens when ideologies run out,' says Krastev. 'Instead of a normative debate about who is right or wrong, they act as a way to divide between "us" and "them". You can't argue with a conspiracy, you're either on one side of it or the other.'

Pavlovsky got on the wrong side of those divides by arguing that Putin should step down in 2011. He was thrown out of the Kremlin. Now he's seen as a double traitor: reviled by both the liberals and the rulers. Which also makes him an object of fascination and the subject of endless comment, a sort of political Everyman, encapsulating all of Russia's hopes and faults.

When Pavlovsky looks at the West today he sees it going through the same changes Russia underwent in the 1990s. A delayed reaction to a similar crisis. 'The Cold War split global civilisation into two alternative forms, both of which promised people a better future. The Soviet Union undoubtedly lost. But then, there appeared a strange Western utopia with no alternative. This utopia was ruled over by economic technocrats who could do no wrong.'

One can pick any number of moments when the 'strange Western utopia' buckled:

The invasion of Iraq put paid to the idea that political 'freedom' was either historically inevitable or desirable . . .

The financial crash made a mockery of the idea that free markets were leading us to an ever-better future . . .

Maybe everyone has their own moment of disillusionment. I remember the immediate shock of the Brexit vote. For a moment it seemed all my old reference points had collapsed. I considered myself a European. What was I now? This can't be compared in terms of scale and trauma with Pepperstein's moment of the 'sky opening up' in the Soviet Union, but there was an echo. In the weeks after the referendum I would find myself in intense meetings with powerless people, plotting to turn back the vote. At one moment I realised this had nothing to do with politics – it was some sort of blind alley of pseudo-therapy.

Other changes were more incremental and perhaps more fundamental. For the last thirty years British pollsters have been finding that our ways of classifying society have been shifting almost as radically as in Pavlovsky's Russia.

Back in the Cold War one used to define the electorate along simple lines of economic class: ideological left versus ideological right, *Guardian* readers and *Telegraph* readers. Then, during the 1990s and early 2000s, when politics was reduced to just another consumer product, pollsters would draw on the categories provided by marketing companies: New Labour would target categories like 'Ford Mondeo Man', and try to satisfy that person's economic desires. Now that too seems outdated: people don't vote along simple categories of consumer choice, as the Brexit referendum so forcefully informed us. Nor do newspapers or parties necessarily represent clear social categories. Circulation of legacy media is so low it's barely representative; people move casually between parties in every election. It's as if the vessels through which we used to channel our social identities have burst, releasing a flood of data points: credit rating scores and shopping habits, football passions and porn preferences. For several years in the early 2010s it became fashionable to define the nation along psychological types, substituting economic class with 'open' and 'closed' personalities, based on the notion that childhood experiences determined political choices. There's even a 'psychological' map of Britain, which looks at each constituency in the country and assigns it a psychological profile. The result maps vaguely onto the Brexit vote ('closed' for Leave, 'open' for Remain) – though this technique becomes frustratingly blurry in the swing areas where accurate polling matters most.

In this flux of identities and ideologies, political campaigners in the West have adopted strategies that are strikingly similar to Pavlovsky's, though they have now been enhanced by social media and big data.

Consider Thomas Borwick, the clever and chatty chief technology officer of the Vote Leave campaign, who explained to me how the vote was won, revelling in the nerdy detail of his craft. Borwick comes from a family of Tory grandees (his mother a former MP for Kensington, his father a baron), and he approaches his work like a precocious schoolboy solving a puzzle or playing Risk.

His job as a campaigner is to gather as much data as he can about voters, calculate on a scale of zero to five which groups are most likely to vote for his side, and then work out the one thing that will motivate those different groups to vote. Is it animal rights or potholes? Gay marriage or the environment? A country of 20 million, he estimates, needs seventy to eighty types of these targeted messages. Social media allows him to target messages with an accuracy a Pavlovsky could only have dreamed of in the 1990s. Borwick's job is then to connect individual causes to his campaign, even if those connections might feel somewhat tenuous at first.

In the case of the vote to leave the EU, Borwick confessed that the most successful message had been about animal rights. Vote Leave argued that the EU was cruel to animals because, for example, it supported farmers in Spain who raise bulls for bullfighting. Even within the 'animal rights' segment, Borwick targeted even more narrowly, sending graphic ads with mutilated animals to one type of voter, and more gentle ads with pictures of cuddly sheep to another.

In the years since the referendum Britain has been trying to work out which ideological reasons drove the vote. Was it nationalists standing up to globalists? Or was it socialism fighting neoliberalism? Was it all because of immigration? Austerity? Of course all of these issues were important. But the search for a single grand ideological narrative misses the point. In the modern day the well-being of bulls can be just as important to politics as any of the above.

Pavlovsky needed to unite his disparate audiences and causes with an emotion each could project their cause into, and so did Borwick. He succeeded with 'take back control', the wonderfully spongy phrase that could mean anything to anyone, with the EU and its 'establishment' the enemy conspiring to undermine it.

'I believe that a well-identified enemy is probably a 20 per cent kicker to your vote,' he told me, always keen to add a data point to any statement.

'Facts' in this environment become secondary. You are not, after all, trying to win an evidence-driven debate about ideological concepts in a public sphere of rational actors. Your aim as a propagandist is not deliberative democracy, but finding a discourse which seals in your audience and breaks down any engagement with the enemy. Social media doesn't merely catalyse this process, it creates an independent demand for it.

Scrolling through Twitter now is like being at one of Rubinstein's cryptic readings. When Russia's covert digital-influence campaign in the US is equated with a new Pearl Harbor, or when criticism of

Trump is labelled 'McCarthyism', historical references have become so shorn of context they feel like library cards thrown into a crowd.

Inside the dynamics of online causes, the only facts that matter are the ones that confirm existing biases. We go online looking for the emotional boost delivered by likes and retweets. It really doesn't matter if the stories you share come from dodgy sources, you just want to get the most attention possible from like-minded people. 'Online dynamics induce distortion,' concludes Walter Quattrociocchi of the University of Venice, who studies the emotional dynamics of social media echo chambers. The way these communities work, with their introverted systems of interpretation, brings to mind Pepperstein's description of 'Medical Hermeneutics'. Alt-right groups, for example, have developed their own signs and codes, complete with an alternative right-wing Wiki to communicate their ironic fascisms. Coherence becomes possible again – but only by fully giving yourself over to a closed community, the experience of which is as schizophrenic as Pepperstein's micro-social groups. One of the funny, tragic stories of the last US elections was the prevalence of 'fake news' farms, which fed audiences crazy conspiracies about how Hillary Clinton performed satanic rites or ran child prostitution rings out of pizza parlours. In 1990s Russia, Pavlovsky had to foist wild conspiracy theories and fake news onto audiences – now they demand them.

And in any case why would anyone want the 'facts' if all they communicate is disappointment? That your kids will be poorer than you; that you will never afford an apartment. That Americans could elect someone like Donald Trump – a man with so little regard for making sense, whose many contradictory messages never add up to any stable meaning – shows just how many American voters no longer felt invested in evidence-based, rational progress. Instead of coherence Trump offers impulses, which satisfy the raw emotions of voters: he is xenophobic one moment and wants to help Syrian kids the next; isolationist in the morning and interventionist in the afternoon. Emotional ego-peaks fill in for information. His speeches could be replaced with a series of emoticons and they'd have the same effect.

Trump is far from alone in discarding logic in favour of emotion and physical performance – again mirroring the example of the Russian art scene of the 1990s. Like the Actionists, many of the most successful, attention-generating, often social media-driven politicians are performing on a stage now devoid of meaning. From the trigger-happy Rodrigo Duterte in the Philippines to Donald Trump in the US, through Boris Johnson in the UK to Vladimir Putin himself, politicians are substituting making sense for making a scene. They may as well be down on all fours growling.

'I think that Russia was the first to go this way, and the West is now catching up in this regard,' Pavlovsky remarked to me, wryly. 'In general, the West can be considered to follow a proto-Putinism of sorts.'

Will this last? Always contradictory, Borwick says he misses the politics of big ideas. He thinks they may make a comeback for a good reason. The problem with audience-driven, data-intensive election campaigns is that they are expensive. Big ideas are cheaper. That may create a new demand for them.

Pavlovsky on the other hand thinks ideology is done. He agrees with the notion of the 'end of history' – but thinks it horrific. An idea of history gave us the potential to have shared ideals, and through ideals, norms. Now all actions are squashed together, flat, and there seems to be no scope for progress. Phenomena ranging from ISIS to the Donetsk People's Republic exist without the possibility of an objective moral perspective. The results are what Pavlovsky, following his mentor Mikhail Gefter, calls 'Sovereign Murderers'. In the absence of norms we have vacuums, where chaos agents behave according to rules they make up for themselves as they go along, murdering according to their own 'sovereign' logic. There is something very telling that the election of Donald Trump in late 2016 – a great victory for incoherence – took place at the exact time that Russia and Bashar al-Assad were bombing Aleppo to smithereens, shamelessly breaking humanitarian norms established since World War II. For those paying attention to both stories, a sickening montage played out between Trump's television debates, with their breakdown of discourse as we knew it, and the non-stop video evidence of barrel bombs bringing down hospitals and apartment blocks, with babies found in the rubble. Of course humanitarian principles have been broken many times before, but in the past there was usually some attempt to deny, to cover things up, to be ashamed, to pretend ignorance. Here it was done with the shrug of the Sovereign Murderer. We have never had more evidence, more facts, to prove that atrocities are taking place. And never has it mattered less.

This is the great paradox of the end of the Cold War: the future, or rather the future-less present, arrived first in Russia. We are only now catching up. Though maybe there's a simple cultural logic at work here. If our own ideological coherence was based on opposition to the Soviet Union's, when it collapsed we would invariably follow.

The Russian regime finds itself at ease in this environment because it has been acting in it for longer. There's nothing mystical at work in its success: it simply has a head start. Matching its messages to different audiences, constantly capturing attention and conjuring the illusion of strength through spectacle, lying for fun, throwing truth to the wind and reducing facts to feelings – this is all familiar territory for the Kremlin. Some politicians in the West have joined in, but most institutions and bureaucracies are still playing by yesterday's rules.

In a final twist, a nostalgia has arisen for 'normalnost', for a time of stable meaning, which for many, especially among media and intellectual elites in the US, was the Cold War. Perhaps this yearning for a time that still made sense helps boost the spectacular amount of attention Russia now receives in the 'liberal press' and in conversations among those 'resisting' Trump in New York and DC: if the Kremlin becomes the great enemy again, then maybe we will rediscover our own, once victorious, notion of freedom. The more our reality becomes like the new Russia, the more we yearn for the old Soviet Union. ■

KEITH JARRETT
THE KÖLN CONCERT

ECM

TWO KEITHS AND THE WRONG PIANO

Hanif Kureishi

Just before Xmas in 2017, having had a minor operation, I was lying in bed, bored, uncomfortable and in no mood to read, when for reasons I can't explain, I thought I'd listen to Keith Jarrett's *The Köln Concert* all through. I'd played it massively over the years, on record, cassette, CD and now on download. But since I tend to listen to music while doing something else, reading, writing or looking out of the window, I can't say I'd actually *heard* or immersed myself in it for a long time.

I recalled that the double album was recorded live in Cologne in 1975 and a lot of people bought it, even those who would never have listened to anything quick or abstract by Charlie Parker or John Coltrane. Musicians – not novelists, movie or theatre directors or painters – had been at the centre of the culture I grew up in. They were our political and spiritual guides and we considered it crucial to keep in touch with what they were thinking. Despite this, for some unknown reason, I didn't hear the album until around 1987.

I remember being depressed at the time because I told everyone so, and then I left London briefly, to stay with Karen, in Cardiff, Wales. In the early seventies we had been at college in Bromley together, doing our A levels, and she was the first female friend I'd had. It was not a romantic attachment: better educated and more cultured than me, she was right of centre then, argumentative and good fun to be around. She came often to the house and my father liked to talk with her. He encouraged us to start a magazine together, which had one issue.

In Cardiff, expecting her to welcome a definitive account of my depression, I arrived to discover that she had married a Buddhist and become one herself. They were wearing orange robes, burning incense and sitting still for long periods. I was appalled: how happy they were despite being ridiculous, having no drugs in the house and wearing a colour that did no one any favours. I grasped that not only would I receive little attention, but that afternoon they also wanted to see *Raiders of the Lost Ark*, which had just been released. Of course, its optimism hurled me into a blacker mood. A good Tarkovsky might have elevated my spirits.

My mood would turn darker that evening. Buddhists, according to my bias, tended to listen to chanting music or something somnolent suitable for aromatherapy. The new Thatcherite capitalism was depleting and exhausting people. If you couldn't keep up, you could cross your legs and check out. Nietzsche called Buddhism 'a kind of hygiene'. But I was half-asleep already; I wanted to wake up and tune in to the cosmic meaning. That was why I was there.

Karen's husband, whom I had taken against – particularly after the devoted way I saw him hold and caress her foot when we visited a shoe shop – put on *The Köln Concert*, which I knew nothing about. When he informed me that the piece was an improvisation I suspected my visit would be short. In the seventies and early eighties I had worked in the theatre and at that time directors liked to use improvisation to 'free the actors up'. These exercises were interminable; I had never seen an actor achieve anything through improvisation that wouldn't have been better coming from a writer who had thought about what he was doing. But, having no choice – 'the ears have no lids', as Jacques Lacan reminds us – I listened. And those first five notes knocked me out; it was like receiving five firm blows to the head.

That night we had supper and a young woman friend of theirs

came round. When the woman had gone and the Buddhists were in bed I retired to the attic where I was staying, and waited. In those days I was an enthusiast of one-night stands, where a never-repeated intensity and strangeness might occur with an unknown person who would remain mostly unknown – apart from their obscenity. Hoping for what Robert Stoller calls 'reciprocated pathologies', the couple would become and remain a kind of living fantasy for one another. That was the idea.

Earlier, the girl and I had whispered together. Now she came back. We lit candles; I crept downstairs for the record. We lay on the bed together and played it all night.

I curled up. Everything was wrong with me. Suffering from lack of curiosity, I was too fearful and inhibited to have sex with her, if that was what she wanted. Or, indeed, if it was what I wanted. Sex rarely lacks trauma: it is almost always shattering and there are few insignificant sexual encounters, however fleeting.

But I lacked the sense or ability to inform her of how I felt. If speaking is obviously the most important thing we do, I could have tried that. She might, after all, have wanted to hear and respond.

Certainly I had always considered it more profitable and interesting to talk with men than with women. My father and I had been close, and I had witnessed how much he and his brothers liked to talk. In contrast, my mother avoided social situations and conversation. She was already nervous, if not frightened and trapped. Later I understood that the freedom to speak, joke or tease could never be enjoyable for her. Petrified, secluded and busy trying not to go mad, more talk would only disorientate her. She was enigmatic to us, and appeared to have little idea of what was going on inside herself. Not that she wanted to be helped. She didn't think it was necessary that people be interesting, funny or attractive. On the rare occasions when people came by to see us I wanted them to have a nice time and like us. Once, when I was enumerating the qualities of someone I liked, she interrupted to say, 'Why can't people just be nice?' My analyst said that that was a profound remark. Clearly, he was on to something. He's nice himself, but I can't imagine that people pay him for only that.

Yet I had always been fascinated with women's bodies, their gestures, clothes, voices and who they were. But, that night, what I called depression was rigidity and repetition; a taste of bitter nothingness. I was lost and afraid in a dark wood with no capacity to enjoy my own thoughts or those of anyone else. I could enter a tunnel of all-debasing, tantrumy fury where things would get dirty in my head, and I'd be tempted to throw myself under a train. Who doesn't know someone who has killed themselves, and even admired their courage? In these moods you can forget that you are the engine of your own tempest.

The nearly dead certainly lack a sense of humour. The British child psychoanalyst Donald Winnicott calls depression 'smoke over the battlefield', but where exactly was the conflict taking place? Who was the speechlessness – the block, the dire shortage of words – for? How do you begin to understand what is going on inside you? I'd travelled a bit and recognised that we lived – if you were in London, if you'd benefited from the welfare state and were in work – in a relatively free society where the bright new individualism of the sixties was still being celebrated, albeit in a darker form. With me, the sources of oppression were within. I was exerting a reign of terror over myself, while destroying my ability to resist. I had put myself on my back.

Stephen Frears and I had made *My Beautiful Laundrette* and *Sammy and Rosie Get Laid*. I had some money for the first time and not long before had been at the Oscars, sitting next to Bette Davis, who had been kind. Now I was at a crossroads, with no direction home or ahead. I knew I should begin the novel I had been attempting since my teens. It would become *The Buddha of Suburbia*, but I didn't know how to start. I couldn't find the right voice for it. Or a voice for myself.

Having successfully sabotaged the Buddhist couple's weekend and more or less lost Karen as a friend, back in London I bought *The Köln*

Concert on cassette because I needed to know it better. The sound is thin and you can hear Jarrett sighing, foot-stomping and making Glenn Gould-like grunts. He was twenty-nine and exhausted that night. The concert took place late, after another concert had finished, and Jarrett almost refused to play because the young promoter had provided the wrong piano. It was only by chance, apparently, that he played at all, or that the gig was recorded.

The Köln Concert is a textured piece: you can hear in it pop, gospel, blues and a little bit of schmaltz, but Jarrett never stays anywhere long enough to settle. He is all over the place. Not only did I understand that the music was original and somehow visionary, but that it was so rich – carrying in it the compressed history of everything Jarrett ever knew – that even today I can detect hidden corners in it. And who couldn't acknowledge that it took a wild confidence to sit in front of a thousand people and invent music that didn't exist five minutes before? Rapturous, possessed by music, he had – and yet hadn't – exposed himself to an exhilarating danger. How could anyone be that free? Nietzsche, himself a keen improviser on the piano, has something to say about this in *The Gay Science*:

> One is reminded of those masters of musical improvisation whose hands the listener would also like to credit with divine *infallibility* although here and there they make a mistake as every mortal does. But they are practised and inventive and ready at any moment to incorporate into their thematic order the most accidental tone to which the flick of a finger or a mood has driven them, breathing a beautiful meaning and soul into an accident.

It also struck me, as I drank in the record – whose beauty slowly began to convince me I needn't kill myself that afternoon – that satisfaction and happiness wouldn't happen for me today, or for a long time. My response to the music had reminded me that concealed inside myself was a more excitable and open self raring to get out. But I knew it could take years to chase away one's defences and live more freely. You couldn't take a pill for it. You had to *do* something. I had read in the Freudian literature that you had to 'work it through'. How did you begin to do that?

My Beautiful Laundrette had been about two aspirational, gay oddballs – a skinhead and a mixed-race kid – who become entrepreneurs almost by mistake. It matched its time: extreme neo-liberal capitalism was gathering speed; society was being sorted into winners and losers. Where there had been once, at least, generational solidarity and a sense of shared, countercultural values – for the liberalisation of the West – there was now, in this new era, the cry of 'no future' and the banal mantra of celebrity and accumulation. Not only that, this was the era of self-help. You were supposed to retool yourself for the new era. In the light of this, even I grasped what was stimulating the Buddhists. If all was acquisitiveness, competition and entrepreneurship, sitting on your ass could seem like rebellion.

I was too restless and ambitious for extended meditation, and I regret that I probably still am. But I began to think about something related to meditation. Suppose you put aside, or entirely gave up, ideas of success and failure, and only proceeded experimentally, following your interest and excitement? What if you retired what Rousseau calls 'the frenzy to achieve distinction'? Didn't that resemble what Jarrett was doing when he turned up not knowing what would turn up? Wasn't that a lateral, Buddhist act?

When I was at school we were neglected when we were not being punished. But now there were fresh horrors for children, and new forms of discipline. Every day had become a test. Goals were set. The young were harried and made to pursue some spurious ideal of excellence and achievement. Putting all this together, and recalling that refusal makes us human, I had been thinking of writing a story about someone who one day rejected the idea of duty and obligation, and decided to proceed only according to his pleasure, following what you might call 'alternative selves', seeking an 'alternative life', re-evaluating his values. He would, of course, soon exhaust the obvious indulgences. If he didn't insist on making himself crazy like Dorian Gray, how might he proceed? Where would it take him, this commitment to surprise, and what would happen as a consequence?

I never found a way to order this story. But I wanted to try and write a book about my own discordance. Despite my state of mind, most of the time my discipline hadn't deserted me. It would always come and go, but most days I would drift across to my desk, read a bit of what I had written previously and cross it out. Usually something kicked off then. Beginning a new piece created some hope and optimism. I embarked on the novel because I had to, starting it simply with the most elementary statement, having the protagonist announce himself, as we did in workshops. 'My name is Karim Amir and I am an Englishman born and bred, almost . . .'

A few days ago, after listening to *The Köln Concert*, I was prompted to glance again at Keith Johnstone's teaching book *Impro*, which we'd used at the Royal Court, where Johnstone had worked. Despite my scepticism with regard to exposing others to your improvisations unless you were Keith Jarrett, this paean to fluency and spontaneity made me so enthusiastic I read it again. I have to admit I adore books that contain instructions.

Freud was always a moralist. Trying too hard to be obedient or good, we become masochistic, because morality in its purest, Kantian form is pathological and asks too much of us. Winnicott, in *Playing and Reality* (1971), discusses the idea of the child being asked to give up their spontaneity in favour of compliance, and what the price of such obedience is. Published in 1979, Johnstone's *Impro*, with its hippy edge, is an immaculate guide to not doing the right thing, to being careless, indecent – and altogether crazier. Wisely, Johnstone calls education 'an anti-trance activity', and suggests that by forgetting your manners and being less impressed by the rules, you can allow surprising things to happen. True speech might even emerge if we remember that speech isn't something you can rehearse; it really is always an improvisation, and the more digressive the better.

However, unlearning is a risky art. If art is controlled madness, then lack of control, and following pleasure, could take you anywhere. Could you be sure you wanted to go there, particularly with other people? Pleasure is an energy, and once you understand that it is a creative force – or rather, *the* creative force – you might begin to get somewhere. I saw that pop had always used this as a creed.

It would be a while before I realised that a series of indifferent relationships weren't experimental. They weren't even relationships. I was narrowing my mind, if not mortifying myself. And after studying Jarrett, I saw that some artists – particularly musicians like Prince, whom I would think about when I began my second novel *The Black Album* – never stopped producing.

But the idea of becoming more productive wasn't *it* either, because I was beginning to see that although being an artist seemed to represent the ideal life – you follow your imagination and get paid, if not praised – it could never be sufficient. Talent can become an obstacle, and making art can become a way of retreating to a bunker where you would feel safe. I wondered if Jarrett had made that mistake with his work, and if he had learned from it.

Most of the time you have to be a person with another person, and if you're lucky you can play with them, making demands and expecting demands back. New things emerge from this exchange. But facing other people straight on in their reality, with their odd, if not strange pleasures – and what, if anything, do they want? – could be too much. Racism, misogyny and other forms of inequality are intended to modify this impact by already diminishing the other. They come to you already filtered so you know what they are. Status is a form of protection, and equality the horror to be avoided. If speaking is a performance, then this form of improvisation is an attempt to find out what is unknown about oneself and others. And the unknown is, as the two Keiths knew, where the excitement lives. ■

CONTRIBUTORS

Josh Appignanesi is a film-maker whose directing credits include the feature films *Female Human Animal, The Infidel, The New Man* and *Song Of Songs*. He is a lecturer in Film at Roehampton University, and teaches at the London Film School and other institutions.

Chloe Aridjis is the author of three novels: *Book of Clouds*, which won the 2009 *Prix du premier roman étranger* in France, *Asunder* and *Sea Monsters*. She writes for various art journals and was a guest curator at Tate Liverpool. In 2014 she was awarded a Guggenheim Fellowship.

David Baddiel is a comedian, screenwriter and television presenter. After graduating with a first in English from Cambridge in 1986, he started a PhD at University College London, but gave up after writing 90 per cent of it for a career in comedy. He has, however, always wondered about his lost career in academia.

Devorah Baum is associate professor in English literature at the University of Southampton. She is the author of *Feeling Jewish (A Book for Just About Anyone)* and *The Jewish Joke*, and co-director of the documentary feature film *The New Man*.

Josh Cohen is a psychoanalyst in private practice and professor of literary theory at Goldsmiths, University of London. He is the author of numerous books and articles on modern literature, cultural theory and psychoanalysis, including *How to Read Freud, The Private Life* and, most recently, *Not Working*.

Jennifer Croft translates from the Polish. She is the recipient of several grants and fellowships, as well as the inaugural Michael Henry Heim Prize for Translation, the 2018 Found in Translation Award, the 2018 Man Booker International Prize and a Tin House scholarship for her novel *Homesick*, originally written in Spanish. She is currently translating *The Books of Jacob* by Olga Tokarczuk.

William Davies teaches at Goldsmiths, University of London. He is the author of *Nervous States, The Happiness Industry* and *The Limits of Neoliberalism*.

Anouchka Grose is a writer and psychoanalyst practising in London. She is a member of the Centre for Freudian Analysis and Research, where she regularly lectures. Her works include the non-fiction *No More Silly Love Songs, Are You Considering Therapy?* and *From Anxiety to Zoolander*, and the novels *Ringing for You* and *Darling Daisy*.

Bernd Hartung is a German photographer. His work has appeared in *Amnesty International, Die Zeit, i-D* and elsewhere.

Max Houghton is a writer, curator and senior lecturer in photography at the London College of Communication. She is a scholarship doctoral candidate in the Faculty of Laws at University College London.

Hanif Kureishi grew up in Kent and studied philosophy at King's College London. His novels include *The Buddha of Suburbia*, which won the 1990 Whitbread Award for First Novel, *The Black Album, Intimacy* and *The Last Word*. He has been appointed Chevalier de l'Ordre des Arts et des Lettres and is a Commander of the Order of the British Empire. His next book, *What Happened?*, a collection of essays and stories, is published in 2019.

Nick Laird is a poet, novelist, screenwriter and former lawyer. His poetry collections are *To a Fault, On Purpose, Go Giants* and *Feel Free*. His novels are *Utterly Monkey, Glover's Mistake* and *Modern Gods*. He is a writer in residence at New York University.

Benjamin Markovits grew up in Texas, London, Oxford and Berlin. His novel *You Don't Have to Live Like This* won the 2015 James Tait Black Prize for Fiction. 'Picking Up Nathan from the Airport' is an excerpt from *Christmas in Austin*, forthcoming from Faber & Faber in 2019. He was named one of *Granta*'s Best of Young British Novelists in 2013.

Fabián Martínez Siccardi was born in southern Patagonia, Argentina. He is the author of *Patagonia iluminada, Bestias afuera* and *Perdidas en la noche*. He lives in Buenos Aires where he works as a writer, translator and journalist on culture issues in both Spanish and English.

Diana Matar is an artist working with photography, testimony and archive. She is the author of *Evidence* and *My America*. Her works have been exhibited or collected by Tate Modern, the Museum of Contemporary Photography Chicago, the Victoria and Albert Museum and the Museum of Fine Arts Houston.

Hisham Matar's debut novel *In the Country of Men* was shortlisted for the 2006 Man Booker Prize and the 2006 *Guardian* First Book Award. His 2016 memoir, *The Return*, was the recipient of many awards including the 2017 Pulitzer Prize, the 2017 PEN/Jean Stein Book Award and the 2017 Rathbones Folio Prize. He is a Fellow of the Royal Society of Literature. A version of 'The Guests' was delivered as the 2018 Edward W. Said Memorial Lecture at Columbia University.

Margie Orford's works include *Water Music, Daddy's Girl* and *Gallows Hill*. She is a member of the executive board of PEN International and PEN South Africa, a Fulbright scholar, a Civitella Ranieri Fellow and an honorary fellow of St Hugh's College, Oxford. She lives in London.

Yvonne Adhiambo Owuor is a writer from Nairobi, Kenya. She is the author of the novels *Dust* and *The Dragonfly Sea*.

Adam Phillips was formerly Principal Child Psychotherapist at Charing Cross Hospital in London, and is now a psychoanalyst in private practice and a writer. His most recent work is *In Writing: Essays on Literature*.

Peter Pomerantsev is a Kiev-born writer and TV producer living in London. He is the author of *Nothing Is True and Everything Is Possible*, an account of contemporary life inside Putin's dictatorship. His writing has appeared in several publications, including the *London Review of Books*, the *Atlantic* and *Newsweek*.

Alissa Quart is a poet, journalist and the executive director of the non-profit the Economic Hardship Reporting Project. She has written five books, the poetry volume *Monetized* and non-fiction including *Squeezed* and *Branded*. Her poetry has appeared in the *London Review of Books* and the *Nation*, among other publications.

Poppy Sebag-Montefiore has worked as a broadcast journalist in the BBC's Beijing Bureau and reported from China for *Channel 4 News*. She has also worked as an investigative film-maker for *Newsnight*. She teaches modern Chinese fiction at King's College London and is currently at work on a novel.

Olga Tokarczuk is the author of eight novels and three story collections. Her novel *Flights*, in Jennifer Croft's translation, won the 2018 Man Booker International Prize and was shortlisted for the 2018 National Book Award for Translated Literature.

Joff Winterhart is an artist, writer, film-maker and dog fan. He has made two graphic novels, *Days of the Bagnold Summer* and *Driving Short Distances*. He also plays drums and writes songs in the band Bucky, and lives in Bristol.